DEATH OF A
SIX-FOOT TEDDY BEAR

This Large Print Book carries the
Seal of Approval of N.A.V.H.

A BARGAIN HUNTERS MYSTERY, BOOK 2

DEATH OF A
SIX-FOOT TEDDY BEAR

SHARON DUNN

THORNDIKE PRESS
A part of Gale, Cengage Learning

Detroit • New York • San Francisco • New Haven, Conn • Waterville, Maine • London

GALE
CENGAGE Learning·

LIBRARY OF CONGRESS CATALOGING-IN-PUBLICATION DATA

Dunn, Sharon, 1965–
    Death of a six-foot teddy bear / by Sharon Dunn.
        p. cm. — (A bargain hunters mystery ; #2) (Thorndike
    Press large print Christian mystery)
    ISBN-13: 978-1-4104-1112-9 (hardcover : alk. paper)
    ISBN-10: 1-4104-1112-5 (hardcover : alk. paper)
    1. Large type books. I. Title.
PS3604.U57D44 2008b
813'.6—dc22   2008031982

Published in 2008 by arrangement with Multnomah Books, a division of
Random House, Inc.

Printed in the United States of America
1 2 3 4 5 6 7 12 11 10 09 08

*For my kids: Jonah, Ariel, and Shannon
because you inspire me everyday
to do my best.*

People who want to get rich fall into temptation and a trap and into many foolish and harmful desires that plunge men into ruin and destruction. . . . Some people, eager for money, have wandered from the faith and pierced themselves with many griefs.

1 TIMOTHY 6:9–10

ACKNOWLEDGMENTS

Special thanks to Julee and the great staff at Multnomah including my editor, Diane. I owe a debt to Greg at the Squirrel Lovers club for answering my squirrel behavior questions. Hope this does squirrels and the people who love them some justice. To the Scleroderma Foundation for the information they provided: you helped me create a character of strength and beauty. To my supportive husband who puts up with being married to a "creative" person and all the baggage that goes with that. Finally, to my summer oasis in Idaho and the ladies who meet me there every July. Your support, love, and brainstorming ability mean so much to me.

ONE

Other than the fact that her fingers were on a computer keyboard, there was no real evidence that the woman behind the counter would be able to get Ginger and Kindra checked in. Tanned skin contrasted with a sequined zebra-print leotard. Blue feathers sprouted out of the top of her head. Her hair had that recently electrocuted look of a supersized bouffant.

Ginger Salinski strode toward the counter, pulling her rolling suitcase behind her. The suitcase contained twin sets, sandals, and a very crabby cat named Phoebe. Big hair and a skimpy outfit weren't going to put her off. She was a woman on a mission and time was running out.

"I don't think the AC is working." Kindra Hall's face glistened like a solar panel as she turned a half circle in the lobby of the Wind-Up Hotel.

Ginger stopped short and closed her eyes,

as if that could shut out yet another piece of bad news. She opened one eye. That would make it only half as bad, right?

People perched on lobby couches, wiping their faces with tissues and sopping wetness from their eyes. Across the expanse of black-and-white checkerboard floor, the bellboy, pushing a luggage rack that was shaped like a Radio Flyer wagon, stopped to unbutton his sweat-stained shirt. The brochure had said that the Wind-Up had a classic-toy theme. A stream of moisture trickled down Ginger's temple. She had been so focused on getting checked in that the tropical temperatures hadn't affected her until now.

"I've seen worse." *Like inside a kiln.*

"I'm sure it's only a temporary thing." Kindra stood on her toes and bounced.

At least the kid still had some pep and that was a good thing. Of course, the endless stream of lattes Kindra had consumed on the drive from Vegas to Calamity, Nevada, probably had something to do with her exuberance.

"They can't charge a hundred bucks a night for a room and not have air conditioning." Perspiration had caused Kindra's blond hair to lie flat against her head.

Ginger winced. The last thing she needed was to be reminded of the cost of this hotel.

She had never paid that much in her life. She could always find discounts and coupons, but not for the Wind-Up. She reminded herself that the best deal, at the expense of relationships, was not a good deal. They needed to be at the Wind-Up so her husband could network.

Ginger cleared her throat. "Let's get Earl checked in so he keeps his booth at the Inventors Expo. We'll go up to our rooms and wait for Suzanne and Arleta. At this point, I could sleep in a sauna."

The woman with the showgirl look and poufy hair glanced up from her keyboard, batting blue eyelashes. "Yes, can I help you?" Thick stage makeup coupled with the heat gave her features a melting-wax quality.

"Are you . . . are you the one who checks us into the hotel?" *Or maybe I have fallen down a rabbit hole.*

The woman slammed a fist on her hip. "For now. I am afraid the regular help has quit. No surprise there." Her booming voice almost overpowered her loud outfit. She leaned over the counter as though sharing a confidence, but spoke at an even higher volume. "Our illustrious owner, Dustin Clydell, has alienated yet another employee. I told him not to blame her for the AC

13

problem. He didn't listen to me when we were married; he doesn't now. I don't know why I keep hoping." She pointed at her chest and nodded. "So who gets stuck with the admin duties? You guessed it. Good old, dependable Tiffany."

"We're in a little bit of a time crunch." Kindra's voice was apologetic, barely above a whisper. "We need to get checked in to reserve her husband's spot at the Expo."

Tiffany wiped her temple and a line of dark brown extended from the corner of her eye to her hairline. "Oh, sorry, honey." She put her hands on the keyboard. "I just needed to vent. This AC mishap is only the tip of the iceberg. This place is going down like the *Titanic,* baby." Tiffany stopped typing and turned. She waggled alternating fingers in the air like dueling pistols. "He just better give me the alimony he owes before this ship sinks."

Ginger clutched her chest. *Titanic* metaphors were not a good choice at this point. "Please, we just need to get checked in."

"I'm so sorry. I did it again." Tiffany tilted her head side to side. "Yak yak yak, that's all I do. I'm sure you folks have enough to deal with already."

Understatement of the century.

"You don't need to listen to me bellyache." Tiffany placed her fingers back on the keyboard. "See, I'm being good." She mimed tapping the keyboard with alternating fingers. "Focus, Tiffany, focus. What did you say your name was?"

"I'm Ginger Salinski. My husband, Earl, is registered for booth 29 at the Inventors Expo. Our contract said that we had to be here by three o'clock Thursday or our spot would be given to someone on a waiting list." She pointed to the clock on the wall behind Tiffany. 2:48. "And we made it." *Took almost an extra day, but we made it.*

"You sure did, sweetie." Tiffany clicked away at the keys. "Let me just get this printed out, so you can sign it." Ginger leaned back on her heels and stood up a little straighter. With everything that had gone wrong, at least Earl would have a shot at getting attention for his invention. Today was the first full day of the convention, so they hadn't lost that much time.

Kindra rested elbows on the counter. "We reserved two rooms. One of them should be under our friend's name, Suzanne Thomas."

Tiffany held up a finger. "Just one moment, dear." She bent closer to the printer, as if listening for sounds of operation. "I can only do one thing at a time. I'm not really a clerk. I just play one on TV." She

15

laughed at her own joke, causing the feathers on her head to shake. "Let me just get this agreement printed up for you. Dustin has been a real stickler about paperwork for the Expo. He's got a waiting list a mile long, mostly local people who can be here in ten minutes, but a few people are waiting in other hotels. The success of the Expo is the one thing that has gone right."

A sudden wind blew past Ginger. A rather large woman dressed entirely in lime green materialized. The woman tapped her white plastic sunglasses on the counter. "I want to report a theft. Someone has taken my diamond tennis bracelets, right out of my room no less."

"I am sure you are mistaken." Tiffany's hands shook like aspen leaves. "You probably just misplaced them. This is a nice hotel —"

Ginger's hand lurched protectively to her own costume jewelry.

"Nice, ha. My friend Gwen has *misplaced*" — the woman did an air-quote thing with her fingers — "her ruby ring and antique emerald and sapphire brooch last night. I think you know that." She leaned closer. Her eyes became slits. "Aren't you the one who took the theft report?"

Tiffany picked up a blank piece of paper

and folded it over and over. "I'm . . . I am helping this woman right now." Her gaze jerked up to the large lime green woman, then back down to her origami project. "Could you come back in just a few minutes?"

The woman exhaled, showing teeth. "I'll be back. You can count on that." She waddled away and disappeared into the sweating masses.

Tiffany crumpled the paper in her hand. "I'm sorry you had to hear that." She tossed the paper toward a garbage can. "We don't have a theft issue at the Wind-Up." She blinked rapidly.

Ginger would bet a fistful of two-for-the-price-of-one coupons they had a big theft problem.

A cacophony of clinking silverware and idle chatter spilled into the lobby as the doors to the hotel restaurant swung open. The sight of the $3.99 buffet sign cheered Ginger. Such a deal.

A tall man with square shoulders sauntered through the door. His clean-shaven face, angular features, and perfectly sculpted hair reminded Ginger of a Ken doll.

A woman barely out of her teens rushed up behind him with a takeout box. She half curtsied as she handed him the leftovers.

Ken doll leaned close and whispered something in her ear. The young woman laughed and fanned her neck with her hand, bending toward him flirtatiously.

The man trapped Tiffany in a laser-beam stare and ambled in her direction.

Two

Though the activity in the lobby did not come to standstill, it had slowed. That whole dramatic hush thing really did happen. People craned their necks toward the handsome man and then whispered to their companions.

Before he made it to the check-in counter, a maid and a bellboy greeted him. The maid was blushing by the time her conversation finished, and the bellboy walked away, chin held a little higher, back a little straighter.

Tiffany had stopped her paperwork and stood at attention when he slipped behind the counter.

He buttoned his tailored suit coat and adjusted his cuffs. He half glanced back toward the open doors of the restaurant where an older woman in a hot pink pantsuit stood, arms crossed and scowling. Then his blue eyes rested on Ginger. Maybe it was just his good looks, but she felt hypnotized by his stare. He held out a hand. "I'm Dustin Clydell, the owner and manager of the Wind-Up."

Ginger introduced herself and Kindra. He offered her a firm handshake.

Dustin touched Tiffany's arm. "What is going on here, Elise?"

Elise? Ginger exchanged a glance with Kindra as Tiffany or Elise or whatever her name was pulled the agreement out of the printer and placed it on the counter. "These folks are here for the Expo. They just made it before the deadline." Tiffany's smile was genuine. After what they had been through, it was nice to have someone be excited about their one triumph.

Ginger's pen hovered above the agreement. But before she could touch ink to the signature line, the Ken doll snatched the paper and frowned as he scanned it. "Which one of you is Earl?"

His smooth voice lulled her. She took a deep breath and tried to get her brain fired up. "Earl is my husband. He stayed behind in Las Vegas. The airlines lost our booth display."

The man made a clicking noise and waved the paper twice. His lids slipped over his eyes, almost snakelike as he turned toward Tiffany. "May I speak to you privately?"

Butter would still melt in his mouth, but Ginger detected a subtle aggression that hadn't been a part of the grand entrance and introduction.

What now? Her palm pressed into the countertop.

Tiffany and Dustin stepped away from the counter, their backs to Ginger. Dustin whispered in Tiffany's ear. She turned so her profile was visible, planted a hand on her hip, and opened her mouth to protest. He raised a finger. She scowled. Then he touched the back of her neck making tiny circles with a single finger. Her stiff posture softened, and she leaned toward him. Finally, she nodded.

Tiffany returned to the counter and took a deep breath before saying, "Earl Salinski signed the original contract; he needs to sign the check-in agreement. It's a" — she glanced over at Dustin — "it's a policy."

Ginger had a hard time processing what she had just heard.

"I'm sure you understand about policies, Mrs. Salinski." Dustin's tone was comforting, like water trickling over rocks. He said the most devastating things in the nicest way. "The booth will go to the next person on the waiting list."

Ginger saw herself slipping down a mountain, sharp rocks digging into her skin as she grasped for something to hold on to. "Please, we've come all the way from Montana."

Tiffany took a sudden interest in the vacation brochures on the display rack.

Kindra pounded the counter. "Where in the contract does it say that Earl has to be the one to sign? Where?"

How could this be happening? She wasn't about to give this up without a fight. "Please, I have ID. I can prove that I am who I say I am." *Don't take my husband's dream away, please.*

Dustin placed a piece of paper he'd been holding into Tiffany's hand. "Give the spot to the next person on the list."

Tiffany said something under her breath that sounded a little bit like, "This is no way to run a business." Her voice was subdued, and she didn't look at Dustin while she spoke. "It's not this lady's fault that you double-booked with the Squirrel Lovers convention and we're overcrowded."

Dustin put his finger to his lips. "I did not make that mistake." He moved from behind the counter. "My former, incompetent staff did."

Tiffany must have been tapping her foot because the whole upper half of her body vibrated, yet she said nothing.

"I have every confidence that you can take care of things, Elise." He shot her one final piercing backward glance.

He glided across the lobby floor. Three people stopped him before he disappeared down the hallway. He offered hand holding to all and comments that made each one of them smile or laugh.

Tiffany unfolded the piece of paper Dustin had given her. Her face didn't quite drain of color — given the amount of makeup she had on that was physically impossible — but a shadow crossed her features and her lips tightened. She refolded the letter.

It didn't take a rocket scientist to figure out what had happened. Dustin was one of those people who got other people to do his dirty work for him. Ginger knew the type.

Ginger cupped her hand over Tiffany's. "I appreciate that you tried."

Tiffany stared at Ginger for a long moment, batting her blue eyelashes. "Most people don't —"

"Don't what, dear?" Ginger had been fooled by Dustin Clydell's smooth demeanor for maybe two minutes. People like him were usually on infomercials pushing the latest lose-one-pound-a-day program while pretending to be your best friend.

"Most people take his side." Tiffany smiled, and new light came into her eyes. "This is not right. I'll get you out on that display floor somehow." She slipped the letter into her sequined purse. Ginger had assumed that the paper must be the people on the waiting list. But why would Tiffany put something like that in her purse?

"Do we lose the room too?"

"No, I can still get you in there." Tiffany clicked the keyboard.

"That Dustin guy called you Elise." Kindra pressed her shoulder against Ginger's, her way of offering support, emotional and physical.

"Tiffany Rose is my stage name. Who would be interested in seeing a dancer who was billed as Elise Rosemond?" She snorted. "It sounds like a librarian's name." Her voice had ratcheted back up to full volume. The old Tiffany was back. She looked at the computer screen. Her eyes grew round. "No. No. No." She tapped the keys, increasing speed and glancing from the keyboard to the screen. "No, please. Don't." She pounded the counter by the computer. Tiffany offered them a smile that was more like a muscle spasm. "It's going to be just a second. The system is down again."

24

The final thing, the possibility of sleep, tumbled down the mountain along with all of her and Earl's dreams. Ginger swayed backward. Kindra's arm wrapped around her, propping her up.

Tiffany patted the top of the monitor with feverish intensity. "What did I tell you? *Titanic.*"

Ginger squeezed her eyes shut. "Please, quit talking about that boat."

"Oh sorry, hon." Tiffany slammed her fingers against her lips, as if to keep more sinking-ship metaphors from escaping. "If you want, Mrs. Salinski, you can have a seat in the lobby until the system is back up. I've sent one of the bellboys down to the Wal-Mart to get some fans. The AC should be working in the rooms . . . once you get to yours. They're on a separate system."

Kindra kept her arm around Ginger's shoulders, obviously thinking she was still in need of propping. "That sounds like a good idea."

Tiffany glanced at the clock. "Oh no, I have to be in the chorus line in five minutes." She bent down behind the counter and produced a pair of shoes with heels that would increase her height enough to put her in the running for a basketball scholarship. "It's a short number. I'll be back in a few minutes." With that pronouncement, she disappeared through some swinging frosted-glass doors.

Kindra guided Ginger toward the lobby couches. "Something doesn't make sense here. If Tiffany hates Dustin so much, why is she working for him?"

The gears inside Ginger's head squealed to a halt. It was rather curious, but she couldn't even formulate a theory as to why Tiffany would be employed by her ex-husband. The way he had manipulated her was disturbing.

Kindra placed her hands on Ginger's cheeks. A gesture that Ginger usually did to Kindra when she was sad about something. It seemed they had exchanged roles. Now Ginger had become the kid in need of comforting. "I'm going to find us some espresso. We didn't come all this way for nothing. Tiffany said she would help us get out on that floor." Kindra managed a very brief, very plastic smile. "We still got the outlet stores and the buffets."

Her attempt at cheerfulness was admirable. "Thanks for trying, kiddo. I just really need to sit down." Ginger wrapped her fingers around the handle of her carry-on-turned-cat-carrier and dragged herself past a row of slot machines occupied by people with pale skin and glazed eyes. She collapsed into a chair. Phoebe peeked out of the suitcase. The poor thing's real cat carrier had been run over at the airport. Fortunately, Ginger had been holding Phoebe at the time. Just one more item on the list of things that can go wrong on vacation.

Kindra made her way across the lobby and out the door.

Phoebe emitted a pathetic meow from a small unzipped opening in the suitcase. "You got it even worse than me, don't you, baby? Can't take that fur coat off." She had tried to leave Phoebe at home. She'd done a dry run with a cat-sitter. After the poor woman threatened a lawsuit over the number of scratches she had, it just seemed easier to bring the monster cat.

Ginger tilted her head. The ceiling was a checkerboard too.

She stared down at her palm. She'd promised God she would live her life with an open hand, that she would let Him have control of the money. They'd taken out a second mortgage to manufacture the invention and pay for this trip. She had trusted God, and now He seemed to be taking away even more, pushing her to an even scarier place. If Earl's invention didn't take off, they could lose the house. She closed her hand into a fist.

A woman walked by with a placard that invited people to see Binky the water-skiing squirrel tomorrow at 2 p.m. at the dock. How had they had managed to make the squirrel in the photograph look like he was smiling?

An inset picture showed a skinny man with kinky hair holding Binky.

A man dressed in a white contamination suit with an Expo pass around his neck raced past Ginger's field of vision. She absorbed the strange scene as if she were watching a ballet performed by duckbill platypuses.

Phoebe meowed again, and feeling sorry for the feline, Ginger unzipped the carry-on and pulled her out, just as a man in a gray bear suit sat down beside her.

The bear nodded at her, crossed his legs, and picked up a newspaper.

Ginger gathered Phoebe into her arms and leaned close to her furry ear. "Phoebe, I don't think we're in Montana anymore."

A shrill alarm shattered the quiet hum of the hotel lobby. Phoebe dug her claws into Ginger's forearm. Her body tensed, preparing for another calamity in Calamity.

THREE

For a brief moment, Ginger closed her eyes and enjoyed the refreshingly cool spray of water on her face and body.

A muffled voice said something about fire, and she was forced to her feet when she was lifted up at the elbows. People squeezed in all around her. The crowd moved as a single unit toward the open doors of the Wind-Up, sweeping her along with it. She was pushed and shoved, sucked forward and back. She pressed Phoebe closer to her chest.

The terrain changed from tile to pavement. Heat enveloped her. Her eyes narrowed to block out the sun's glare. People spilled out of the open doors onto the sidewalk and out into the street.

Wrapping both arms around Phoebe, Ginger stepped back and tilted her head, looking for signs of fire in the ten-story structure. Poor Phoebe was so panicked she was shedding wet fur by the pound.

"I don't see anything, do you?"

The bear stood beside her. Only he had taken his head off. Even with his dark, nearly black hair matted from sweat, he was a good-looking kid, about Kindra's age. Small silver hoops adorned both ears. He had high cheekbones and caramel-colored skin.

Ginger glanced up at the chrome and glass structure. Two signs hung above the doors of the Wind-Up. The doors were the same color scheme as Bazooka bubblegum wrappers. The larger sign read INVENTORS EXPO. Made perfect sense. In ornate swirling letters the smaller sign read WELCOME SQUIRREL LOVERS. Ginger squinted and leaned toward the doors. They weren't swirling letters. Cartoon drawings of squirrels formed the words.

"I don't see any signs of fire." The hotel design included two vertical cylinders with a rectangular entrance in the middle. The brochures had boasted that each of the cylinders housed huge convention floors and rooms that provided views of those convention floors.

Heat hung in wavelike shimmers around the Wind-Up Hotel, which was next to another hotel that looked like a multistory

Italian villa. The ten stories of the Wind-Up dwarfed the discount bait shop on the other side of it. A huge lake accented with emaciated vegetation glistened behind the hotels. A neon sign advertised gondola rides at the Little Italy Hotel.

"Fire could be in the basement or the convention halls," the bear said. "Or on the side that faces the lake."

"Yes, I suppose." Ginger nodded. People jostled around them. The conversation had an odd feel to it. So casual. Like they were having a tea party in the middle of the Battle of the Little Bighorn.

The young man tapped his furry chest. "You're wondering, aren't you?"

Ginger readjusted Phoebe in her arms. Poor thing looked half her normal size with her wet fur. The animal was more fluff than flesh. "Well, I —"

"It's for a PR stunt. I'm a Steiff bear, the kind antique dealers collect." He pointed to a label on the ear of his bear head. "The whole hotel is done in a classic-toys theme, right?"

Ginger nodded.

"Anyway, tonight, right before the first full day of the convention closes, I'm supposed to dance through it, me and a bunch of other toys. Then Dustin, he's the hotel's owner, comes down in the glass elevator and gives a welcome speech to the convention-eers."

Ginger managed an "Oh." She was sway-ing again, and her head felt like it was stuffed with cotton balls.

The kid shook his head. "I trained as a Shakespearan actor, did some off Broadway, got a degree in theater. I just never thought my life would get to this low point so soon." His face hardened. "Dustin Clydell makes lots of promises he doesn't keep."

The bear had misinterpreted her exhaus-tion as somehow being a judgment of his current acting job. "I'm sorry to hear Mr. Clydell was deceptive." Sorry, but not surprised. She patted his furry shoulder. "I understand about things not going the way you planned. Boy, do I understand . . . and I have met Mr. Clydell."

The young man's expression warmed, and then he held out a paw. "I'm Xabier Knight."

Seemed the fastest way to make friends around here was to acknowledge the truth about Dustin.

"Ginger Salinski." Phoebe was feeling heavier by the moment. "Xabier, that's an unusual name."

"It's Basque. I'm originally from northern

Nevada. My great-great grandfather came over from Europe to herd sheep."

Ginger shifted the soggy Phoebe to the arm that hadn't fallen asleep.

"You here for the convention?" His smile showed perfect and blindingly white teeth. "You don't look like a squirrel lover."

"Well, I was . . . My husband and I —" She sighed and closed her eyes. "It's a long story. And it'll make me cry if I tell it. That Dustin fellow gave our booth away even though we made it by the deadline."

"Don't feel bad. Dustin makes lots of people cry." His jaw tightened and venom flowed through his words. "Sometimes I think I would kill the guy if I got a chance, but I would probably have to take a number."

"He seems to irritate some people and have the complete adoration of others."

Xabier shifted the bear head from one hand to the other. "I — I was just kidding . . . about the killing thing."

They had a moment of awkward silence when they looked up at the hotel for signs of fire. Xabier smiled at the cat in her arms and patted Phoebe's head.

"I think this is a false alarm." He tugged at some loose fur on the bear ear. "Wouldn't be the first thing that has malfunctioned in this million-dollar dive."

"He's got to be making money. He charges a hundred dollars a night and doesn't offer any discounts."

"If you ask me, I think he cut corners on the functional stuff to pay for the glitz and glamour. All that licensing and special manufacturing had to have cost him a pretty penny. It's not like you can trot down to Home Depot and get a hot tub shaped like a Frisbee."

The initial panic of the crowd had subsided. People spread out along the sidewalk chatting. Some had crossed the street to the parking lot. Kindra's voice rose above the mumble of the groups.

"Lattes coming through."

Xabier lifted his head and scanned the crowd. "Ah, the international distress signal for people in need of an energy boost."

"That's my friend's voice." Ginger searched the sea of faces for Kindra. She wouldn't be hard to spot, one dry person among the soggy masses. Her gaze gravitated toward two plastic cups moving above a sea of bobbing heads. Ginger waved to get her friend's attention. Kindra came into view.

"Cute blonde."

"She needs to finish college first, Xabier."

Ginger's reprimand came with a smile.

The actor raised a protesting paw. "I just said she was cute."

Kindra sidled up beside Ginger. "Triple-shot twenty ouncers, iced, can you believe it? Things are looking up already."

Ginger shifted Phoebe, who was doing her sack-of-potatoes routine, to rest inside the crook of her elbow before she took a cup the size of a small barrel.

Kindra pointed at Xabier with her straw. "Who's the bear?"

"I'm Xabier Knight, bear extraordinaire." An electric sparkle passed between them. "And your friend has informed me that you need to finish college first."

Kindra rolled her eyes, then rested her head on Ginger's shoulder. "She looks out for me."

Ginger wasn't so old and hadn't been married so long that she'd forgotten what that little electric charge during eye contact meant. She took a sip of coffee. She had never tasted battery acid, but she was pretty sure this coffee had a similar flavor. All the sugar couldn't mask the bitter intensity of the caffeine kick.

Kindra elbowed Ginger and held out a hand to Xabier. "I'm Kindra Hall, physics major and bargain hunter extraordinaire, and I only have two more years college of left."

Xabier touched his matted hair. "I look a lot nicer when I haven't been rehearsing in this suit." He tugged the fur on his chest. "It makes me sweat."

"You don't look bad to me." Kindra chewed on her straw. "Not bad at all."

The doors of a balcony on the second floor of the hotel opened. Fanfare music spilled out.

All three lifted their heads and stepped toward the street to see better.

Dustin Clydell stepped out onto the balcony and waved.

"Give me a break," said Xabier. "He's so over the top."

The man standing next to them commented, "Who does he think he is, the queen of England?"

Dustin ran a palm over his perfect hair and lifted his chin. "Ladies and gentlemen, please accept my apologies." Despite the distance, his voice was loud and clear.

"He must be miked." Xabier rubbed his neck.

Dustin continued. "It seems we had a glitch in our alarm system. There is no fire. You may return to your rooms. Remember, you want to wind up at the Wind-Up."

Somebody in the crowd yelled, "Hey, what about the AC?"

"Not to worry. Not to worry. We'll have that working soon enough. In the meantime, enjoy the many amenities that our hotel offers. Don't forget about the underground outlet shopping and the upcoming World's Largest Garage Sale." He raised his arms even higher. "And welcome, inventors and squirrel lovers!"

"He is some piece of work. I bet he had makeup on too. Everything is an opportunity to grandstand." Xabier continued to shake his head. "That looks like about the second floor. He must be in Victoria Stone's suite."

Kindra shaded her eyes. "Who's Victoria Stone?"

"You know, Little Vicky. She was a child actress."

Ginger shook her head.

"I guess she wasn't that big a star. She had a hit song. Someone told me her manager made good investments for her." He glanced up. "Most of the second floor is hers. I tried to get in to talk to her to see if she could give me some pointers about acting, but she had lots of servants, lots of security."

Dustin continued to wave and smile for a

moment before backing through the French doors. People meandered back into the hotel.

Xabier mentioned something about a rehearsal and excused himself.

Ginger took a sip of her coffee. Waking herself up via caffeine was probably a bad idea. She would just be exhausted once it wore off. "Maybe they have our room ready, huh?"

Kindra nodded. "Suzanne and Arleta called me. I told them about Earl's losing his booth . . . temporarily. They had to park like a million miles away and walk back to the hotel. The close lots are sectioned off for the vendors to set up for the World's Largest Garage Sale."

"I wonder how Earl is doing. I'll have to call him and tell him the bad news."

Kindra gripped Ginger's wrist. "Don't do that just yet. Maybe we can find a way to get him out on that floor. He never has to know this happened. Tiffany said she would help."

Phoebe had fallen asleep in Ginger's arms. "I got to get her some food and water." Once again, they made their way back into the hotel.

The clerk, who wasn't Tiffany, checked them in by filling out forms by hand after

Ginger showed him her Internet reservation confirmation and the credit card bill with the room deposit on it. No one was going to accuse her of not having her paperwork in order.

"There is only one room available at this point," said the clerk.

"But there are five of us . . . and a cat. We reserved two rooms."

The clerk, a college-aged man in a white T-shirt and jeans, shrugged. "Right now, one room is open. You can try another hotel if you want."

Ginger closed her eyes. "We'll take the room you have. I want the deposit back on the other room."

"The good news is the room next door belongs to Binky, the water-skiing squirrel." He pressed the stapler against the papers. "Who would have thought you'd have such a brush with fame." He wiggled his thick eyebrows.

The clerk's sarcasm was not lost on Ginger. She spoke through tight teeth. "Little Vicky and Binky the Squirrel. This place is just crawling with celebrities."

The clerk pointed to the poster on an easel. "And don't forget Fiona Truman from the Shopping Channel."

Kindra crossed her arms. "Binky the *squir-*

rel is in the room we were supposed to have?"

"And his trainer," said the clerk. "We only have one floor that allows pets. With the squirrel lovers here, those rooms came at a premium."

Ginger shook her head. "I don't care. It doesn't matter at this point. Let's just go upstairs and get some sleep. If I can get a nap, I'll be able to problem solve."

The other half of the BHN, short for Bargain Hunters Network, Suzanne and Arleta, stumbled into the lobby. Ginger couldn't quite come up with a metaphor for what her friends looked like. She pictured them being run over repeatedly and then shoved into a paper shredder and rolled in mud. Suzanne's sleeveless blouse was buttoned crooked. The geometric purple print didn't match the floral red and yellow print of her shorts. Hadn't Suzanne been wearing something with sleeves the last time she'd seen her? Suzanne's mascara had melted, giving her an appearance that fell somewhere between deranged raccoon and ghoul.

Arleta, who normally had posture like a board, was bent into the letter C. Her tight silver bun veered to one side on top of her head.

"I am not walking that far to get to the rental car again." Suzanne placed a hand on her hip. "I'm looking forward to the garage sale, but this is ridiculous. The sales don't start until Saturday."

"I saw campers moving in," Ginger said. "They must stay there while they set up."

Suzanne rooted through her purse. "I got my mom-in-law to watch the kids. This was supposed to be my vacation, my girl time."

Ginger and Arleta gave Suzanne sympathetic smiles and patted her back.

"Look at the bright side, Suzanne," Kindra said. "Things have gone so horribly wrong, they couldn't possibly get any worse."

Ginger managed a laugh. Leave it to Kindra to notice the pretty colors of the lava flowing from the erupting volcano.

Suzanne pulled a compact out of her purse and flipped it open. Her head jerked back. "Ouch." She slammed the compact shut. "Why didn't you guys tell me I look so scary?"

Ginger fished through her purse for a handy wipe. Earl had given her this travel purse last year. It had a secret compartment to hide valuables, but it was special because Earl had given it to her to begin their *life of adventure* as empty nesters. She unfolded the handy wipe. "You look better than all of us put together."

"Ha." Suzanne leaned forward and closed her eyes so Ginger could wipe off the worst of the melting makeup.

Kindra's attention seemed riveted on the hotel restaurant. "My stomach's growling. That buffet has my name on it."

"Don't you ever need to sleep?" Ginger patted the area around Suzanne's eyes with the cool cloth. Then she pulled out another handy wipe and washed her own face.

"I'm with Kindra." Arleta touched her flat stomach. "I haven't had any real food since we left Las Vegas. Those burritos we got at the minimart don't count."

"I'm in," Suzanne said.

"Sorry kids, I pick sleep over food." Ginger peeked at the handy wipe, which was saturated with red and black.

"We'll bring you up something from the restaurant." Arleta squeezed Ginger's shoulders. "You know, when my David was alive and we would go on digs, sometimes things didn't go as planned, but we ended up finding even better artifacts than we had hoped for."

"Thanks for the encouragement." If nothing else, Ginger was glad the BHN was here with her, so they could all be miserable together.

After good-bye hugs, Ginger found Phoebe's suitcase carrier untouched but soaking wet in the lobby. Pulling Phoebe in her makeshift cat mover, Ginger walked past a room filled with people at slot machines. She wasn't even a gambler. Yet she'd come to Nevada and lost everything. She stepped onto the elevator, checked her room number, and pushed five. She still had a bed to sleep in. That was something. The thought of a nap in a room by herself put a spring in her step.

The elevator jolted to a stop, but not on the fifth floor. The doors did not open. Ginger tapped her fingers on the handle of her cat carrier. She pushed five again. Nothing. She drew in a slow, deep breath and then pressed the number over and over until her finger hurt.

Surprise, surprise.

The elevator was broken too, and she was trapped inside.

FOUR

Ginger picked up the emergency elevator phone. No dial tone.

She took an inventory of the nourishment she had with her: cat food and maybe some old candy. It could be days before someone figured out she was here. Gum with lint on it and a side dish of Life Savers stuck to the bottom of her purse was about as appealing as shopping at a store with no clearance rack.

She turned a half circle, examining the ceiling panels.

The cat meowed a protest.

"They do it in the movies." *Of course, they have stunt doubles.*

She yelled once. Who was going to hear her? She slumped down on the floor and sat cross-legged.

She was trying to remember all of Psalm 23 when the elevator jolted and the doors slid open. She scrambled to her feet, and yanking Phoebe's carrier across the threshold, she bustled out of the elevator. A row of closed doors and an expanse of bright blue carpet greeted her. She had no idea what floor she was on. She wandered down the carpeted corridor. All the rooms were four hundred numbers.

The elevator doors opened behind her. Ginger spoke to the unoccupied space. "You tease. You are not getting me back in there. My cat and I will be taking the stairs." The doors slid shut.

Ginger padded down the long hallway. The quiet was broken by the sound of an ice machine and footsteps on the stairs. She headed toward the stairs but stopped when she heard a woman's voice.

"So is that it? Have you resorted to stealing the guests' jewelry?" The voice was Tiffany's, the dancer from the front desk.

"No, of course not. Come on, Leesy, you know me." And that voice would belong to the infamous Dustin Clydell, the man with the smooth, hypnotic tone.

"I have had two more reports. That means I am up to five since the conventions started. Really valuable stuff. You have access to all the rooms. You're desperate for funds. Who else could be doing it?"

"Leesy . . ." His voice filled with sensual,

persuasive warmth.

Ginger stared at the ceiling. Phoebe did the same thing.

"Leesy . . . ," he repeated.

Here we go again. Ginger resisted rolling her eyes.

"Don't you touch me. I am tired of your manipulations and your promises." Tiffany spoke in mocking tones, "Oh, we're going to get back together, Tiffany. Just help me get the hotel shaped up." After a pause, she pleaded, "How long are you going to string me along? How long?"

"I am not stringing you along. I told you. I am about to come into a big windfall that will fix everything."

"Is this it? Is this your big windfall? Five reports, Dustin, five."

Ginger pressed herself against the wall. Tiffany seemed to be gaining some strength where Dustin's manipulations were concerned.

"First you sell invention booths off to the highest bidder and now this!"

Is that how it worked around here? Ginger squashed swelling anger with three deep breaths. Dustin had destroyed Earl's chances at being a famous inventor so he could make a little more money.

"I'm telling you. I am not stealing the

jewelry."

Yeah, but he didn't deny selling off the booths.

"Let's get one thing straight. I've put up with a lot for you, but I'm not interested in being married to a thief." More stomping up stairs. Abrupt stop. "By the way, the ice machine on the fifth floor is broken. Somebody has been using a ton of it. That's why I came down here. Do you suppose you could get one thing in this hotel to work right?"

"Leesy, come on. Please, honey."

Ginger slipped into the vending machine room. Tiffany's footsteps faded. Ginger counted up to eleven Mississippi before she saw Dustin's back as he made his way down the hall.

She stepped out. "Mr. Clydell, you sold off my husband's dream to the highest bidder."

He whirled around to face her.

A guest emerged from her room. The woman walked slowly past, listening to their conversation. Dustin smiled at the older woman, and she lowered her head coyly. Did this guy ever give it a rest?

"Is that what you did?" Her voice sounded weak, like a vapor. She needed to recover her gumption if she was going to help Earl.

"I'm sorry, I don't remember you." He threw his hands up. "I just talk to so many people."

She'd seen a flash of recognition in his eyes. This was just one more way he wiggled out of a confrontation. With one decision he had swept away all their plans, put their home, their future, their savings in jeopardy. And he didn't even remember her? A twinge of rage pinched a nerve behind her right ear. "You gave my husband's booth away to someone else. Apparently because they were willing to pay more money." She managed to keep her voice level.

The woman disappeared into the vending machine room. Ginger listened to coins tinkling against metal and waited for Dustin's response.

Dustin aimed his laser-beam gaze on her. Charismatic Ken doll was back. He could turn it on or off with the flip of some internal switch. Was he even aware of it? "I don't know what you have heard, but I didn't sell off your booth. My ex-wife has issues." He leaned closer and whispered. "She's paranoid."

Only hours into her stay at his hotel, and she had already concluded problems were always someone else's fault in Dustin's world. "You stole my husband's dream."

She couldn't help herself. Despite her best effort, her voice slipped into a higher octave; anger colored every syllable. She took a step toward him. "We worked so hard and risked so much to get here." She jabbed a finger into his chest. "And you took it from us in an instant."

Dustin stepped back and held up his hands. "Mrs. Salinski, I understand you are upset." He touched his hand to his chest. "But please don't threaten me."

The woman from the vending machine room sashayed past, holding a bucket of ice and three Almond Joys. If she moved any slower, she'd be going backward.

"I didn't threaten you."

"You touched me." His eyebrow cocked up slightly.

Vending Machine Woman hesitated at her door and then disappeared inside.

Tears warmed Ginger's eyes. "I am too upset to deal with this right now. But you just wait, mister." She planted her feet. "And this is a threat. Once I have had a nap, I am going to see to it that my husband gets his booth back one way or another."

Dustin held up his hands again and then turned his back. He ambled toward the elevator and pushed a button.

Once he was inside and the doors zinged

shut, Ginger said, "I hope it gets stuck."

Phoebe meowed.

"I know. It's wrong to want bad things to happen to your enemies." She tilted her head toward the ceiling. "Forgive me, Lord." She grabbed the carrier and trudged toward the stairs. "It's just that I have had enough of Dustin Clydell. Just about enough."

Ginger heard a gasp behind her. She whirled around. Vending Machine Woman drew her fingers up to her mouth.

Ginger stepped toward her, ready to explain why she was so angry with Dustin.

The woman's eyes widened with fear. She slammed the door shut. The lock clicked in the bolt.

FIVE

Ginger stepped out onto the fifth floor. She turned the old-fashioned skeleton key in the lock and opened the door of room 517. One wall of the room was a window that looked out on the convention floor. Afraid she would see the booth that was supposed to be Earl's, she couldn't bring herself to even glance out the window. She drew the curtains.

She parked the Phoebe holder by the bed and tossed her travel purse on the night-stand.

The room was nice, done in bright colors. The only signs of the toy theme were the teddy bear lamps and the Raggedy Ann doll shower curtain. Nice, but ordinary. At a hundred bucks a pop, she'd expected a gold-plated hot tub and her own massage therapist.

She got food out for Phoebe, then poured water into a cup and set it beside the food dish. Phoebe meowed a thank you.

Ginger pulled her laptop out of the back of her suitcase and set it on a table. The computer fired right up. Thank goodness for waterproof fabric. She and the girls had started a blog called Livin' Large on the Cheap. They hadn't gotten any advertisers to help finance the trip, but they had quite a few readers. No surprise there. Bargain hunters wouldn't pay for something they could get for free.

Ginger collapsed on the bed. Maybe later she would update the blog. She touched her ringlet curls. They had completely lost their spring. Earl said the hairstyle made her look like she was auditioning for a movie of the week, *Shirley Temple: The Later Years.* When the curls weren't deflated like this, she thought they suited her. She had managed to dye them back to the shade of ginger brown that, if memory served, she was pretty sure was her actual hair color.

Ginger massaged her sore, sunburned feet, the result of spending half a day standing on the Vegas tarmac in a hundred-plus degree heat waiting for the lost display booth materials to show up. From now on, she would remember to SPF her tootsies. She probably looked worse than an accountant on April 16. After a long flight and driving fifty miles without benefit of makeup retouches and getting an unwanted shower from the hotel's sprinkler system, a glance in the mirror might cause a coronary. The handy wipe cleaning she'd done in the lobby might have helped a little, but it still seemed risky.

She turned onto her side. Phoebe crunched her food. Ginger pulled her legs up closer to her chest. Her mind drifted, and her eyelids grew heavy; she thanked God for the blessing of a comfortable bed. The crunching grew softer, more distant.

In her dreams, she was a squirrel gathering her acorns into a pile. Over and over, she built up a good supply of food and a nice nest. Then bears and other squirrels invaded her tree, took everything, and messed up her straw bed.

Women's whispering voices and the padding of feet on carpet stirred her awake. She opened one eye. Phoebe purred on her head. Heavy, heavy, her eyelids, her head, her arms, they were all lead. Phoebe moved off the bed.

And Ginger was swinging back and forth, back and forth, like in a hammock. Someone hit the light switch. In the dark room, she rolled over and fell into a deep sleep right after a tender hand rubbed her back and a female voice told her to rest.

Kindra sat down on a bench by the outlet shops. Suzanne and Arleta had gone up to their one and only hotel room to give Ginger her meal and see if she wanted to join them. The maps of the Little Italy and the Wind-Up showed that the underground outlets for both hotels were connected by one continuous tunnel.

That meant that she had a moment to catch her breath. She and the other bargain hunters had eaten a slow meal and then spent hours exploring the streets and above ground shops so Ginger could get some sleep. They had gotten Ginger some food once they thought she would have had enough sleep. It had to be close to nine by now. Kindra had pushed past the need for sleep and had entered the giddy stage of exhaustion. She couldn't conk out if she tried. She was too wound up. No biggie. Staying awake all night was standard operating procedure during finals week.

She crossed her arms, closed her eyes, and thought about what kind of blog entry she would do for Livin' Large on the Cheap when it was her turn. Something about outlet shopping adventures or . . .

She opened her eyes. Across the corridor

by the candy shop, a bear paced, holding his bear head in front of him. The magnetic pull of attraction caused the sensation of a thousand warm pinpricks all over her skin. She'd recognize that cute teddy bear anywhere.

Xabier Knight's knitted brow was evident even across the corridor. His paws curled into fists. He shook his head at some internal dialogue. The store behind him advertised discounted European chocolate with a special on Belgian chocolate. When he looked up at Kindra, his features smoothed out. He stepped across the corridor to the bench where she sat.

"Hey."

"Hey," she said back. Oh great. The vocabulary champions were in the house. Kindra scrambled for something clever to say so she could quit nodding like a bobble head.

"What are you doing?" He leaned a little closer toward her.

She swung her legs back and forth but stopped because it probably made her look like she was eight years old. Not the impression she was going for. "I'm waiting for some friends. We're going outlet shopping."

" 'Least it's cool down in the basement, huh?"

"No AC is a little hard to take." She really wanted the conversation to get to a deeper place.

He set his bear head on the bench. "You get to see me when I'm not sweaty. I just put the suit on."

"You look good either way."

Xabier hung his head and kicked at an imaginary object on the concrete. How cute and endearing. He did everything but say, "Ah shucks, Miss Hall, I ain't nothing to look at." Xabier was definitely something to look at. She pointed to the bear head. "You getting ready for your performance?"

"Yes." The scowl returned to his face. "This is not my idea of a real acting job."

"You seemed kind of upset a minute ago."

"I don't want to dump all my problems on you. It's just . . . well, have you ever made a plan, had a scenario in your head of how you thought something was going to turn out, then it turns out to be the exact opposite?"

Kindra crossed her legs, hoping to create a look of sophistication. "This whole trip has been like that. Earl, that's my friend Ginger's husband, had a vision for what the outcome of this convention would be. He had everything planned. I'm starting to think that maybe God doesn't want us to make plans."

"God, huh?"

Kindra reached over and touched the bear head's soft fur. Xabier tugged on the ear. He hadn't had a strong reaction either way to the God reference she had dropped. "Are you angry? 'Cause a moment ago over by the candy shop, I noticed . . ."

"I am angry." He shook his head. "No, that's not it. I'm — I'm disappointed in someone. I don't know why I let myself get hopeful that things would be different. Why did I hope?"

"You're human, aren't you?" She moved her finger toward the bear's ear. His hand brushed over hers. His touch sent a little spark through her.

Xabier touched his furry bear chest. "Yeah, I'm human."

They both laughed. She liked the way he could get past a bad mood so quickly.

He picked up his bear head and walked backward so he could stare at Kindra. "I'm glad I saw you." He stopped, glanced at the floor, then the ceiling. He bent his head but never made full eye contact. "Listen, ah . . . the Little Italy Hotel has a nice rooftop garden." He swayed from side to side. "Maybe you could meet me up there, say around eleven?"

Kindra bounced twice on the bench. "I'd like that."

"Cool, cool." He nodded. "There's a bench with a trellis over it."

"I'll find it."

Xabier waved a paw at her. She waved until he disappeared around a curve in the corridor. She gripped the bench and swung her legs back and forth. Yep, that Xabier made her stomach smolder. But there was more to love than just physical attraction. She needed to be practical here. After all, she was a future physicist. Now she knew what she would write in her blog entry:

Some things are worth paying full price for. When choosing a boyfriend, don't go to the clearance rack of relationships. I think it's possible to think so little of yourself that you keep downgrading what you think you need. It starts by saying, "I don't need someone who is sold out for God, just a guy who goes to church." Next thing you know, you start to think the guy who lives with his mother and bids for baseball cards on eBay all day is a pretty good catch. I don't come from the healthiest family in the world. My folks didn't talk to each other for three years once. Not the best example of a good marriage. I just know some things should not be bought on sale. Go for the top of the line where men are concerned. Pity is not a good thing to base a relationship on either. I always feel real sorry for that mustard-colored down jacket that is left on the clearance rack. But I don't look good in mustard. Some guys are mustard-colored down jackets. Leave them on the clearance rack and hold out for a designer man.

Ginger would never let her do an entry like that, but it made her smile. Xabier was certainly designer caliber and sweet. Next time she saw him she would have to ask him if he had any interest in the price of baseball cards on eBay.

When Ginger opened her eyes, the room was completely dark. The aroma of grease and salt made her mouth water. A takeout box rested on the table. Ginger sat up on the bed. Phoebe wasn't beside her. She called for the cat but didn't hear a reply. After turning on the light, she checked under both beds and in the makeshift carrier. Hmm. That cat had to be somewhere.

Her growling stomach drew her to the table by the window. She opened the foam box. Cold hamburger and french fries never tasted so good. She clicked on the overhead light to read the note beside the box.

"Sleeping Beauty, we are too wound up to sleep. Gonna hit some of the underground outlets. All the shops are open late. Took the laptop. We'll do the blog entry. The BHN."

Ginger never thought she would see the day when she wasn't leading the charge to an outlet store. She opened a ketchup packet, squeezed some onto the foam carton, and dipped a fry.

Feeling better equipped to deal with the convention sites after a good rest and food, she opened the curtains. The convention floor buzzed with activity. Now, where was booth 29, the booth that was supposed to be theirs? The hotel had sent her a map of the convention floor when they had first signed up. Her eyes scanned over robots, objects too small to discern arranged on display, and what looked like an ordinary washing machine, only larger. There it was. Booth 29. A man stood folding and unfolding a ladder while several other men watched.

Ginger leaned a little closer to the window. Was she seeing right? Earl, her Earl, was out on the convention floor not far from booth 29. She couldn't make out his features from this distance. It was his straw hat with the peacock feather that she recognized, his way of standing back on his heels. He spoke to someone who was hidden behind a display board that said Wesson Electronics. Even at this distance, the slicing motion of his hands communicated anger. She gave herself one guess as to why her hubby was mad.

Ginger rested her forehead in her hands. She didn't think he would get here so fast. The last message she'd gotten from him said he was still waiting for the plane with their lost luggage to arrive. She should have been the one to break the news to him.

Earl disappeared behind a sign.

Watching the convention floor was like picking a scab. She turned away and took another bite of burger. "Phoebe. Kitty, kitty, kitty. Mama's got a burger." No reply. The bathroom door was closed. Phoebe liked sleeping in bathtubs.

She finished the last bite of her burger. When she checked the bathtub, Phoebe wasn't there. Her rib cage tightened. Okay, she was a little worried about Phoebe. The cat might have slipped out when the girls came up to drop off the food. She turned around to grab another french fry and caught a glimpse of Earl pacing the convention floor, head lowered. She needed to get down there, to be with him.

Music muffled by glass played on the convention floor, probably a march. Led by the gray teddy bear, the toys, an assortment of dolls, soldiers, and stuffed animals, wound through the convention floor. Ginger hoped Xabier was better at Shakespeare than he was at being a dancing bear. The other toys waved and twirled, stopping long enough so people could read the signs they carried.

She leaned a little closer to the window. The only word she could make out on the signs was *Wind-Up*. Most of the inventors had at least one toy dance past their booths. Xabier appeared at one end of the convention floor, dashed straight across the main aisle, and disappeared through the exit doors.

The music stopped. A recorded Darth Vader-ish voice boomed so loud she could hear it clearly, "Welcome to Inventors Expo." Confetti and balloons fell from nets attached to the ceiling. The toys cheered, clapped, and jumped up and down, looking toward the glass elevator. The music from *2001: A Space Odyssey* played.

The elevator did not move. The last of the balloons drifted to the floor. The toys' leaping and clapping subsided. The elevator remained immobile. The Velveteen Rabbit gave a final hopeful hop. One of the toy soldiers kicked a balloon.

The inventors returned to their conversations, some with glances back up to the elevator. No Dustin. There must have been a change in plans.

Ginger scanned the floor again but couldn't see Earl.

She touched her palm to her chest. She'd have to search for Phoebe later. Right now she needed to be down on that convention floor with the man who just found out his well-planned dream was not going so hot.

Six

"The convention floor closes in less than half an hour, and you don't have a badge." The man with S E C U R I T Y written across his chest in white letters pointed a thick finger at Ginger's chest where her badge should have been.

She curled her toes over the edges of her flip-flops, the only shoes she could stand to wear with feet hurting like they did. "Please, I have to get in there." She stood on tiptoe to see above the sitting security guard's flat hairdo. Activity on the convention floor didn't show any sign of slowing down. A toy soldier sauntered by, holding the hand of a troll doll. A man demonstrated his invention by placing a cabbage on top of a device and pushing a button. The cabbage shook violently and then was sucked into the device.

"I have to find my husband." She angled her head to one side to get a better view.

The guard rose from his stool and stepped into her field of vision. "Rules are rules." He crossed his arms over his chest, which made it look like he was wearing a plain black T-shirt. S E C U R I T Y disappeared.

"Please, by the time I find someone who can issue me a badge, the floor will be closed. I saw my husband from the window of my room. He looked upset, and it's my fault. I didn't think he would get here this fast. I just need to talk to him. Please."

Except for a bulge in one eyebrow, the man's square face showed no reaction. "Look, lady, I was told not to let anybody in without a badge. Those people paid a fee to be in there."

"I paid that fee." Ginger tapped her lobster red toes. No matter how long she stood here pleading, this guy wasn't going to budge. She slammed her fist on her hip. Budge, smudge. There had to be another way in. She glanced around and considered options. "I don't suppose you saw him leave. He was wearing a straw cowboy hat with a peacock feather in it."

The elevator doors opened and a small man in a bathrobe stepped out.

"Lots of oddly dressed people come and go in this place. I can't say that I remember him," the security guard said.

The short man in the bathrobe made a beeline toward them. He brushed past Ginger.

Water dripped from his fuzzy hair. He wrung his hands while he talked. "Someone has taken my Binky."

The security guard cleared his throat and added the extra measure of massaging his Adam's apple, as if trying to force the words out. "Your . . . umm . . . umm, pacifier?"

Under normal circumstances, such comments would have confused Ginger as much as it had the security guard. These were not normal circumstances. "You mean the water-skiing squirrel, right?"

"Yes, my Binky is missing." He cinched up the belt on his bathrobe. "Both him and his exercise wheel were not in the room when I got out of the shower. Someone has taken him. He's got a big performance tomorrow."

Ginger was having a hard time imagining what the motive would be for squirrel abduction. "I haven't seen him. I'm so sorry." She did feel empathy for him. Phoebe was missing too. But telling him that her hunting cat was also loose in the hotel would only increase his fear.

The security guard checked his watch. "Why don't you report your problem to the hotel desk, Mr. ah — ?"

"Simpson. Alex Simpson."

"Mr. Simpson, why don't you inform the front desk of your loss?" He made the suggestion as though he were reading it from a cue card. This guy probably checked his watch every twenty minutes, counting down to when his shift in Weirdville would be over.

She imagined he had a very normal life: playing golf on the weekend, mowing his lawn. She pictured him with two kids, named Hannah and Joe, and a wife who drove their Volvo to her part-time job at Cracker Barrel. His world was not filled with men racing through lobbies in bathrobes, kidnapped squirrels, and romantic interludes between troll dolls and toy soldiers.

The short man untied his bathrobe belt and cinched it up even tighter. "This isn't a diamond necklace that's been taken." He slapped his arm with the ends of the belt, increasing the intensity as he talked. "This is Binky, my Binky, a live animal. Have *you* tried to get help from the front desk? Half the time there isn't even someone there. You have to do something." He clamped a hand onto the security guard's shoulder. "This squirrel is the centerpiece of the convention."

With Squirrel Man occupying the security guard's attention while beating himself silly with a bathrobe belt, Ginger slipped away. There had to be another way onto the convention floor. Xabier Knight, a.k.a. Steiff bear, had run from one end of the floor to the other and then disappeared from view. Maybe there was another entrance. She slowed her pace. And probably there was just another cranky security guard at that entrance who would explain that the rules were the rules.

She passed a murky room where four men and one woman sat at a table playing cards. The elevator doors caught her attention and caused something to click in her brain. The only other way onto the convention floor was that glass elevator. She'd watched the glass elevator for a long time waiting for Dustin to make his grand entrance. She estimated that it was one floor above her room. She hesitated, remembering her last ride on an elevator. This was for Earl. She stepped inside the lobby elevator and pushed six. The numbers sped past without a glitch.

The doors opened, and she stepped out into another lobby area, very different from the walls of doors that led to hotel rooms on the fifth floor. Plush Victorian couches lined a wall done in antique red and gold roses. The carpeting was a rich red with gold threads running through it. Wooden doors occupied either side of the waiting area. The intent of the decorating was probably to create an effect of tasteful sophistication, but overkill made it come across as gaudy. One of the wooden doors was slightly ajar.

"Dustin, is that you?" The voice lilted slightly. "Did you bring me my Belgian chocolate?" The voice was almost singing. The door swung open. A woman of about sixty held her hands aloft theatrically. She gave Ginger a quick head-to-toe and then let her arms fall by her side. "You're not Dustin."

"No, I umm —" Ginger scrambled for an explanation. To come clean or try to find a way to get to that elevator that had to be on the other side of the door? That was the question. She had the feeling she had stumbled onto a private residence. But Xabier had said that Little Vicky lived on the second floor. Yet, something about this woman screamed former child star.

The woman had thinning, dark hair that had been teased to give it volume and unsuccessfully hide bald spots. For an older woman she appeared to be in fairly good shape. Her tight-fitting purple jogging suit revealed no extra pounds. Except for the penciled-in eyebrows and long purple fingernails, she wore no makeup. Washed-out features and pallid skin gave the impression of a soft-focus photograph.

Honesty seemed the best choice. "No, I'm not Dustin." Okay, vague, stating-the-obvious honesty. "You were expecting him?"

"We were supposed to meet. This is his place." She traced her collarbone with her finger and then tugged on her ear. "We had something rather important to discuss." She glanced at the wall clock. "Our meeting was for ten. He should be here by now."

Dustin seemed to be missing a lot of appointments tonight. "He was bringing you chocolate?"

"He knows Belgian is my favorite." She clasped her hands together and shrugged. The woman took a small step back, and a shadow crossed her expression. "I'm sorry, who did you say you were?"

"My name is not important." *Only my mission.* Oh please. She sounded like 007. "I came up here because I need to ride the glass elevator down to the convention floor."

"But the glass elevator is not for public use. This is a private residence." A tone of hostility entered the child star's voice. "How did you get up here?"

"I just rode the Ordinary Joe elevator up and stepped out." Ginger's feet pulsated. She slipped out of her flip-flops and rubbed one foot against her calf, which did nothing to alleviate the sunburn pain.

The woman shook her head. "I'll have to tell Dustin his alarm system is malfunctioning again."

"I'm sorry, but I have to sit down. My feet are killing me." Ginger hobbled over to the couch and plopped down. "So this is Dustin's place?"

"Please don't get too comfortable. I will have to ask you to leave. Dustin should be here any minute. We have important things to discuss." Again, she tugged on her ear.

Ginger pulled a travel-size Aloe vera out of her purse and slathered it on her smoldering feet. "If I could just ride down that elevator, I would be out of your hair." She closed her eyes and enjoyed the cooling effect of the gel.

"I can't let you do that. This is not my place. I'm on the second floor." She pouted. "I don't have a glass elevator that descends to the convention floor."

Second floor. She'd had a feeling. Ginger pulled out the last ace up her sleeve — flattery. "Oh, I know who you are. You're that famous actress. I heard there was a celebrity who lived in this hotel."

Victoria shifted her weight slightly and batted her eyes. Her lips pursed. "Yes, that is me. I am Little Vicky." She squared her shoulders, tilted her head, and placed her feet in second position.

Echoes of *Sunset Boulevard* and someone being ready for their closeup streamed through Ginger's head. Kind of creepy. Victoria eased across the carpet so the ceiling light washed over her face. "Please, let me ride down on the elevator. I don't have much time before that convention floor closes. Earl might be so upset he won't come back to the hotel room for hours."

"You have to know the code to get the elevator to move." Victoria stepped out of her spotlight. "Far as I know, only Dustin knows the code."

Ginger slumped down on the couch. She wasn't going to get to Earl, they had no booth, her cat was missing, and she wanted to amputate her feet to end the pain.

"Who is Earl?"

"He's my husband. We came here from Montana for this convention."

"A husband. I never had one of those." Victoria placed both hands on one hip and lifted her chin. "Had a lot of things. But never one of those."

Victoria talked about spouses like most people talked about bread machines. An item to acquire. Just a little something to display on the countertop. "Can I just look out on the floor and see if I can spot my husband?"

Giving Victoria her closeup moment must have opened some kind of hospitality door. She didn't seem so anxious for Ginger to leave. Victoria glanced at her watch. "I guess that would be okay. Dustin is late anyway."

She ushered Ginger into the suite. Dustin's place also had a wall of glass that looked out on the convention floor. The uncluttered simplicity of the apartment caused her to stop. Neutral tones, solid country-style furniture with clean even lines, no neon, no glitz, no trendy accessories. Nothing that said money, money, money.

She passed a bookshelf that had an extensive collection of motivational books. Books on positive thinking and how to be a millionaire in three days. She recognized some of the titles from the books Earl had been reading. There was also an assortment of larger books on decorating, art, and architecture. An entire shelf was devoted to books and magazines about Donald Trump.

A computer stood in a corner; papers were neatly stacked in folders labeled Outgoing and Incoming.

"It takes most people by surprise," Victoria said.

An open door revealed a queen-size bed with a tattered quilt on it, a nightstand with a lamp, and two books. "After meeting the guy, it's just not what you expect." An old black-and-white movie played on the television in the living room. She picked up the DVD box on top of the television, *A Stolen Life*. "Are you in this one?"

Victoria giggled and touched her cheek to her shoulder. "No, Dustin and I both like old movies. I just started watching it while I was waiting. He doesn't let very many people up here." Victoria trotted behind Ginger while she circled the simple apartment. "He's got a fancy office on the main floor where he conducts business."

Ginger turned slowly to face the child star. "But he doesn't mind if *you* wait for him in here?"

"Dustin and I are friends" — she ran her finger along a countertop — "old friends."

The word *friends* had a ring of untruth to it. Something bonded Dustin and Victoria together, but it wasn't friendship.

Ginger glanced out at the convention

floor. The activity had slowed. No potential distributors strolling around from booth to booth. Only inventors and family members lining up their products and straightening their booths. She scanned the floor from one end to the other. The entrance and exit doors had been closed. No Earl. No Earl anywhere.

The number 29 on a lighted pole showed where she and Earl and the girls should be right now: making sure the stuffed bear was angled to look threatening, lining up the Pepper Lights to create an eye-catching display. She rested her forehead against the glass. Earl was probably wandering around the hotel distraught. Could she even hope that he would come back to their hotel room?

Victoria pulled a pitcher of orange juice out of the refrigerator. "Did you spot him?" Cold steam billowed out of the freezer when she retrieved a bag of ice. Little Vicky certainly knew her way around Dustin's place.

Ginger shook her head. "Thank you for letting me look." She sighed and looked toward the door.

"I wonder where Dustin is." Victoria pounded the bag of ice on the countertop with vicious intensity, then she grabbed a pick from a utensil canister and stabbed at it. "He knew this meeting was important to me."

Ginger took one final look out on the convention floor. Six, maybe seven, people still wandered around the floor, and four of them had carpet sweepers and vacuums. Victoria continued to attack the ice, allowing pieces to fly across the counter. She unzipped her velour sweat jacket and hung it on a stool. Her sleeveless camisole revealed muscular upper arms.

She must have noticed Ginger staring. She touched her bicep and said, "Tae Bo and weightlifting."

"I do water aerobics myself. We'd have to get a microscope to see my muscles."

"I have to soak in a hot tub after my workout," she confessed. Ice cascaded into her glass.

The two women shared an ain't-getting-older-fun laugh.

"I have a private spa room in the hotel fitness center. You should join me sometime for a workout and massage."

The invitation took Ginger by surprise. Maybe being the resident celebrity got lonely sometimes. "That sounds like fun. I'll have to take you up on that before we leave." She turned her attention back to the convention floor.

Victoria tossed ice into the blender on the counter. "Would you like a smoothie? I make them for Dustin all the time."

That explained why she knew her way around Dustin's kitchen. Maybe Victoria wasn't so strange. "Sure, that sounds good." She wasn't in a hurry anymore. After she called the front desk to report her missing cat, she would just have to wait in the room. Earl would have to come to her.

Ginger walked over to the wall of glass, her attention now drawn to a booth that had a snake in an aquarium. The words The Reptile Catcher written in hot pink were displayed next to a picture of what looked like a spoon with rounded claws on it. Talk about a limited market. Pet-store owners and kids with lizards.

Ginger's breath caught in her throat. She leaned a little closer to the window. "Do you have some binoculars?"

Victoria took a gulp of smoothie. "There's a pair on that stool by the elevator. Dustin likes to watch the convention floor."

Ginger grabbed the binoculars. Her heart pounded. Phoebe strutted toward the reptile display as if she owned the convention floor. Most of the cleaning crew had on head-phones or were moving with a rhythm that suggested music fed through ear buds, so they did not notice the cat on the hunt. Phoebe stopped in front of a cage that probably had snake food in it, live mice. She flicked her tail.

"I think I'll skip that smoothie."

Ginger rested her open hand on her ever-tightening chest. A deep breath would be nice. Phoebe jumped on the counter that contained the mice and then up on a railing where a bushy-tailed water-skier rested.

"I need to get down to that convention floor fast."

SEVEN

Commander Laughlin looked up from his Sudoku puzzle. His nineteen-year-old niece stood in the doorway of his office looking like she was biting her lips off. She held a single piece of paper in her limp hand.

"Problem?" He put his pencil down. His chest ached with a sensation somewhere between heartburn and firecrackers going off. He had been dealing with the pain since he hired his niece.

Ashley crossed and uncrossed her arms. The paper she held fluttered. "I just got a call from the Wind-Up Hotel —"

"And?"

"I've been looking at the list of dispatch codes you gave me to follow, and there is no number that goes with what the call is about." Ashley studied the paper. So deep was the furrow in her brow that he feared her face would crack, splintering off into a million pieces and revealing the empty space inside. "I was thinking it fell somewhere between a lost dog and a kidnapping. So I thought maybe I should just make something up. You know, a new code."

The commander took a sip of cold, oversweetened coffee to push the scream traveling up his throat back down into his stomach. He had promised his sister he wouldn't shout at her daughter. Megan had explained that Ashley was a sensitive girl. "This is not a creative writing exercise. The dispatched officer won't know what you're talking about if you give them a code that doesn't exist."

The teenager stared at the ceiling. "Well, what am I supposed to say?"

"What was the nature of the call?"

Ashley gnawed on a fingernail. "Somebody at the Wind-Up phoned and said that a squirrel has been stolen . . . or kidnapped."

Laughlin rubbed his bubbling stomach. There was only so much shouting he could swallow before he got another ulcer. "A squirrel? For real?"

"I thought I would send Officer Drake. I looked at the map and that's his patrol area. There was a call earlier from the Wind-Up about stolen jewelry. Officer Spurgen was on duty then."

Two calls in one night from the Wind-Up.

For Calamity, that was a crime wave. Weird that they were both coming from the same hotel.

"I just don't know what the procedure is for a squirrel-napping." Ashley nibbled on her fingernail with focused intensity. Maybe he should offer her some salt.

Laughlin batted his pencil around the desk with coffee stirrers. So many choices here. Do you even treat a call like this seriously? He decided two things. First, they weren't busy. And second, sending his best detectives on such a call would be the source of much humor at company picnics. He cleared his throat and spoke in his best *Dragnet* voice. "For a kidnapping, you want to send the detectives right out there. The sisters are on duty tonight, dispatch them, you don't have to give it a number, just tell them what's going on."

"The sisters?"

His niece was too new to know about the department joke. "Detectives Mallory and Jacobson are both named Cindy. Well, Mallory goes by Cynthia. You know, with a Y. So we call them the sisters or the Cindys."

"Oh." Ashley nodded like she understood. Then she gripped the trim on the doorway and leaned into his office. "So are they sisters?"

Laughlin clenched his teeth. Nepotism was almost always a bad idea.

Ashley turned so he saw her in profile. She fingered the piece of paper. Again, she snacked on her lower lip.

"Something wrong?"

"Uncle Glen, I don't think I'm right for this job." She pivoted on the balls of her feet.

Glen Laughlin suppressed a hallelujah yelp. Ashley would be gone, and he would still be invited over to Megan's for Christmas dinner.

"I've been thinking I would be more suited for aeronautical engineering."

Laughlin slapped his hand on the desk. "Now that's something to think about, Ashley."

On a bench outside the Gap outlet, Kindra slumped against Suzanne. Shopping bags surrounded them. A small crowd milled down the hallway. Arleta sat in the coffee shop across the corridor with the laptop open. "What do you suppose she's going to blog about?"

Suzanne shrugged. "We need to post something. We haven't made an entry since we left Montana. Ginger had the laptop open, but she didn't post."

"You notice how every piece of clothing Arleta buys is shiny?"

Suzanne wiggled on the bench. "Don't go giving her a hard time. She spent all those years being the professor's wife wearing safe colors, gray and navy. I'm glad she found her inner showgirl. The woman is entitled to a hot-pink-and-sequins phase."

Kindra pulled her blond hair out of its ponytail. "I just hope I'm that feisty when I'm her age." Even at this distance and through the coffee shop window, Arleta's blouse glistened.

"I don't think *feisty* is the word for it. The woman has better marksmanship skills than a marine sniper. Would you take a shooting class when you were seventy-five?"

"I hope so." Kindra kicked one of her shopping bags. "Shopping isn't as much fun without Ginger."

Suzanne pulled out her cell phone. "I don't know if Ginger is going to feel like shopping at all . . . considering."

Kindra leaned close to Suzanne to see what she was looking at on her phone. Suzanne flipped through pictures of her four kids. "We got this long tunnel filled with stores of marked-down stuff. How many times in a life does that happen, and we can't even enjoy it because of everything that's gone wrong."

Suzanne touched the picture of her baby, one-year-old Natasha. "This is my first vacation since I started having kids. The whole time I was packing and they were dragging things out of my suitcase and getting chocolate stains on my silk blouses, I couldn't wait to get on that plane. Now that I'm here, all that I can think about is them." Her voice faltered.

"Don't be sad." Kindra scooted a little closer.

"I'm okay." Suzanne rested her head against the wall. "I just didn't think I would miss my babies so much. I'm not usually this emotional. The lack of sleep is catching up with me."

"Me too. I hope Ginger was able to rest." Kindra wrapped her arm around her friend. "We might have to sleep in shifts if we don't get another room."

"It would be nice if we could all get on the same body clock before we left. The trip certainly isn't matching up to what I thought it would be."

"You make plans and God makes plans; guess who has seniority in the planning department." Kindra pulled a white T-shirt out of one of her bags and held it up.

A bear walked by on the other side of the

hallway that divided the stores. Kindra jumped to her feet. "Hey, it's Xabier." Earlier, a toy soldier and a showgirl with a headdress and tail feathers had gone into the coffee shop. Nobody craned their neck at the bear. Weird was the new normal around the Wind-Up.

Suzanne rearranged her bags around her. "Xabier?"

"This cute actor Ginger and I met earlier. He invited me to get together with him later." Kindra waved and bounced on her heels. "Hey, Xabier." He wasn't more than twenty feet away. Why wasn't he responding? "Xabier. Hey."

The bear turned in the direction of the shouting and then turned away. Kindra's hand fell limp at her side. He had looked right at her and not waved. So much for blossoming romance.

"He kind of ignored you." Suzanne tucked a strand of wayward brown, curly hair behind her ear. "Are you still keeping your date?"

"It's not a date." Already her heart was sinking to the vicinity of her loafers. "Okay, it's kinda sorta a date. Of course I'm going. At the very least, he has to tell me why he just treated me like I was invisible."

The bear glanced behind him. His shoulders jerked up. He took big strides. Again, he craned his neck and then ran down the corridor.

Kindra slumped back down. "Maybe he didn't hear me."

"Everyone in Calamity heard you." Suzanne rested her head against the wall again.

Kindra crossed her arms and slipped even farther down on the bench. "That means Xabier did hear me and didn't want to say hi to me. Not the option I wanted to pick. If he doesn't like me, why would he invite me up to the rooftop garden?"

"You like him?"

"He seemed kind of sweet. His eyes were all warm when he looked at me."

"Is he a believer?"

"I only talked to him for like five minutes. He didn't take the bait when I mentioned God, but how do you know? Unless you meet a guy in church or on the mission field, it's not like the first thing you bring up."

Suzanne touched Kindra's arm. "Check out those two."

Two men dressed in sports coats and slacks strode through the corridor. One of them was short, middle-aged with a paunch. The other bore a resemblance to Frankenstein: tall, square shoulders, square features.

They wove through the tunnel peering in shop windows, each working a different side of the hallway. They looked at each other and nodded, some signal passing between them.

"It must still be seventy degrees above ground. Those guys could use a tank top and shorts." Just watching them made Kindra sweat.

The middle-aged man lifted his chin, indicating something in front of him to Frankenstein. They increased their pace but did not break into a run. Even with their attempt at nonchalance, they stood out like a hot pink suit among navy and gray. They were on some kind of focused mission. Everyone else was wandering.

Suzanne whispered in her ear. "Kindra dear, you can't hide a gun with a tank top."

Kindra inhaled a sharp gasp of air. "No way."

"Didn't you see the bulge?" Suzanne patted her hip. "This may not be Vegas, but it is Nevada."

Kindra stood up and peered down the curving concrete corridor. "You don't think they're chasing after the cute teddy bear, do you?" She massaged the back of her neck, attempting to ward off the rising anxiety.

"He was the only one running."

Kindra slumped back on the bench. What kind of trouble was Xabier in?

"Do you mind if I sit here?"

Arleta looked up from her laptop at a woman whose primary feature was big, brown eyes. Even slightly shadowed by a leather beret the woman wore, the penetrating intensity of the eyes was the first thing Arleta noticed. "Oh sure, dear. I'm just blogging." She liked saying that word. Blog, blog, blogging. It made her feel hip and with it. Hanging out with Kindra and Suzanne did that for her.

The coffee shop buzzed with late-night activity. The seat beside her was the last unoccupied one in the house. Through the window, she could see Suzanne and Kindra resting on a bench, surrounded by shopping bags.

Arleta looked at the woman over the top of her glasses. She had had twenty-twenty vision all her life, and now at seventy-six, she had to break down and get these geezer glasses. She took comfort in the fact that the spectacles were just for reading and that they had jewels on them.

The woman slumped into the chair beside Arleta. Her leather jacket had a patch on it that made reference to a Christian motorcycle organization. "I like your glasses."

Arleta touched the rhinestones on her cat's-eye frame. "If you're going to go blind, you might as well go blind in style."

"I won't bother you for long." The woman angled her head to get a better view of the counter. "They're a little backed up. I'm just waiting for my hot tea and Italian soda. I get tired if I stand too long." The woman took her hat off. The clarity in her eyes overpowered her distorted features. The effect was subtle, but it looked as though her skin had been pulled and stretched over her skull.

The woman touched Arleta's wrist. Her fingers were puffy and blue. "I'm sorry. I didn't mean to freak you out. I have a disease that causes my skin to thicken and my hair to get thinner." Her lips seemed frozen.

"You didn't —" She must have shrunk back from the woman without realizing it. "Okay, you did freak me out . . . a little."

The woman laughed a sort of trilling laugh, like birds singing. "I've been looking at this face in the mirror for a while. I forget that it shocks other people." She put the hat back on. "So are you from Calamity?"

"Just visiting. We came for the outlet shopping, and one of my friends has a husband who was supposed to do the Inventor's Expo."

"I live in northern Nevada. Came here to have a talk with my ex-husband about our son. I don't know why I'm telling you this." The woman shifted slightly in her chair. "I don't know anyone else in this town, and you have a kind face. I have to have one of those difficult talks with my ex. I'm meeting him at a bench out by the gondolas. This place is so busy all the time. He said it would be quieter out by the lake. I'm sorry, I am babbling because I'm nervous."

Arleta patted her hand. "It's all right."

The woman traced the grain of the wood in the table. Her finger moved in slow hypnotic circles. "I suppose it all happens for a reason, even these difficult talks. It all works together for good. That's what God says, anyway."

Arleta straightened in her chair. "That God guy again."

"What do you mean?"

"You ever feel like God has your phone number, and He just keeps hitting redial?"

"Oh yeah."

A man behind the counter yelled, "Number sixty-four, Italian soda and mint tea."

"That's my order." The woman rose to her feet. "It was nice talking with you —"

"Arleta, Arleta McQuire."

"I'm Gloria. Gloria Clydell. Maybe I'll see you around the Wind-Up. My ex-husband is the owner." She held out her hand.

Arleta opted out of giving her opinion about Dustin Clydell. There was probably a good reason she was his ex-wife. Gloria's handshake was like a vapor passing over Arleta's palm. "Is it fatal, what you have?"

"It can be. It's spread to my lungs, the thick skin, so I have to be careful." She leaned a little closer to Arleta. "Don't look so glum. I've had scleroderma for fourteen years. The pain was awful at first, but it has sort of evened out."

Arleta felt like she'd just run a long way in a hailstorm. Her skin tingled with cold and pain, and she didn't know why. "I'm sorry, I — I don't know what made me ask that."

Gloria's gaze did not flicker. Such kind eyes.

Gloria negotiated her way through the crowd to the counter. She emerged a few seconds later holding one plastic cup and one foam cup and returned to Arleta's table. She wrapped the Italian soda in napkins. "Cold irritates the swelling in my hands. The napkins help. You have fun blogging."

She turned toward the door and then pivoted back around. "You might want to pick up that phone the next time it rings. You know, the God phone."

Arleta mimed a phone to her ear. "I'll think about it." She watched until the crowd outside the coffee shop enveloped Gloria and she disappeared from view. She clicked open a file and typed:

I am sitting in a coffee shop near the Wind-Up Hotel surrounded by shopping bags but suddenly, the nifty sweatshirt I got with the sequin embroidered cat matters very little to me. Our trip has spun off in unexpected directions that I am sure Ginger will share about later. I have had so much fun buying a whole new wardrobe and finding a flashier new me. But I am still the same old me on the inside. My soul needs some sequins and a little sparkle too. A conversation I had with a stranger reminded me that you can shop all you want, fill your life full of stuff, but in the end you die just like everyone else. I am pretty sure I got another twenty years before the warranty expires on this old ticker. But in the end, I am not the one who gets to decide that, am I now? We live in a world that says if you got a problem, throw money at it: from deodorant to Botox, to those TV ads for all those pills (half of which I have no idea what they are for). From stinking armpits to aging, anything that makes us slightly uncomfortable can be warded off by buying the right thing. But we still can't buy our way out of death. It comes to us all, no matter how rich or important we are.

Arleta read over what she had written. How depressing. She pressed the Delete button and watched the cursor eat the text until the blank screen stared back at her.

With her heart pounding like a basketball under Michael Jordan's control, Ginger peered through binoculars as Phoebe jumped on the railing and stalked toward the celebrity squirrel. "There must be a way to make that elevator work."

Victoria rooted through cupboards until she pulled out a bag of almonds. "Only Dustin knows the code." She tore open the package of nuts.

"Please, the lives of a very important squirrel and a cat that I dearly love depend on it." If Phoebe killed Binky, the squirrel lovers would demand a death for a death. "Those doors to the convention floor are locked. The cleaning crew isn't going to hear me knocking. You know Dustin. Can't you guess at the code? People usually use their birthdays or something like that."

Victoria rolled her eyes. "All right." After tucking the bag of almonds under one arm, she swept past Dustin's desk and grabbed a Day-Timer. "I have a couple of guesses." She stepped into the elevator, placing the snack on a chrome shelf. "I am only doing this because I am mad at Dustin for missing our appointment."

She didn't care if Victoria's motivation to help her was revenge. She'd take what she could get. "Thank you." Ginger stepped in behind her.

"It's a six-number code. I know that much." Victoria grabbed a handful of nuts out of the package and munched. "Let's try the address for the Wind-Up." She pushed six numbers on a small panel the size of a calculator. Ginger held her breath. "Nope." Victoria grabbed another almond and popped it in her mouth.

Ginger bit her thumb nail counting each nibble Victoria took. She was up to four. How could she be getting her snack fix at a time like this?

"What about Dustin's birthday?" Even without binoculars, Ginger could see

Phoebe slithering across the floor in hunter mode. Hunched down, the cat took six or eight steps and then stopped, ready to pounce. Her tail sliced the air like a switchblade.

Victoria flipped through the book. "Hmm. He's got his ex-wife's birthday on his list of dates to remember."

"Tiffany Rose?"

"No, that's his second ex-wife."

"How many ex-wives does he have?"

"Two that I know of. He's got Gloria's birthday on here. That's his first wife. I'll try that date." Victoria pressed the buttons on the panel. A whirring sound signaled the start of a motor. "What do you know." Victoria stepped out of the booth. "Enjoy your magic-carpet ride."

"Thank you." The door closed, and Ginger pushed the number one on a larger panel on the elevator wall.

Her heart slammed against her rib cage. She pressed her hand hard against the glass. The floors slipped by.

Please, God, don't let my cat kill that squirrel.

EIGHT

The doors of the glass elevator slid open, and Ginger stepped out. None of the cleaning crew even lifted their heads in her direction. She raced toward the reptile catcher display, scanning the shelves and the railing above. No sign of cat or squirrel.

A flash of gray by a doorway caught her peripheral vision. A woman with her back to Ginger vacuumed about ten yards from where Phoebe had disappeared. Ginger scampered across the carpet and tapped the woman on the shoulder.

The woman jumped. Arms flew up. She whirled around and pulled her ear buds out. She clicked off her vacuum. "Goodness, you near give me a heart attack."

"I'm sorry." Ginger read the name on the woman's light blue smock. "Cheryl, can you tell me where this hallway leads?"

"To the other convention hall." Cheryl bent back, causing bones to crack somewhere in her body.

"Where the Squirrel Lovers' convention is?"

"Yep." The woman massaged her lower back and tilted her neck side to side. "Those squirrel lovers, they are something else, aren't they? Nice folks."

Any other time Ginger would have delighted in small talk about furry tree dwellers and the people who loved them, but right now the clock was ticking. "Is it open?"

"Oh sure, sure. I always unlock the doors first thing so the crew can move on through." The cleaning lady studied Ginger. "Who are you?"

My name is not important, only my mission. She cupped the woman's shoulder. "Thank you." Before the cleaning woman had a chance to become suspicious, Ginger bolted for the dark hallway. She felt along the rough-textured wall, moving toward the faint light that must be the other convention floor.

Ginger blinked and waited for her eyes to adjust to the brightness of the convention floor. Looked like the squirrel lovers had called it a night too. A stage with a podium occupied one corner of the floor. A sign reminded squirrel lovers that the keynote speaker, Martha Hillstrong, squirrel expert and founder of the club, would be speaking tomorrow. Clear plastic tubes circled much of the convention hall. It took her a moment to figure out that the scratching noises were squirrels running through the tubes.

Ginger slowed her pace through the convention hall. "Here, kitty, kitty, kitty." The other squirrels might have distracted Phoebe from her intended target. She walked past a table that displayed everything squirrel: squirrel bookmarks, stuffed squirrels, squirrel identification books.

Ginger turned, surveying every dark and shadowed space. Listening. Memories of the screams she heard in the night when Phoebe caught a rabbit caused her shoulders to bunch up to her ears. "Here, kitty." Her voice faltered.

She studied the tubes. The squirrels were only faint impressions moving through the murky plastic. When it came to hunting, Phoebe was a lot like Ginger at a store sale, very focused. The cat probably hadn't gotten distracted by the other squirrels.

From a far corner of the convention floor, she heard a yowl that chilled her. Phoebe was afraid of something. "Phoebe, Phoebe. I'm here." Ginger ran in the direction of the cat's yowl.

Phoebe stared down from a high window.

"Come on down," Ginger pleaded. No dead squirrel in Phoebe's mouth. That was a good sign. "Come on, baby. Come on down."

Phoebe lifted her furry chin and disappeared through the window. The window faced the backside of the Little Italy and Wind-Up Hotels, by the lake. Ginger ran to the door nearest to the window where Phoebe had escaped. Locked. That meant she would have to get a cleaning person willing to open it for her.

She raced back through the connecting hallway to track down Cheryl.

Detective Cynthia Mallory's mouth watered as she stood in front of door number 515 of the Wind-Up Hotel. "Can you please not wave that thing under my nose?"

The other Cindy, Cindy Jacobson, drew the jelly doughnut toward her chest. "They were free down in the hotel lobby." She took a bite. "I could have grabbed you one."

Cynthia Mallory stared with longing at the sugar on the younger detective's cheek. "That's not the point. You know I'm doing Atkins. You're like Jack Sprat's mean sister."

The boxy blazer Cindy Jacobson wore didn't hide that she was the poster child for skinny minnies. "Who's Jack Sprat?"

"Nursery-rhyme character." Even before she had decided to do Atkins, food had been a source of tension between them. Jacobson ate constantly and never gained a pound. Depending on the hour, their shift usually involved one trip through a fast-food drive-thru and a stop at a bakery or coffee shop. Mallory carried a Ziploc baggie with deli ham. "Skinny Jack Sprat and his fat wife."

Jacobson's eyes were uncomprehending. "Sorry, never heard of the guy. My parents had me reading Shakespeare by the time I was seven."

Mallory thought about the complete collection of *The Andy Griffith Show* on DVD she had at home. Just one more way that she and Jacobson were polar opposites. In college, she had thought it was an accomplishment to get through a Shakespeare class without jumping off a building.

Being partners with someone who never had a bad hair day and could eat anything caused her own insecurities to rise to the surface. But she could live with it. Jacobson was the best partner Mallory had ever had in her thirty years as a cop.

"Never mind." Mallory's fist hovered over the door. "I dream about cake and fudge at night. I get arrhythmia when I go past a candy shop. Could you please just not eat sugar in front of me?"

Jacobson wiped the red jelly off her mouth and held up the doughnut. "No problem, but may I finish this?"

Mallory nodded. Again, she lifted her hand to knock on the door. "This is a first for us, huh? A missing squirrel."

"We did have the one lady who lost her champion poodle." Jacobson took a luscious bite of the doughnut and chewed for a moment. "You remember that?" She licked the sugar off her lips.

Detective Mallory's mouth watered. Oh the torment. She leaned a little closer to her partner. The aroma of doughnut was intoxicating. "Squirrel abduction. You ever feel like you've been sucked into some alternative universe that is being run by cartoons?"

Cindy Jacobson shrugged. "It's a job."

"I forgot to check the roster. Was Elmer Fudd on patrol tonight?"

Jacobson laughed. "Could be worse. Could be dealing with all the messy crime down in Vegas. We just get the weird stuff here."

"Into every life a little weirdness must fall," Mallory said.

"Let's see if we can get to the bottom of this before my shift is over. The Wind-Up has had a busy day. Spurgen took a jewelry theft report earlier. How hard can it be to find a squirrel? My money is on the little critter having escaped and this all being nothing."

"I say it was Colonel Ketchup in the library with a toaster oven."

"Miss Chartreuse in the sauna with a towel." Mallory drew her hand back from the door. She closed her eyes.

"What are you thinking?"

Again, she appreciated that Jacobson could almost read her thoughts. "I know this is funny to us. But the man cared about the squirrel enough to phone it in. For his sake, we need to take this seriously."

Jacobson nodded.

Mallory rapped hard on the door of 515. A man with fuzzy hair and whitish skin opened the door. The rims of his eyes were red. Mallory put him in his midfifties. Not terribly muscular. Little guy. "Mr. Simpson? You phoned in a report about a missing squirrel?"

"A kidnapped squirrel." Simpson nodded, causing the excess skin on his face to shake.

Mallory held out a hand. "I'm Detective Mallory. This is my partner, Detective Jacobson." She noted that Simpson had no calluses on his hand. Probably worked in an office. Unless, of course, a performing squirrel provided enough income to live on.

The door swung open wider to reveal a woman hunched over the table by the window. The bright floral-print muumuu cascaded down her large body in an explosion of color. Long, lackluster hair framed a round face. Plastic-frame glasses nearly consumed a small nose.

"This is Martha Hillstrong. She's the organizer and keynote speaker for the convention." Simpson sniffled.

Martha rose to her feet and held out a hand to Cynthia Mallory. "I'm here to offer support to Alex . . . Mr. Simpson. Binky meant a lot to all the squirrel lovers."

Mallory took note of the I heart Squirrels button pinned to Martha's chest. She cleared her throat. "Mr. Simpson, why don't you tell us exactly what happened, and we'll see if we can find that squirrel for you?"

Jacobson took out a notebook and pen. That her partner was willing to be the silent detail-taker while Mallory focused on reading the body language of the person she interviewed was one of the reasons they worked so well together. Mallory nodded and listened to Mr. Simpson's woeful tale. He'd been taking a shower. Binky was exercising in his ball.

"Do you have that exercise ball?"

Simpson shook his head. "It was taken too. It has his name on it."

Martha Hillstrong scooted to the bed where Mr. Simpson slumped. She patted his back while he recalled the details of the kidnapping.

Mallory continued to nod and listen, moving about the room taking mental snapshots. The oddest thing in the room was the excessive amount of ice buckets, all in various stages of melting. She counted five in all. She scanned the bureau for liquor bottles. No signs of Mr. Simpson being a heavy drinker. She'd like to get a peek in his minifridge. Maybe he had a more sedate party of root beer and Sprite planned.

Jacobson coughed and patted her chest. "May I have some water? That doughnut seems to have caught in my throat."

It was nice to have a partner who read your mind. Simpson retrieved a paper cup, walked to the bathroom, and turned on the faucet.

"Do you have some ice to go with it?" Jacobson took two steps toward the bathroom, a move that put her in full view of the refrigerator.

Simpson returned. "I know, it's hot in here."

Sure enough, Simpson ignored the buckets

of ice, opened the fridge, and pulled ice out of the little freezer.

Jacobson thanked him for the water and sipped.

Mallory asked the question of the hour. "So what do you think the motive for taking Binky would be?"

Simpson rested his face in his hands. "Do you know how long it takes to train a squirrel? Binky was valuable. He had lots of bookings."

Martha Hillstrong straightened her back. "Maybe someone who didn't like squirrels took him. There are people like that . . . squirrel haters."

Simpson gripped Martha Hillstrong's flabby arm. "Yes . . . that could be it."

"Thanks for all your information. We'll be in the hotel awhile longer. It would be nice if we could find that ball Binky was rolling around in."

They left just as Martha wrapped an arm around Mr. Simpson.

Mallory and Jacobson walked silently down the hallway and entered the elevator. Once the doors closed, Jacobson spoke. "There was more ice in the fridge, only it was red. No soft drinks."

"Like made out of Kool-Aid or something?"

Jacobson nodded. "The guy seemed genuinely upset about the loss. I just noted that all that ice seemed like an irregularity."

"Probably nothing," said Mallory.

"Probably." Jacobson touched her stomach. "I don't know about you, but that $3.99 buffet looked pretty tempting."

"Jacobson." Mallory protested.

"I'm sure they have a side of beef for you."

Cheryl the cleaning lady jingled the keys in her hand. "I'm only doing this because I'm a cat person."

"Thank you." Ginger struggled to get a deep breath. Time was of the essence. With Phoebe outside, she might never find her. Or worse, her cat would wander out into the street and be hit.

"Of course, those two-for-one coupons at the Steak House were a nice bonus." Cheryl winked.

Never underestimate the power of a discount to open doors and dispel suspicion. "You're so welcome."

The cleaning lady sorted through her keys. "Hate to see anything bad happen to that squirrel either." She pushed the door open. "There you go. I'll be locking this behind you, so you won't be able to come back in this way. These convention halls are supposed to be secure."

Darkness and desert-night cold greeted Ginger. Water lapped against the shore. Anchored boats banged against one another. Her feet pounded along the boardwalk. She ran toward the backside of the Little Italy Hotel.

Light spilled from a downstairs room as did the aroma of Italian spices. The clinking of silverware and quiet chatter floated out from a covered terrace. Ginger exhaled. Up ahead on the boardwalk, Phoebe sat beneath a street lamp grooming herself.

"Phoebe." She trotted across the wooden sidewalk. "Phoebe, come back here."

Phoebe lifted her behind and swished her tail. Then she scampered into darkness out onto the pier. Gondola boats were tied and lined up along the dock in strings of three and four. The farther Ginger ran down the pier, the darker it got. Phoebe's white paws showed up in the dim light. The cat was leaping from boat to boat.

"What I do for you." Ginger kicked off her flip-flops and stepped into the first wobbling boat.

One gondola banged against another and she nearly sailed headfirst into the water. Her fingers got stuck between two boats rocking together, a Ginger sandwich. She pulled her fingers free and shook out the pain. Four boats away, Phoebe posed at the front edge of one of the boats, head tilted, tail tucked under.

"Here, kitty. Come to Mama."

The cat didn't so much as flinch.

"Tell me you haven't killed that squirrel. Any squirrel but that one."

Ginger crawled into Phoebe's craft. The cat leaped to the bottom of the boat. Ginger gathered Phoebe into her arms. Phoebe purred against her chest. "I thought I was going to lose you."

Across the water several boats away, she saw a circle of light. Somebody was in one of the boats. Holding Phoebe, Ginger scrambled back onto the dock and ran until she was parallel to the string of boats. In a gondola, the farthest vessel from shore, a man bent over as if staring at something.

"Yo, who's out there? What are you doing?" *Yo?* Where did that come from? She sounded like a sailor or one of those hip-hop fellas.

A familiar voice floated across the water. "Is that you?"

"Earl, Earl, I am so glad I found you. I have been looking for you all night." Ginger walked to the edge of the dock and leaned over to see better. Earl's light bobbed up and down. "What are you doing out here?"

Water lapped against the shore. Laughter, soft and distant, rose up from the restaurant. On the other side of the hotels, cars rolled over concrete.

A shiver trickled down Ginger's back. "Earl?" At the same moment she spoke, Phoebe squirmed free, scratching Ginger's hand in the process. Ginger recoiled from the sting of broken skin and the warm seep of blood. "Earl, what is it?" Phoebe scampered up the pier, but Ginger remained frozen by some unnamed fear.

Earl stood up. The flashlight cast a circle of light on the boat next to the one he stood in. Ginger focused on the sound of her own exhale and inhale until it seemed to match the rhythm of the water licking the shore. *Breathe in. Breathe out.*

Earl's voice floated across the water. "You might want to go inside and get security." He turned, directing the light toward the front of the boat. "There's a man in a bear costume, and as far as I can tell he's not breathing."

NINE

The scent of roses greeted Kindra as she stepped out onto the rooftop garden of the Little Italy Hotel. She spotted the trellis with vines around it and the bench beneath, just as Xabier had described. Soft solar lights were dispersed between the rose-bushes and other greenery. A few couples wandered around. She was the only person by herself.

Kindra checked her watch. Already eleven. After burying her face appreciatively in a rosebush, she wandered over to the bench and sat down. A fountain, hidden by plants, trickled and bubbled behind her.

She retied the sleeves of the jeweled cardigan she had over her shoulders, fluffed the skirt of her black dress, and sorted through the coupons in her purse before she dared herself a look at her watch. Okay, so he was five minutes late. *Not a good sign.* She was willing to forgive his ignoring her in the underground outlet mall, and she was open to hearing an explanation as to why he was running from men with guns. But being late for a date? A girl had to draw the line somewhere. That shifted him from the full-price-new-on-the-floor rack to the ten-percent-off section.

Kindra untied her sweater and slipped into it to stave off the night chill. She crossed her arms and stared at the sky. *I am not going to be upset. I am not going to feel rejected.*

She hadn't made a huge emotional investment in this guy. It was no big deal. Her throat tightened. She counted stars. She was up to fifty before she allowed herself a glance at the entrance. A dark head emerged. Kindra stood up. Another head, a woman's, appeared. A couple stood at the entrance holding hands, leaning into each other. Kindra slumped back down on the bench.

Down below, sirens sounded. Couples ran to the brick fence that served as a railing around the garden. Kindra rose from the bench and peered over the edge of the Little Italy rooftop. About twenty people, some of them policemen, scampered like ants who had found a crumb. The location of the morsel seemed to be out in one of the gondola boats where the cluster of people grew. All those police. What on earth could have happened?

Dragging her silk scarf on the ground, she wandered back toward the garden entrance half hoping that Xabier would emerge smiling.

Okay, so she was sad about him not showing up and upset about being ignored in the outlet mall. This guy was not worth her time. Kindra raced down the stairs to find the other members of the BHN for wisdom, consolation, and hugs.

Detective Mallory placed her hands on her hips and surveyed the crime scene. In a few short hours, they'd gone from jewelry theft, to squirrel abduction, to a dead body in a bear suit. The Wind-Up had officially become Calamity's hot bed of illegal activity.

Crime-scene people had set up floodlights along the boardwalk and sectioned off the area with tape. They'd have to work through the night.

Her first observation was that four out of five members of the forensics team were overweight. She patted her own ever-expanding hips. No more muffins and doughnuts in the break room. Wait a minute. Was she becoming some kind of diet

Nazi, pushing her beliefs about nutrition on everyone else, demanding that they eat just like her?

One of the forensics guys crawled out of the boat, hiking up his refrigerator repairman pants and nearly falling onto the pier. He wobbled to his feet, breathing heavily from his effort. Nope, she wasn't a food tyrant. A veggie tray would be good for all of them.

She walked a few paces down the pier. Her second thought was that killing someone in a boat was a lot of work. Let alone in a bear suit. Forensics always trumped speculation, but she suspected the victim had been killed elsewhere and moved, but not too far from here. A guy in a bear suit was pretty heavy.

She assessed the area surrounding the crime scene. Beyond the Little Italy Hotel was a park with a golf course on the other side of it. On the Wind-Up side was a dock for larger boats and an unused atrium with dusty windows.

Maybe the perpetrator had intended to take the boat out in the lake and dump the bear. The part of the pier where the bear had been found was dark enough to allow the suspect to go undetected if he were quiet. All guesses at this point.

Detective Cindy Jacobson conversed with one of the crime-scene crew, a recent female hire named Somebody Smith. Her first name started with a *Y.* Jacobson leaned toward Y. Smith, heads close together, speaking in whispered tones. Jacobson broke the circle of privacy and glanced in Mallory's direction. Y. Smith handed her an evidence bag. Jacobson strode over to Mallory.

"What do you have?"

The younger detective sighed. "They can't ID the body until they get the bear head off. It's latched on. We detained the guy who found the bear." She checked her notebook. "An Earl Salinski and his wife are waiting inside if you want to question them."

Mallory nodded. "It's a place to start. Guess we can move forward when we get the ID. Anything else?"

"There's a Gloria Clydell. She was out here for a meeting with her ex-husband. She says her son was hired to wear the bear costume, some sort of PR thing. She's pretty shook up."

Mallory rubbed her temples. What she really wanted right now was five chocolate chip cookies and a glass of milk and to watch *The Andy Griffith Show.* "Lucky for us we were here, huh?" Oh well. If she had wanted regular hours, she should have become a bank teller.

Jacobson placed a hand on a slender hip. "The Wind-Up is having a busy night."

"Let me know as soon as you get a name on the victim. What's the name of Gloria Clydell's son?"

Jacobson glanced at her notes. "Xabier Knight."

"Why the different last name from his mom?"

Jacobson shrugged. "Remarriage, most likely."

"I guess I'll start with the couple that found the body. What did you say their names were?"

"Ginger and Earl Salinski from Three Horses, Montana. If you want to handle the interview yourself, I can work on getting an ID and start the list of people to question."

Mallory turned to go, but felt the press of Jacobson's stare on her back. "Is there something else?"

Jacobson held up the evidence bag the Smith woman had handed her. "This was found beside the body."

Mallory leaned closer to see what was in it. A ball of fur. "A rat?"

"A squirrel. Forensics is wondering if we

should tag it as evidence or as a second victim."

In her nearly thirty years of police work, Mallory didn't recall reading or hearing about a circumstance like this. The issue had never come up in any of the workshops she had attended. They were off the map on this one. "Let's get an ID on both the bodies and then I'll figure it out from there."

"Is it possible to tell one squirrel from another?"

Way off the map on this one. "We got a hotel full of squirrel lovers. Ask one of them that question." She threw her arms up. "If it is The Squirrel, one of the more sensitive members of the squad will have to inform Mr. Simpson. I don't want this turned into a joke."

Earl hadn't said a word to Ginger since they had been escorted to the conference room by a police officer. She wasn't feeling terribly chatty anyway. A tingling numbness had settled into her bones. That illogical notion that what she was going through was not real kept invading her thoughts.

This conference room was the most generic room she had ever been in. Large conference table, beige office chairs, beige carpet, and beige walls. Not even a picture on the wall.

Earl squeezed her hand and then pulled away, crossing his arms over his chest. "Things sure haven't gone like I thought they would."

Ginger nodded. She didn't want to think about what had just happened. The bear costume looked like the one Xabier had worn. The thought of someone that young dying made it hard for her to breathe.

How much longer did they have to wait? After staring at the floor and then at the ceiling, which was also beige, she opened her purse, looking for something to do, anything to keep her mind from returning to the same horrible thoughts.

She pulled her coupons out of their book and spread them out like they were cards. She organized them by the amount of discount they offered. Then she arranged them by category: food, clothing, entertainment. Reading the coupons, thinking about how much money she would save, calmed her down. If she didn't have her coupons, she'd be counting ceiling tiles. She just needed to do something.

She slapped down a coupon for fifty cents off butter substitute. Maybe next she could arrange her coupons by most dominant color. "I hope the police come soon."

Earl answered with a grunt. She brushed her fingers over his razor-stubbled cheek. He hadn't said anything about losing the booth. He must have found out when he was on the floor. Their setbacks seemed small in the face of this terrible thing.

The door burst open. Earl jerked his head up and rubbed his eyes. A woman dressed in a gray suit nodded at them.

"Earl and Ginger Salinski? I'm sorry to have kept you waiting." The woman massaged her forehead. "I'm Detective Mallory."

She sat down at the conference table opposite them, unbuttoning her blazer, which was tight through the arms and shoulders. She was fiftyish with auburn hair. Ginger recognized the shade as Spicy Red #114. Her own hair had been that color once. "I know it's late and you're probably tired. I would like to ask you a few questions if I could."

Both Earl and Ginger nodded.

"Mr. Salinski, can you describe for me how you found the body?"

Earl straightened in his chair and folded his hands on the table. "I heard noise out on the pier. It was dark." He pulled one of the Pepper Lights out of his jacket. "So I used my flashlight to go down there."

"That's awful brave of you, Mr. Salinski."

Ginger gathered her coupons into a pile. She didn't like the way Detective Mallory's tone implied that Earl was guilty of something.

"The other end of the light is self-defense spray. I figured if it was anything bad, I could deal with it." He rolled the Pepper Light across the table to Mallory. "The ends have different textures, so you won't go to turn on the light and accidentally spray someone."

Mallory rubbed her finger over the hard-plastic pepper-spray nozzle. "I haven't seen one of these before."

"I invented it." Earl beamed. "There are others on the market but none as good as mine."

Ginger cringed. Earl was so proud of his invention. They had to find a way to get it to customers.

Mallory nodded and rolled the light back to him. "And what were you doing out on the pier at night?"

"I just pulled into town fifteen minutes earlier. The guy at the desk said I wasn't registered, but he gave me a complimentary pass." He touched the badge he had around his neck. "I couldn't find my wife to find out what was going on, so I stepped out back for some air."

Nerves in Ginger's neck pinched. She did a double take at her husband. Mallory lifted her head from her notes. Why had Earl lied about the time he got into town? She had seen him hours earlier on the convention floor. He had a badge and everything.

"Mrs. Salinski, is something wrong?"

"No, no, I'm just fine . . . considering."

Mallory laced her fingers together on the table. "Yes, considering. Can you tell me what you were doing out there, Mrs. Salinski?"

"I was out there looking for my —" Ginger shot straight up from her chair.

"Ginger, sit down," Earl said.

Phoebe. She needed to find Phoebe. Ginger rubbed the strap on her travel purse. With all the hoopla, she'd forgotten that her cat had run off again.

"Everything all right, Mrs. Salinski?"

"Yes, I just . . ." She plunked down into the chair. "Is this going to take much longer?"

"I have a few more questions. Did you see or hear anything unusual before your husband found the man in the bear costume?"

Ginger shook her head. Her thoughts tumbled over one another like a toddler's building blocks. The bear costume had looked like Xabier's. *What if . . .* "Is there anyone else who wore a bear costume besides Xabier Knight?"

"We don't have an ID on the body yet." Mallory studied Earl and then Ginger.

Ginger touched her collar and then broke eye contact. Her guilty conscious was getting the better of her. The detective looked at them like they were somehow involved.

Mallory leaned back in her chair, pushing her palms against the rim of the table. "You folks look tired. Why don't you get some sleep?" Her gaze did not waver.

Ginger pushed her chair away from the table. The detective made her feel like she was specimen under a microscope. "I have things to do."

Mallory traced over something she had written. "You are staying around for a while, aren't you?"

There was that look again from the detective, a slight narrowing of her eyes. She must have been able to tell that Earl was lying. She couldn't change that, and it didn't feel right to say anything to Mallory until she talked to Earl. All she could do was tell the truth from here on out. "We booked the room through the end of the convention on Sunday."

Earl rolled the Pepper Light back to Mallory. "You can keep that if you like."

How could Earl be thinking about marketing his invention at a time like this? Was he so focused on his goal that what had happened here tonight didn't matter to him? Maybe he had lied because he thought an investigation would interfere with finding a distributor for his invention. Had it really come to that? It just didn't seem like Earl, but . . .

Mallory pushed her chair back and rose to her feet. Ginger and Earl stood at the same time. Mallory offered a backward glance before leaving and closing the door behind her.

"She thinks we had something to do with the murder."

"You were acting kind of nervous, Ginger," Earl said.

"Me?" She touched the palm to her chest. "Here's the key to our room. I don't know where the girls are. You might have to fight someone for a bed."

"Why don't you come up with me? It's been a long day for all of us." He touched her hand just above the elbow.

Involuntarily, she pulled away. Why had she done that? This was her husband, her Earl. Of course he wasn't a murderer. She knew his character. Still, he had lied about when he had gotten into town.

Ginger took another step back. "I need to find Phoebe. I don't like the thought of her being out there in the cold."

Earl slipped the key in the hole and pushed the door of room 517 open. Both beds were occupied, one with Arleta and one with Suzanne. No sign of Kindra. He knew from his last camping trip with the grandkids that he was too old to sleep on the floor. Maybe the hotel had a spare room.

When he stepped into the hallway, a woman in a dress that looked like a paint store had exploded on it slipped out of room 519. She dabbed her eyes with a Kleenex.

"Ma'am, are you all right?"

"Haven't you heard the news?" She tore the Kleenex in half and continued to dab.

"Oh, about the body?" What other news could she be referring to?

A new crop of tears sprouted in her eyes. "Yes, they think it might be Binky." She shook her head and whispered, "I just feel so guilty."

Binky? What kind of cruel parent would name their kid Binky?

"I can't sleep." The woman wiped the rims of her eyes. "I'm going to go downstairs to wait for any news."

"I'm headed downstairs to see if they have another room available. I would be glad to walk with you."

"That's so nice of you to offer. What is your name?"

"Earl Salinski."

She held out a hand. "I'm Martha Hillstrong. I am the founder and president of the Squirrel Lovers Club."

Hmm. Maybe Binky wasn't human.

"Thanks for the offer, but Mr. Simpson in 515 said he would go down with me." Her voice cracked. "Binky was his squirrel."

Martha dug in her pocket and produced a key. "I know they don't have any more rooms. With two conventions, the hotel is full." She placed a key in his hand. "You've been kind to me. Why don't you take my room? I won't need it for a while."

"Thank you. I just need a couple hours' shut eye and I'll be back on my game," he murmured.

A man with fuzzy hair opened the door to 515 and nodded in Martha's direction.

Detective Mallory stared at the piece of salami and celery sticks in her Ziploc baggies. Living with a growling stomach appealed to her more than downing this snack.

It was nearly two in the morning. She collapsed onto a couch in the lobby. A college-age blonde in a black dress slept on the couch opposite her. The young woman used her pink cardigan as a blanket.

Jacobson was supposed to meet her here with an update. Something must have delayed her. Mallory closed her eyes. Her muscles relaxed. Her thoughts drifted. Cartons of chocolate chip mint ice cream floated around her. Bowls of it with chocolate sauce were set in front of her.

She sensed that someone was staring at her.

Jacobson had slipped noiselessly into the chair kitty-corner from her. Like part of a Vegas magic act, she had just suddenly appeared.

"What have you got for me?"

"Sorry for taking so long to get here. We had some setbacks" — Jacobson cleared her throat — "but we have an ID on the body."

"The suit belonged to a Xabier Knight, right?"

The blonde on the opposite couch stirred, rolling over on her side but not waking.

"Correct. It was his costume, but it wasn't Xabier who was in the suit. The victim is a Dustin Clydell; he owns the Wind-Up. Dustin's first wife, Gloria, identified the body. We have been unable to locate Xabier Knight."

"Let me do the math. Xabier, who is missing, has a different last name than his parents, one of whom is dead."

Jacobson nodded.

The blonde stirred again, pulling her sweater toward her chin.

"Does the ex-Mrs. Clydell know where he is?"

Jacobson shook her head. "She's pretty shook up. Plus, she's weak from a chronic illness. I didn't want to push her."

For lack of something better to do, Mallory pulled a celery stick out of her baggie. "You said something about setbacks?"

"Two things. I sent a uniformed officer up to tape off Dustin's apartment, and it had been ransacked. Two, we took the bear suit off the victim. Forensics bagged it. Somewhere in transport, someone lifted it."

Mallory bit into her celery stick. "Have a uniformed officer watch the apartment. I'll get the crime-scene people up there when they're done outside." She rubbed her temples. What sort of comment do you make about a stolen bear suit? "Is there anything else?"

"I've started to put together a list of people we need to question. Gloria Clydell and Xabier when we find him. Dustin had another ex-wife, Elise Rosemond, a.k.a. Tiffany Rose, chorus-line dancer."

Mallory rose to her feet. "Good, we got an ID and a place to start. Let's all go home and get a couple hours' sleep."

Jacobson checked her notebook. "You might want to question Earl and Ginger Salinski again. We have a witness who says Ginger threatened Dustin, something about a dispute over a spot on the conference floor."

Cynthia Mallory cupped Jacobson's shoulder. "Good work. Let's get a little sleep." She stumbled toward the entrance but turned. "I totally forgot to ask. What does the prelim exam suggest the cause of death is?"

Color rose up in Jacobson's cheeks. "I didn't tell you because I didn't quite know how to put it. Of course, we'll know for sure after full autopsy."

"Cause of death?"

"They found . . . fur in his mouth."

Mallory connected the forensics dots. "Death by squirrel. You, ah . . . don't see that every day." She *had* been sucked into an alternate universe. *Just keep it as official as possible.* "Suffocation?" Did she want to hear this?

127

Jacobson nodded. "We do have bruising on the neck and some petechial hemorrhaging, so the exact sequence of events has to be worked out." Jacobson threw her arms up. "Into every life, a little weirdness must fall."

Mallory stared across the expanse of checkerboard floor. How angry did you have to be to use a squirrel as a weapon?

TEN

Ginger slumped down on a bench beside the lake. She managed one more lackluster cry for Phoebe. Stars twinkled in the night sky, and a soothing breeze came off the water. Heaviness seeped into her muscles. She bent forward, resting her elbows on her knees. Time to give up.

Part of the dock area was still sectioned off with police tape. Traffic noises from the other side of the street increased in volume, and people bustled by on the boardwalk surrounding the lake. She could see the lights of the park and golf course that bordered the lake on the far side of the Little Italy Hotel.

The Calamity strip stirred to life when most people were long past ready for bed. She closed her eyes. *I will not think about Phoebe dodging speeding cars.* What was God doing? Now even that stupid cat had been taken from her. If they didn't find a distributor and see a return on their investment, they might not be able to make payments on the second mortgage. They could lose the house.

Footsteps sounded on the wooden pier. "Do you mind if I sit by you?" The voice was female, with a warm quality.

Ginger scooted over to make room. She cleared her head of the thoughts of being homeless and turned her attention to the person beside her. The dim light provided a silhouette of a woman with a hat and gloves on. She wore a leather jacket. The hat brim shadowed her face.

The desert night could be chilly, but the winter getup seemed like overkill or a sign that the woman was a couple slices short of a loaf. "Lots of room on this bench." Ginger inched toward the edge.

The woman tilted her head toward the night sky. "Did you come out here to pray too?"

Pray? Why was that always the last thing she thought to do? Ginger rested her forehead in her palm. "My cat ran away. I can't find her."

The woman's voice was filled with compassion. "I am so sorry." She scooted a little closer and patted Ginger's back. "We get attached to our pets."

This lady seemed pretty normal. Ginger regretted her initial judgment. "What a night." She slumped a little on the bench. "I'm sure you've heard the news."

"I heard." The woman paused. Her breathing was raspy and shallow. "I was afraid it was my son Xabier. It was his costume. I just found out it was my ex-husband. I didn't think it was possible to feel relief and unbearable pain at the same time."

Ginger's troubles suddenly paled beside this poor woman's. "I am sorry. I didn't realize you knew the victim. We met Dustin's ex-wife. You're not Tiffany. You must be Gloria, the other wife."

"Dustin has . . . had made his personal life very confusing. How did you know my name?"

"It's a long story. You know Dustin's glass elevator? Your birthday is his code."

A small laugh that was more of a sigh escaped Gloria's lips. She shook her head for a moment. "He never forgot my birthday. Always sent a card, even after we were divorced. It's a blessing to know I was on his mind enough that those were the first numbers he thought of." Gloria sat up a little straighter and turned slightly toward Ginger. "That was sweet of you to share that with me."

A family from the veranda of the Little Italy's restaurant stepped out onto the pier and walked by the two women. The father put his arm around a boy of about eleven while mother and daughter trailed behind. Gloria folded her hands in her lap, then unfolded them and tucked them under her skirt. She bent her head.

The intensity of Gloria's pain was almost tangible in the cool night air. Ginger leaned into Gloria's shoulder. What could she say? A year ago, she had lost her best friend at the hands of a killer. She knew from experience that the last thing she needed to do was offer clichés. "It is peaceful here at night, isn't it? I see why you like it."

Gloria nodded and then tugged at the puckers in her skirt. "My son Xabier has disappeared. No one has seen him since the body was discovered. He hasn't spent much time with Dustin in the last ten years. He wanted to reconnect with his father. I'm afraid that the reality of being with his dad didn't match the fantasy. I tried to warn him." She shuddered. "The last time I talked to Xabier, he was angry."

Ginger focused on the water lapping against the shore, choosing her words carefully. "So many unknowns in your life right now. Sometimes it's easier to deal with bad news than an unknown."

"Yes, true. Waiting to hear if I had a chronic illness was way worse than knowing what I had."

Maybe the winter clothes had something to do with her illness.

"I don't think my son is capable of murder." Gloria hugged herself and leaned forward. "Then again, Dustin has this . . . had this ability to drive people to do things they never thought they would do."

"I noticed that about Tiffany. He makes her angry and yet she's working for him."

"My ex-husband is . . . was poison of the sweetest kind. My guess is that he filled Tiffany's head full of promises and strung her along, worked his charm on her. I warned Xabier that that would happen, but he wanted a father so badly."

"I think I saw some of that sweet poison."

"I don't know if this makes any sense, but Dustin was like a drug. You hate yourself for staying; you leave in a rage. But then you start to crave his sweet talk, so you go back. It took me years and lots of prayer to get him out of my system, to not fall under his spell. It made me nuts that he was one person out in public, Mr. Make Nice, and an entirely different person in private. He could be . . . pretty ugly to Xabier and me when we didn't live up to his fantasy of what a good Christian family should be. The hardest part is that he wasn't so self-absorbed when we were first married. I kept waiting for the old Dustin to come back."

"I think I understand." Ginger shifted on the bench and hugged her travel purse to her chest. "Poor Tiffany is probably in the midst of withdrawal."

"Thank you for listening to me rant." Gloria touched Ginger's arm. "What's your cat's name?"

Considering what Gloria was going through, she was touched that she showed interest in something as silly as a cat. "Phoebe."

"That's a pretty name for a cat."

"Thank you. I met your son when we had that alarm problem. He's a real nice boy. I think he likes my young friend Kindra." It seemed a bit odd that Xabier hadn't acknowledged that Dustin was his father. And why was Xabier's last name different from his parents? She wanted to know, but this was not the time to ask.

"I think he said something about a Kindra." A tremble permeated her words. "I did the best I could with Xabier."

Ginger put her hand over Gloria's gloved fingers. "Parenting is never easy. I have four kids myself. And you did it alone."

In the distance, a boat motor sputtered. A group of people carrying champagne bottles burst out of the back doors of the Wind-Up laughing and chattering. Their revelry faded as they made their way to the street.

"Okay, boys and girls, let's play a game called Calamity PD Profiler." After four hours of sleep and a cheese and onion omelet, Cynthia Mallory's confidence had returned. Alex Simpson had identified the dead squirrel as his Binky a few hours ago. Forensics was going over the last place Dustin was seen alive, the backstage areas of the inventors convention floor. Unfortunately, they had to close down the convention. The investigation was moving along.

She paced Dustin's ransacked apartment and addressed her audience of two, Jacobson and a uniformed officer. "Crime-scene people combed through this place early this morning. There is no reason to believe the murder, and we are calling it murder at this point, took place here." Mallory pulled a piece of gum from her back pocket. Gum was almost like food; at least you got to chew. "Dustin Clydell's apartment is still useful to us for two reasons. Jacobson, what are those two reasons?"

Jacobson stepped forward, embracing the role of eager student. She addressed the officer. "One, the apartment tells us what kind of a person the victim was. Two, the apartment was gone through around the time of the murder, so the murder and the B and E may be connected."

Mallory turned toward the officer, who leaned against the door. Her experience was that the more the uniformed officers felt like they were part of the crime-solving process, the more likely they were to bother pursuing leads they ran into on patrol. "So why would someone do this to the victim's place after he is dead?"

The officer planted his feet shoulder-width apart, straightening his posture, a pose suggesting a military background. "Leftover rage or looking for something."

"Excellent." Mallory took note of the officer's nod and smile. "Let's face it. Stuffing a squirrel down someone's throat is a crime of rage."

Mallory continued to pace, hands linked behind her back, chewing her gum in rhythm to her steps. Desk drawers had been opened and dumped and books pulled off shelves. Towels, silverware, crackers, and boxes of chocolate had been dumped on the counter. Her guess was that it wasn't about rage; the destruction appeared to be a search for something specific and small. Enough books were scattered across the floor to suggest that the ransacker was looking for something flat, a document, maybe.

"No doughnut this morning, Jacobson?" The comment was filler while she paced and tried to think of the next line of questioning.

"I ate it before you came, and I had the $2.99 breakfast buffet. They have really good —"

Mallory held up her hand and chewed her gum with furious intensity. "Don't go there."

"What if I only mention protein products?" Jacobson raised her eyebrows.

A moment of shared humor passed between the two detectives. Mallory rolled her eyes. She was taking this diet thing too seriously. It was making her hostile in weird ways. What kind of person forbids other people to mention certain kinds of food? Mallory circled the room. "Let's go back to our first reason. These are less-than-perfect circumstances, but pretend like everything is in its place. What does this apartment tell us?" Mallory swept her arm across the room. "What kind of a guy designs a hotel around a classic-toys theme?" The officer looked like he was barely out of his twenties. "There are no wrong answers here. Brainstorm with me."

He shifted his weight, ran his hands through his hair. "A guy who is still a kid inside." His words were measured out with careful pauses.

"Good one," Mallory said.

The compliment must have given the officer some confidence because he blurted his next comment. "Maybe he didn't have much of a childhood."

"Yes, exactly." Mallory wandered over to a window that looked out on the convention floor. She checked her watch. It had been almost eight hours since the body was discovered. "Jacobson, what can you tell me about the guy based on the type of books he read?"

Jacobson scanned the bookshelf and then the volumes scattered across the floor. "Big on self-improvement. Turns everything into math."

Mallory cocked her head. "What?"

"Seven secrets of this, five ways to get rich quick. Improve your life in three minutes a day. Six unhealthy habits of mediocre people."

The officer grinned. Jacobson was in good form this morning.

"Got a lot of books about Ted Turner, Donald Trump, Sam Walton, and Bugsy Siegel, the guy who had a vision for Vegas. Empire builders." Jacobson rose to her feet and continued to inventory the shelves. "No fiction. No poetry. No books about art and architecture. The guy wanted to improve every part of his life but one."

Mallory shook her head.

Jacobson stood back. "Lots of how to make your business better, but nothing on how to make your relationships work." The younger detective placed her hands on her slender hips. "My shelves at home are filled with how to make your marriage better and get along with your kids and neighbors books."

The revelation that Jacobson read books on relationship improvement surprised Mallory. Jacobson's life seemed so perfect, two kids and a supportive husband. Mallory had two failed marriages under her belt and a daughter who called on Mother's Day and made a guest appearance at Christmas.

Mallory stalked toward the desk. "Walk around, people; tell me if the room reveals anything else about this guy."

"There's nothing showy about the place." The officer stopped beside a stack of magazines. "The guy is on every regional magazine he can get his face on. Total publicity hound. You would expect his place to be more ostentatious."

Ostentatious? The officer must have read his word-of-the-day calendar this morning. He disappeared into the bedroom.

Mallory turned a half circle. "We surround ourselves with what feels comfortable. Plain and simple felt comfortable to Dustin in private."

"Look what I found." The policeman emerged holding a Bible. "It was in his nightstand drawer."

Jacobson stepped toward him. "Does it look like he read it every night?"

"The pages are crisp. I thought it was interesting because there's a photo of a lady and a kid." He paused on the inside cover. "There's a dedication dated four years ago." He angled the Bible to read. " 'Dear Dustin, hope this helps you find your way home. Love, Gloria.' " The officer handed the Bible to Mallory.

The photograph had to be of Gloria and Xabier. It was old. She'd been told that Xabier Knight was twenty-three. The boy in this picture was maybe ten. "My guess. If he wasn't reading it, he kept it close because it was a gift from his first wife." She flipped through it and saw yellow. A single highlighted verse in 1 Timothy 6. " 'Some people, eager for money, have wandered from the faith and pierced themselves with many griefs.' "

Mallory set the Bible on the desk where disheveled stacks of paper collected. She picked up the Day-Timer. Interestingly, Dustin's last appointment was at ten-thirty at night with someone named Edward Mastive. He had penciled in a Victoria Stone for ten o'clock and the word *speech* for nine-thirty. Dustin's body had been found around eleven. She handed the planner to Jacobson. "We need to find out who Edward Mastive is. He may have been the last one to see Dustin alive. Track down this Victoria Stone too."

Jacobson recorded the names in her notebook.

A single piece of paper tacked to the small bulletin board caught Mallory's eye. Written three times in block letters was the phrase WALT DISNEY DID IT.

Jacobson moved closer. "What did you find?"

Mallory yanked evidence gloves from her back pocket and pulled the tack out of the piece of the paper. She held the paper up and read it out loud. "I guess our crime is solved. We'll just pick up Walt on our way to the station house." She retrieved another piece of paper that had Dustin's signature on it off the floor. The handwriting was the same as the accusation directed at Walt Disney.

Jacobson kneeled on the floor and flipped through a volume on wine. "You got that faraway look in your eyes, boss. What are you thinking?"

Mallory leaned against the desk. Nothing but the uneasiness in her stomach told her the note was significant. It had been her experience that sharing gut feelings did very little to impress other officers, especially male officers. Mallory pushed herself off the desk and waved the note. "I was just wondering if Mickey and Minnie know anything about the murder."

Ginger closed her eyes, focusing on the rhythm of Arleta moving the oar of the gondola boat through the water. Midmorning in Calamity was still cool enough to enjoy being outside.

Suzanne slapped at a mosquito on her shoulder. "Tell me again why we're out here."

Kindra adjusted the tie of her cotton, wide-brimmed hat and slathered sunscreen on her legs. "Because Ginger and I thought this would be more private. No one can overhear us while we're on the water."

"Couldn't we at least hire a gondola driver so Arleta doesn't have to do all the heavy lifting?" Suzanne asked.

Ginger spoke without opening her eyes. "The gondola drivers cost extra. We are way over budget already." She didn't want to open her eyes. Right now, life felt like way too much to bear. The breeze and the rhythmic sound of the oars soothed her.

"I don't mind rowing," Arleta said. "It's good exercise."

The robustness of Arleta's tone cheered Ginger. Not much got the senior member of the BHN down. Today Arleta was dressed in white cowboy boots, white skirt, and turquoise, western-cut jacket. The sequins and grommets on the jacket caught glints of morning sunlight. Ginger opened her eyes. *Time to deal with life.*

"Last night, Kindra overheard that lady detective talking about Earl and me. They say I threatened Dustin. Because Earl was found leaning over the body, they think we are up to some kind of funny business."

"You mean they suspect you of murder?"

Ginger cringed. She couldn't bring herself to think the thought or say the word. But leave it to Suzanne to blurt it out. "Maybe they just want to ask us more questions."

"So did you threaten Dustin?"

Ginger raised her arms. "I guess. He just made me so mad. I didn't kill the guy, and I sure didn't ask Earl to."

Kindra adjusted herself on the narrow wooden seat. "That's all we need to know." She slipped into her gauzy, long-sleeve blouse.

"Kindra, why don't you wear a parka?" Suzanne slapped another mosquito.

"I burn easily, okay?" she snapped back as she buttoned her blouse to the neck.

Arleta stabbed her oar in the water and pushed it through. "Ladies, ladies, we all know that none of us is getting much sleep. Let's not get at each other's throats just because we're tired."

Kindra crossed her arms. "At least you guys had beds to sleep in. Ginger and I caught our ZZZs out in the lobby."

Ginger placed a steadying hand on Kindra's forearm. It was a technique she had learned teaching Sunday school. A soft touch calmed an agitated child. "The couch wasn't uncomfortable." But it was lonely. She hadn't been able to find her husband.

Kindra's spine collapsed, and she sighed. "I'm sorry, guys. I am not mad at you. I am worried about Xabier. He's disappeared. I

144

don't know why he didn't tell me Dustin was his dad." Her shoulders jerked up slightly. "I kind of liked him. We sorta had a date that he missed."

Suzanne wrapped an arm around Kindra. "Kind of, sort of, this sounds serious."

Kindra touched her chest. "I know there has to be more to a relationship than attraction, but when he looks at me something goes off in my heart like Fourth of July sparklers.

The rest of the BHN offered an assortment of "oohs" and "ahhs."

Ginger stared out at the glassy lake. Arleta stopped rowing and took a seat beside Ginger. The rest of the BHN stared at Ginger. Her friends were here to help her, and that was something. She cleared her throat.

"When the police come to question Earl and me, we need to show why we are not guilty. All of us saw different things last night that may or may not be important. Let's put the story together. I'll start with what I know. Dustin missed his big speech a little before ten; he missed his appointment with Little Vicky after that. He died in the bear costume that belonged to Xabier."

Kindra added. "I talked to Xabier when he was still in the bear costume — that was when Arleta and Suzanne were up dropping off Ginger's food. And I am sure it was Xabier; he had his head off. That must have been a little after nine."

Suzanne lifted her water bottle off the bottom of the boat. "Kindra and I saw the bear racing by with two men after him close to eleven. The bear might have been Xabier, or it might have been Dustin."

Kindra undid the top button of her shirt. "It was probably Dustin. I can't believe Xabier would have run by without a wave — or something — when he saw me."

"A little after nine," Ginger said, "I saw the bear run across the convention floor. It could have been Dustin, or it could have been Xabier. That would have been after Kindra saw Xabier and before the bear was chased by those two guys." She shifted on the wooden seat. "Dustin told Tiffany he was about to come into a windfall that would solve all their problems," Ginger said.

Kindra bounced on her wooden seat. "Oh, and . . . that woman told Tiffany that her jewelry and her friend's had been stolen from their rooms."

"We know that Binky the squirrel was found dead with Dustin and that my cat was chasing him." Ginger made eye contact with each member of the BHN, waiting for them to burst out laughing. But they smiled and nodded as though she were sharing a recipe for pineapple upside-down cake.

Suzanne nudged Ginger in the shoulder. "That could be important . . . the squirrel thing."

"At least it's something for Earl and me to bring to the police. Maybe they can find those two men who were chasing the bear. They might be why Xabier has disappeared or Dustin is dead."

"Where is Earl, anyway?"

"I don't know. I haven't seen him since right after the body was found." Her jaw tensed. She pressed her palm against her chest and stared at the water rippling around the boat. "I don't know what has become of my husband."

And that worried her more than anything.

ELEVEN

Mallory and Jacobson waited at the open door of Dustin Clydell's office. A woman with sandy-colored eighties hair stood at the file cabinet, her back to them. She zipped open a drawer, yanked out a file, examined it briefly, and tossed it on the floor.

Mallory slipped into the office. Framed magazine covers and newspaper articles about Dustin covered one wall. Civic awards cluttered glass shelves along with framed pictures of Dustin with assorted celebrities. The opposite wall was a window that looked out on the lake.

Mallory cleared her throat to cover the sound of her growling stomach.

The woman spun around. Except for the poufy hair, her appearance was office chic: cream blouse, slacks, subtle makeup. Hardly the showgirl they had been expecting. Tiffany Rose was probably in her early thirties.

Jacobson flipped open her notebook. "We were told we could find Elise Rosemond here."

The woman raised her hand as if she were in second grade. "That's me, but I have decided to go by Tiffany Rosemond. Sort of a combo of both my names. Sounds more businesslike, don't you think?" She turned toward Mallory. "What can I do for you, sweetie?"

Mallory tried to remember if anyone had ever called her *sweetie* in her life. Nope. Nothing in the database on that one. Not even by one of her ex-husbands. "You are Dustin Clydell's second ex-wife?"

Tiffany raised her hand again and rocked heel to toe. "Guilty. I was married to Dustin for two years."

Saying the word *guilty* was usually not a good idea in the midst of a murder investigation. Mallory tilted her head toward the file cabinet. "So are you running the hotel now?"

"I was practically running it before Dustin died. He was all show and no do." She stepped over the heap of files that had accumulated around her feet, slipping on a stray one. She recovered and sat on a corner of the huge mahogany desk. "I've got a lot to do. The police have closed down the inventors convention, trying to figure out if Dustin was killed there. Huge loss for the hotel." Tiffany leaned forward as though sharing a juicy bit of gossip, but her voice grew even louder. "Money is flying out the window as we speak, but I think I can fix it."

"Did Dustin leave you the hotel?" Jacobson took a step toward Tiffany.

Tiffany crossed her legs, leaned back on her palms, lifted her chin, and shook her hair, supermodel style. "The specifics of Dustin's will haven't been released. He told me a while ago he was going to give me the hotel. I'm the only obvious choice. His first wife wouldn't be interested in this sort of thing, and he didn't get along with his only child." She uncrossed her legs and sat up straight. "You're not from Dustin's lawyer's office, are you?"

Mallory noted the hopeful glee in Tiffany's voice. "We're detectives."

"Oh." Tiffany hiccupped the word. She hopped off the desk and wandered toward a bay window that looked out on the lake. "I guess that means you want to ask me some questions . . . about Dustin's death." She combed her fingers through her hair.

Mallory paced a half circle hoping to cause Tiffany to turn so she could read her reactions while they did the interview. "So why were you working for your ex-husband? You must have had a good relationship with him."

"A good relationship?" Tiffany released a forced laugh. She picked up a mug that had been sitting on the bay window and turned again so Mallory had a clear view of her back.

"All the staff we interviewed seems to have liked him."

"That's because they didn't know him. Dustin could be quite charming at arm's length." Tiffany stepped closer to the window. *She is slipperier than a river trout.* Mallory raised an eyebrow in Jacobson's direction. Jacobson closed in on Tiffany so she would have no choice but to look at Mallory. Tiffany offered both of them a clear view of her profile.

Mallory leaned sideways, nearly touching the wall, to get some level of eye contact with Tiffany. "Did he make you crazy, Tiffany?"

Tiffany turned to one side and then to the other and then slipped out from between the two detectives, so they had a clear view of each other. Mallory did an "after you" gesture, and they both followed Tiffany across the room.

She walked over to the mahogany desk, picked up a sequined purse, and then put it back down.

"You were divorced from him. Why didn't you just leave if he upset you so much?"

"He owed me money as part of our divorce settlement." She sauntered from the file cabinet to the window and then back to the file cabinet. "He promised he would pay what he owed me if I helped him with the hotel."

Mallory stepped closer to Tiffany. "We estimate that he died between ten and eleven last night. His last official appointment was with someone named Edward Mastive. Do you know who that is?"

Tiffany shook her head.

Jacobson flipped through her notebook. "Can you tell us where you were between nine and midnight?"

"I was sleeping, and no one was with me. I had to get up early to run the front desk." She drifted across the room and fingered the glittery purse again.

"You still haven't told us why you kept working for him," Jacobson said.

"You know, I have a lot to get done here." She returned to the file cabinet. Kneeling, she gathered a stack of files and dumped them on the desk, and then she picked up the purse.

Mallory mentally reshuffled her interrogation technique cards. Trying to corner Tiffany was not working. She softened her tone. "We have all been stupid when it comes to men. I'm the president of that club."

For the first time since they had entered the office, Tiffany made eye contact with Mallory. She tossed the purse back on the desk. "Dustin . . . had a way of . . . a way of . . ." She slammed the heel of her hand against her forehead. "I'm not a stupid woman. Please don't think that."

"I'd never think that." Her comment wasn't to win Tiffany over. She had some firsthand experience with being a smart woman who made poor choices in men.

Tiffany picked up one of the files and slammed it back down on the desk. "What I don't understand is that when I looked through the financial records . . . Dustin said he could pay me once the hotel was back on its feet." She crossed her arms and spoke through tight teeth. "I took a few accounting classes at the junior college. This hotel was actually making a profit. Why did he lie to me, and where *was* all the money going?"

Mallory shifted her weight. This was news.

All the employees they had talked to so far were under the impression that the hotel was going under. Where was the money going? That Dustin had a gambling problem was the obvious conclusion, but somehow that didn't fit what they knew about the late Mr. Clydell. Dustin liked to gamble, but not at slot machines. Maybe he had made some sort of bad investment as an aspiring empire builder.

"He kept saying he needed more money. He sure wasn't putting any of his money back into the hotel. This place needs some serious maintenance." Her hand brushed over the purse.

Jacobson asked, "Is there something in that purse you want to tell us about?"

Tiffany's head jerked up. Her face paled. "No, I —"

Good call, Jacobson. "Tiffany?" Mallory made her request as gently as possible.

Tiffany dragged the purse across the desk and unzipped it. "The afternoon before he died, Dustin slipped me a note." She pulled a piece of paper out of her purse and handed it to Mallory. She curled her fingers into fists and shook her head. "Look at me. I'm protecting him even after he's dead."

The note was short, written in the same

block letters as the accusation against Walt Disney.

Leesy, I have struck the deal of a lifetime. Our money problems are over.

Dustin

"Leesy was his pet name for me." Tiffany rubbed her neck with an open palm. "I guess it doesn't matter now. He's dead, right?" She stared at the ceiling, lips pressed together. "I think Dustin was stealing jewelry from the guests. I think the deal he was talking about was with a fence or something." Her words came out in a sudden burst.

"Have the thefts stopped since his death?"

Tiffany nodded. "I reported the thefts. But I should have told someone the minute I suspected Dustin. I don't know why I felt like I had to protect him."

Mallory knew why. Dustin had messed with her mind so much, it would be a long time before she would be able to think straight. She pulled the "Walt Disney did it" note, still in the evidence bag, out of her blazer pocket. "Do you know what this means?"

Jacobson jerked slightly, something Mallory had never seen her do. Did her partner

155

not approve of her showing the Walt Disney note?

Tiffany shook her head. "Dustin was working on his uncle's dairy farm from the time he was five years old. He never got to play much. That's why he liked classic toys. I'm sure he liked Disney stuff for the same reason."

Mallory waved Dustin's note to Tiffany. "We'd like to keep this if that's okay with you."

Tiffany nodded. "All this will be worthwhile once I get the hotel."

The two detectives excused themselves and slipped out of the office. Mallory caught a glimpse of Tiffany resting her face in her hands through a slit in the open door. Jacobson and Mallory walked down the long hallway. Mallory thought the *swish-swish* of her thighs brushing against each other was oppressive in the silence. Her waistband felt even tighter than usual. Maybe she should start working out more.

Mallory waited until the elevator doors closed before speaking. "So Dustin told Tiffany she was going to get the hotel. Material gain is always at the top of the list for motive. But I think I see an even stronger motive."

"Which is?"

"He messed with her mind. Speaking from experience, you can only take so much of that before you either get out or retaliate. I got out; maybe Tiffany made the other choice."

"I'll take your word for it." Jacobson leaned against the brass railing in the elevator. "When I was working patrol, we'd get called in on domestic violence cases. Within ten minutes of our arrival, some of those women were already taking the jerk back. It never made sense to me."

"Dustin didn't use his fist. He was more subtle than that. You got a woman who feels slighted and ripped off, and yet she stays and works for him and protects him from being suspected of theft. Would you like yourself very much if you were that weak?"

"Guess not."

"The rage smolders for a long time, and then there's a sudden outburst." Mallory pushed the number one on the elevator panel.

"Outburst? You mean like killing him?"

Mallory nodded. The doors slid open. "In the meantime, let's keep an open mind. We need to track down the Salinskis for further questioning. I had a feeling when I interviewed them they were hiding something."

TWELVE

Ginger slumped behind the screen of her laptop when the two lady detectives walked by the window of the coffee shop. The heavier one, the one whose name started with an *M,* turned her back toward the window facing the European chocolate outlet store. Belgian chocolate was still on sale.

Kindra glanced at the window and then back at Ginger. "Maybe you should just go talk to them."

Ginger clicked the keys on the computer and waited for her e-mail to open. "In the first place, you said they wanted to talk to both Earl and me." Her throat constricted. Where was that man? "In the second place, I need to find some evidence that points to someone other than us." Ginger watched the counter on the unread e-mails line click up to twenty-four, then twenty-five. "In the third place, I haven't checked e-mail or blogged since we left Three Horses. We told readers we'd post about our bargain hunting adventures."

"We haven't had any bargain hunting adventures."

Her counter was up to forty-three. "And in the fourth place, I want to find my cat before they put me in the slammer." Her voice wavered. "Animal control hasn't picked her up. She has to be around here somewhere."

"Finish your blog, and I'll help you look for her." Kindra took a sip of her iced latte. "Then you can mark that off your list."

Ginger recognized one of the e-mail addresses: inspiredinventor@netland.com. "I can check another thing off my list. I know where Earl is." She read the e-mail.

Sweetheart, having trouble finding you. Left messages at the front desk. Called your room. Invention floor closed, but there is still hope. Fiona Truman from the Shopping Channel is still holding auditions for inventors to market on her channel. Need to do some prep. Auditions are tonight in the restaurant at eight. Can you be there? Could use a cheerleader. See you soon. Love, Earl.

That was it? Come and be his cheerleader? His priorities were pretty clear: invention first, wife second. Despite her feelings of rejection, she would be there at eight. They had to get this invention off the ground. Too much was at stake to give up.

"Ginger, is everything okay?" Kindra's voice seemed to come from very far away.

Kindra was probably not the best bargain hunter to share marital strife issues with. Except for a rather large Beanie Baby collection, the kid lived alone. The stuffed animals probably never fought. The worry had built up enough in Ginger that it was going to spill out sooner or later. "Did I have that 'I have left the building' look in my eyes again?"

"You and Elvis." Kindra's freckles and the blond ponytail always made her look younger than twenty. "We've got two missing guys, Earl and Xabier. At least Earl is sending you e-mails."

Ginger's attention drifted to the coffee shop window. Outside the European candy outlet store, Victoria Stone trotted by. She jogged in place and turned toward Ginger. "Looks like our resident celebrity is out exercising."

"What?" Kindra tore the lid off her latte and licked the foam out of the inside.

Ginger pointed through the window and waved at Victoria.

Victoria darted across the corridor and poked her head in the coffee shop. "You should come with me, Ginger." She pumped her arms and twisted side to side. "I'm doing three miles today."

Ginger pointed at her laptop. "I'm right in the middle of something."

"Some other time then. We'll work out together."

"Definitely, before I leave." Ginger wasn't sure if she could keep up with the likes of Victoria. Water aerobics didn't hold a candle to three miles of running.

"Sounds good." Victoria ran in place for a few seconds before trotting back out to the corridor and jogging out of view.

"Could that shade of purple in her workout suit be any louder?" Kindra pressed biscotti crumbs into the table. "She certainly wants to call attention to herself."

"She's a celebrity. That's what they do." Ginger glanced at Earl's e-mail again. Vicky wasn't the only one trying to get attention. The worry she'd been storing bubbled up and spilled over. "All Earl can think about is getting someone to notice his invention. Financially speaking, we need to do that, but it's like he's lost sight of me." She closed the cover on her laptop and leaned a little closer to Kindra. "I think he lied to the police about what time he got into town. I saw him on the convention floor hours before Dustin was found dead."

Kindra's mouth formed an oval. "This is your husband you're talking about."

"I know he didn't kill Dustin. I think he lied because he thought a police investigation would interfere with getting a distributor for his invention. This dream is consuming him."

"He was kind of bossy when we were getting ready for the trip." Kindra shifted slightly in her chair and stared at the customers milling through the shop. "I just figured the change was temporary. We all know he's a good guy."

Ginger flipped the laptop open again. She clicked the Delete button on Earl's e-mail. "I just don't know what to do."

Kindra shook her head. "You need to have a talk with him. Ask him straight out."

"The advice from the peanut gallery is wise." Ginger turned her attention back to her computer. *One thing at a time.* Deleting e-mails she could deal with. "Arleta and Suzanne can answer some of these comment e-mails from the Livin' Large blog. Where are they anyway?"

"Arleta said something about going fishing, and Suzanne's doing some more shopping."

Ginger lifted her fingers off the keyboard. She reread the e-mail on her screen as the warning hairs on the back of her neck came to attention. "This is interesting."

"What's that?" Kindra angled her head to see the computer screen.

"When I say interesting, I mean interesting in a scary way. This first one was sent the day we left Three Horses." Ginger slid the laptop so Kindra had a better view.

Kindra read aloud. " 'I have been following your blog for some time. Boy, do I need help getting my spending under control. It is so great that you will be in Calamity. I will be there too. Maybe we could meet and you can help me before I spend again. LOL.' "

Ginger tapped the screen. "Now read the one that was sent yesterday."

" 'Where were you? I looked for you and your husband out on the convention floor. There was no booth with a Pepper Light like you wrote about in your blog. Is this some kind of hoax? Are you a liar? I bet your credit card debt is as big as mine. You're just a fake. A big fake.' "

Kindra twirled her fingers around her

ears, the international sign for "This person is one slice shy of a loaf." "She even signed it *Crazy in Calamity.*"

Ginger sighed. "Looks like I have my first cyberstalker. I don't think she or he can track me down."

"Isn't your e-mail address GSalinski?"

There was that pinching at the back of her neck again. She hadn't thought of that. Ginger closed her laptop.

"Aren't you going to blog?"

"And encourage these kinds of e-mails?" Ginger laced her fingers through her curls. Fog drifted over her thoughts. What was the one thing she could deal with?

"I'm sure the rest of our readers are pretty normal."

Outside, Victoria Stone jogged by again. She lifted her chin as though posing for an unseen camera, pivoted, and ran toward the stairs that led back up to the hotel. The two detectives coming down the stairs stopped her.

Ginger yanked on a single curl and let it spring back into place. "Let's go find that cat."

Ten minutes later, Ginger stood at the entrance of the Squirrel Lovers convention. No bulky security guard tried to stop Ginger and demand that she get a badge when she wandered onto the convention floor. While Kindra combed the street and the front side of the hotel with a picture of Phoebe, Ginger had decided to retrace the cat's steps the night she disappeared.

A crowd had gathered around the stage. The woman whose face had been on the keynoter billboard the other night, Martha Somebody, spoke from the podium. "Binky will be dearly missed. He was a bright spot at all our conventions." The crowd nodded in agreement. "We have decided to complete the final days of the convention, but it will now be as a memorial to Binky."

More nods and a flutter of applause.

A large, white carnation bobbed by Martha's ear when she sniffled and wiped her nose. "Mr. Alex Simpson, Binky's owner and trainer, would like to say a few words in honor of this great squirrel." Martha stepped down from the stage, lifting the hem of her muumuu by tugging at the waistline.

Mr. Simpson had shed his bathrobe from last night for a navy suit and pink tie. He began his elegy by resting his head on the microphone. Sniffles and whimpers floated up from the mourners. Slowly, Mr. Simpson raised his head. "Binky was very special to me . . ."

Ginger skirted the edges of the convention floor, calling for Phoebe in low tones. She had hoped to be unobtrusive in her search, but with a funeral going on, that just wasn't gonna happen. Martha stood at the edge of the mourners, craning her neck in Ginger's direction, her eyebrows furled so intensely they had become a unibrow.

Ginger offered a spastic smile and checked under a table that sold squirrel feeders. Maybe this wasn't the best time to be looking for a cat. Her attention was drawn to the poster of the water-skiing Binky on an easel by the door. The advertisement said that Binky would still be skiing in the marina today and tomorrow. Ginger rested her palm on her hip. *Hmm. A dead water-skiing squirrel. That would be something to see.*

"Do you want to know a dirty little secret?" Martha had come up behind her. Her thick glasses made her eyes appear unnaturally large.

Ginger tried to think of a time when a dirty little secret was actually something you wanted to hear.

"I saw you looking at the poster." Martha's carnation dangled precariously below the stem of her glasses.

"Binky is dead. Shouldn't you take it down?"

"The dirty little secret is that there is always a Binky in training." She pulled the flower from behind her ear and tugged at the petals. "He's a huge draw for the conventions, and we get outside revenue from spectators who come to see him. Most important, it's good PR for our squirrel friends. The new Binky is named Leonard."

"A replacement . . . a twin." Ginger made sure she understood correctly. "Like Lassie."

"Exactly. I'm going to miss the old Binky." Martha tore another petal from her flower. "And the way he had to die. I just feel so guilty."

"Guilty?"

Applause rose up from the crowd. Mr. Simpson finished speaking and stepped down from the podium. A slide show with pictures of Binky flashed while a woman played "Danny Boy" on the violin. The music was too loud to talk over. Martha trudged back to the stage. The lights on the convention floor dimmed as a spotlight shone on the violinist. Mr. Simpson made his way toward the back of the convention floor, stopping for a brief hug from Martha.

Ginger stared up at the open window Phoebe had gone through. Phoebe had made a strange sound when she was up on the window sill. Had she seen something that upset her? Maybe the murder had happened out there with only a squirrel and a cat as witnesses and the squirrel had been silenced.

Sad and fearful thoughts about Phoebe invaded her brain. She had poured all the leftover love she had into that cat after her last child left home. What would she do without her Phoebe? Her stomach clenched.

Ginger navigated through the dark room toward the back door, bumping into only one display table. When she pushed the door open, noonday light on the boardwalk nearly blinded her. She shaded her eyes. From the window where Phoebe had sat, she would have had a view of the boardwalk on one side, and on the other side, the dock where the larger boats were housed along the back of the Wind-Up. The boardwalk was too public, but maybe whoever had killed Dustin had met him closer to the larger boats where there had been less light.

The back door swung open again, and Mr. Simpson stepped out. He made eye contact briefly and then turned his back to her. A hand went up to his face. Probably wiping away tears. No need to disturb him.

The boardwalk brimmed with people

sauntering past the shimmering lake. This was the last place she had held Phoebe. An orange cat scampered to the Dumpster behind the Little Italy restaurant. Phoebe wasn't in the habit of hanging out with other cats, but maybe hunger had overridden her antisocial tendencies. Since the cat refused to wear a collar or tags, she would blend right in with the other alley cats. The orange cat sat atop the closed half of the Dumpster. The animal meowed plaintively when she saw Ginger.

"Have you seen my Phoebe?" Ginger stiffened and shook her head. She had to stop talking to cats or she would be a candidate for membership in the nutty old lady club.

The alley smelled of rotting things, dirt, and spicy tomato sauce. Ginger placed a protective hand over her nose and peered inside the Dumpster. The orange cat leaned in as well. Something furry, gray, and motionless was buried beneath the refuse. Her heart pounded. She pushed cardboard and noodles out of the way and tugged.

Not Phoebe. She exhaled. The fur was artificial. The bear suit was the one Xabier had worn, the one Dustin had died in. Someone had taken a knife or scissors and shredded the suit, revealing three layers of fabric. These things were well made. She turned the suit to its satiny lining. Lasagna fell on the concrete.

Her fingers touched something hard, bumpy. She slipped her hands into a pocket and pulled out two necklaces. Near as she could tell, diamond necklaces. Had someone shredded the suit looking for these? That didn't make sense. She'd found them in ten seconds. Certainly the person who shredded the suit would have found the necklaces. They must have been looking for something else. In any case, this could mean that Dustin was the jewel thief. It was the bargaining chip she needed in order to talk to that lady detective.

She hung the suit over her arm and clicked open her purse to put the necklaces in. Feet padded on concrete behind her. She turned slightly. Something hard made contact with the side of her head. Sunspot sparks crowded her field of vision. But this was no migraine. She swayed.

Her view dimmed to blackness.

THIRTEEN

Cynthia Mallory wiped the sweat from her brow as she and Jacobson walked down the stairs of the Little Italy Hotel to the Mermaid restaurant. The cool of the basement was a welcome change. Outside, late-afternoon temperatures had pushed into the low one hundreds. Even though she had long since shed her blazer, her sleeveless button-down was soaked. Jacobson's face wasn't even glistening. What kind of a person didn't sweat when it was over a hundred? She toyed with the idea that Jacobson was a robot. That had to be it. She was a part of some wild police experiment to reduce costs by replacing people with machines.

Jacobson veered her eyes over to her partner after taking a sip of her iced tea. "What are you staring at?" She held up the glass bottle. "It's diet iced tea. I can't do any better than that."

Mallory shook her head. "It's not that." This heat was getting to her. Of course her partner wasn't a robot. "I'm sorry I was such a diet nazi. You can eat whatever you want."

They walked under a flashing neon mermaid into the restaurant where the primary feature was an aquarium that occupied a whole wall. A small shark swam in circles around fish of assorted colors. Restaurant booths featured blue vinyl seats and pink tablecloths. An abundance of plants, in the corners and hanging from the ceiling, flourished. Bright lighting revealed three patrons in the restaurant and only one who matched the description of Gloria Clydell.

The first Mrs. Clydell rose from the booth as they approached. The thick cardigan and floral print dress didn't hide her thinness.

Mallory leaned close to Jacobson and spoke under her breath. "Wish we knew the contents of Clydell's will for sure. Give us more leverage to get her to tell us where the kid is."

Jacobson whispered, "A secretary is a pretty reliable source. She remembers the day Clydell came in and signed on the dotted line."

Gloria moved within a few feet of them. Simultaneously, they lifted their heads and smiled at Dustin's first wife.

"Thank you for meeting me here." Gloria held out a hand to Mallory. "I have sun and cold sensitivities. This place makes me feel like I'm outside."

The haunting impression of Gloria's hand lingered on Mallory's palm, like touching carved wood.

"We can understand that." Jacobson had already pulled her notebook from her purse.

Gloria's hand fluttered to her neck. "Do you two want anything?" She sat down in front of a piece of blueberry pie and a glass of milk. "They have really good desserts."

Both detectives shook their heads. Mallory's mouth watered. The pie did look yummy.

"You said you were supposed to meet your husband the night he died. You weren't in his Day-Timer."

"It was a last-minute thing. He said he had another appointment out on the pier and that he could meet me right after that."

"That must have been Edward Mastive. Do you know who he is or why they were meeting?"

Gloria shook her head. "He just told me to meet him outside."

Jacobson took a seat in the booth opposite Gloria while Mallory remained standing.

"Nothing is official yet. Mr. Clydell's assets will probably be frozen until the investigation is concluded."

Jacobson leaned a little closer to Gloria. "The rumor, though, is that your son inherits the hotel."

Gloria exhaled. "Dustin was full of surprises." She tilted her head. Her face paled. "I suppose this makes things look pretty bad for my son."

"No one can find your son, Mrs. Clydell. Do you know where he is?" Mallory loomed over her.

Gloria's hand trembled when she patted her hair. The trembling might be health related, and it might be nervousness.

Gloria shook her head. "I am not hiding my Xabier. He hasn't been in touch with me. He doesn't own a cell phone." She placed one swollen hand on top of the other. "I'm worried."

Nothing in Gloria's Clydell's mannerisms suggested she was lying.

"What prompted your visit with Dustin?" Mallory leaned against the booth.

"I've been divorced from Dustin for fourteen years. This is the first time in six years that I've seen him. I send him a card at Christmas with a current picture of Xabier, and he sends, I mean sent, me, a card on my birthday. That was the extent of our communication."

Jacobson tapped her pen on her notebook. "Did he say something to you about Xabier, inheriting?"

"He never mentioned his will. Tiffany is under the impression that she gets the hotel. I should have guessed Dustin was playing her."

"So why now, after six years, do you decide to make a visit?" Mallory shifted her weight so she could lean against the booth.

Gloria pushed a piece of pie crust across her plate. "Xabier graduated from drama college. He told me that he thought his dad could get him some acting opportunities. I think, though, that Xabier's real motive was that he wanted to connect with his father." She cut a very small piece of pie and scooped it onto her fork. She chewed slowly. The area around her mouth seemed immobile, stiff. "All of my health problems made me realize I may not . . . be here for long. I wanted Xabier to have someone. I may have encouraged him against my better judgment."

Jacobson flipped a page in her notebook. "Did Xabier find what he was looking for with his father?"

Gloria sat up, resting her arms against the

back of the booth. "Nobody ever got what they were looking for with Dustin. He has . . . had a way of stringing you along, making you think it was just around the corner." She traced the rim of the glass of milk with a puffy finger. "Dustin told Xabier he was going to set up a theater troupe for him. It wasn't my son's dream to be a dancing bear. The last time I talked to him, I think he felt degraded by his dad."

"Hotel records show that you checked in two days ago. Xabier's been here for a month." Mallory sat down next to Jacobson.

"Things between my son and Dustin had gone downhill. I still have a little clout with my ex-husband. I thought I could patch things up."

"What was the attraction between you and Dustin?" Mallory realized the question had nothing to do with the investigation. She just couldn't figure out how two very different people had gotten together.

"When I met Dustin, he was different, beautiful and simple and poor. He pulled me out of a biker bar and drug addiction, introduced me to the Lord." Gloria lifted her head, causing the dark circles under her eyes to intensify. "You feel a debt to the person who saved your life."

Jacobson stopped writing in her notebook long enough to ask, "What changed him?"

"Dustin discovered his gift. People rallied around him and whatever cause he championed. They were drawn to him. He wanted to build a material empire under the guise of building it for God. I just couldn't go there. Just because you put the God sticker on your greed doesn't make it right." Gloria fingered a crocheted shawl on the seat beside her. "He honored my wishes and took God out of his sales pitch. Watching my husband be consumed by his desire to be the next Donald Trump was like watching someone with a meth addiction. Suddenly the man I fell in love with was not there, not inside that body anymore." Gloria rubbed her arms as though she were cold.

Mallory waited a suitable interval before getting back on task. "Please let us know if your son gets in touch with you."

Gloria nodded and stared at the tabletop. The first Mrs. Clydell seemed to be working through some deep pain.

"Why does your son have a different last name than you and your husband?"

"Knight is his stage name. I don't think he was fond of Clydell, didn't want that identity. I wanted him to use my maiden name. He would have been Xabier Espina."

She shrugged. "Kind of like Antonio Banderas."

Jacobson leaned a little closer to Gloria. "You're aware that your son was seen arguing with Dustin?"

Mallory cringed at the question. Gloria was cooperative. They needed to keep it that way. Implying any guilt where Xabier was concerned was a bad idea.

Gloria looked at Mallory, then at Jacobson. "I didn't raise my son to be a murderer, but I —" She shuddered and drew the shawl around her shoulders. "I've just never seen him so angry. I'm sure all this will make sense when he comes forward."

The honesty of the answer took Mallory by surprise. This woman wasn't hiding anything. She pulled out of her pocket the note that accused Walt Disney. "Do you know what this means?"

Jacobson sat up a little straighter and spun the salt shaker. It was her partner's turn to be unhappy with the line of questioning. Jacobson must really hate it when she whipped out the Disney note. They needed to talk.

Gloria shrugged. "When Dustin was trying to work through something, he would write the same thing over and over." She held the note, turned it slightly. "I don't

178

know. Walt Disney was an empire builder too."

"Thank you, Mrs. Clydell. You've been very helpful."

Ginger opened her eyes. She lay motionless, hands folded on her stomach. A canvas roof hung above her, and a light breeze stroked her cheeks. Thoughts leapfrogged over each other. Her senses scrambled to absorb something familiar.

In the distance, she heard the bubbling roar of a river. The aroma of coffee and bacon hung in the air. There were noises. People noises. Someone spoke in Spanish. A car varoomed to life. A car door slammed. A moth flitted by beneath the canvas roof above her. Someone shouted in English about a broken drive shaft. The reply came in a language she couldn't identify, maybe Japanese.

The throbbing at the back of her head intensified when she turned on her side. Tents, lots of tents. Different colors, different sizes. A forest of evergreens circled the tents. Given the international flavor of the conversation, her first thought was that she had been kidnapped by circus performers. Although she saw a woman in a sparkly leotard who could have passed for a trapeze artist, the other people didn't look like performers. Some wore what looked like blue mechanics uniforms. A woman in brown slacks and shirt and checked apron sauntered through the camp.

"Looks like Sleeping Beauty woke up," a bodiless voice, female, said.

Ginger saw legs, old legs, spider-webbed with varicose veins and wearing men's trouser socks that were rolled down on the top. Chunky white shoes, the kind that nurses wear, covered the feet.

"Where am I?" Ginger lifted her head slightly. A hot lead weight seared the back of her head.

The legs sat down on a bench underneath the same canvas Ginger was under. A tinkling sound, someone stirring a liquid inside a mug, filled the air.

The headless voice spoke again. "You might want to rest awhile. You've had a pretty nasty blow to your head."

Ginger closed her eyes. She did remember that part. Someone had hit her just as she was about to put the jewelry in her purse.

She heard footsteps and another voice, this one male and younger. "What shift they got you on today, Ida Mae?"

Ida Mae laughed. "That sounds like a song I might have learned on the piano when I was girl." She sang, "What shift they got you on today, Ida Mae, Ida Mae."

The man slapped his hands on his thighs and tapped his foot in rhythm to Ida Mae's singing.

She continued her tune. "Mr. Fredricks wants me to clean the offices, downtown, downtown. I'll be there from ten to four, ten to four, then I'll collapse on the floor, on the floor."

They both laughed.

"You rock, Ida Mae."

"I don't know about rocking, Donny. I did love to play my mama's piano though." An *aah* sound escaped her lips.

"I can take you in on my bike if you like," Donny said.

"I would love to feel the wind in my hair, but I got to bring my Kirby with me tonight."

Taking care not to lift her head, Ginger turned sideways. "Where am I?" A view of the man's worn high tops was all she could manage.

"Hey, she woke up." The high tops moved toward her.

"Just opened her eyes a few seconds ago."

Ida Mae bent over Ginger. The face Ginger looked into was a very old face. Milky brown eyes floated in a sea of wrinkles.

White hairs sprouted randomly in the furrows of skin. "We plucked you out of the river just like Moses."

"I was floating in the river?"

Ida Mae's head bobbed. "In a gondola boat with a hat over your head."

Whoever had knocked her unconscious must have tossed her in one of the boats and sent her down the river. "I don't suppose there was a bear costume or some jewelry with me?"

Ida Mae's forehead crinkled even more. "Maybe you should rest a while longer." She squeezed Ginger's shoulder.

"Please, I'm not nuts."

Since it was the position that created the least amount of pain, Ginger lay flat and stared at the canvas roof. She could still move her eyes even if she couldn't move her head. The roof was a sort of awning outside of what looked like an army-surplus tent. She'd gotten a glimpse of Donny before the smoldering headache became too much. He had dark, curly hair and an acne problem. She'd managed to absorb some of her surroundings during her brief observation. Assuming this was Ida Mae's tent, she owned a two-burner camp stove and a thirty-year-old Kirby upright.

"You don't understand. I have to get back

to Calamity." Her voice didn't even sound like it was coming out of her mouth.

"Calamity? Is that where you floated out from? I should have known with the gondola boat."

"Where am I now?"

"You're just outside of Las Vegas," Don offered.

"Is this a commune or something?"

Both Ida and Don laughed.

Don got down on his knees so Ginger could see him. "This is a tent city. You're on National Forest land."

Ginger did a miniature shake of her aching head to show she had no idea what Don was talking about.

"We all have jobs in Vegas, but we can't afford the housing costs, so we set up our tents outside the city limits. Our little city has rules. The biggie is you have to be employed."

"And no druggies." Ida put her face close to Ginger. The faint scent of Lysol wafted to Ginger's nose. "You aren't a druggie, are you?"

"No, I'm here for the Inventors Expo. I mean, I was in Calamity for the Expo. Now I have clues about a murder." Given that her sanity was in question, she decided to leave out the squirrel parts of her story. She gripped Ida's spongy arm. "I have to get back to the hotel. I have to tell the police what I found. I have to help Earl with his invention, or we'll lose our home."

"Sure you do, dear." Ida patted her arm.

Don said, "We can take you into Vegas, but priority for the rides has to be for people who have a shift to work. I'm the transportation coordinator."

"She's a skinny thing. I bet we can just squeeze her in with me."

"Maybe. I think some of the girls that work the Bellagio got to go in at nine," Don said. "If you don't mind going in an hour early, there's space in Taheer's van."

What was she thinking? She could just call somebody. Earl or one of the girls could come and get her. "My cell phone is in my purse. Can you hand me my purse?"

Both of them shook their heads.

Ida Mae leaned over her. "Honey, you didn't have a purse when we found you."

She had no money, no ID, no credit card, and no cell. And she had lost the precious travel purse Earl had given her. "Does anyone in the camp have a cell?" Her voice was faint.

"We don't have brick and wood homes. Cell phones are not exactly high on the list for our next purchase." Don sat down on

184

the bench by the two-burner camp stove. "Somebody in the camp might have one. I can ask around. Probably not going to get decent reception out here, though."

No cell phone. How did she end up in this strange world with nothing that would get her back to the one where she belonged? "Sorry, I guess I wasn't thinking."

Ida stretched her arms so they touched the canvas roof. "If she rides out with me, that gives her four hours to sleep and maybe heal up."

Heal up probably meant "come up with a more believable story for why she was floating down the river in a gondola." The story she'd given, the true story, was too weird to be taken seriously.

Ginger felt herself drifting back to sleep while Don and Ida Mae chatted. Like being sloshed back and forth in a boat. No phone, no money, no credit card . . .

She awoke briefly in darkness to the aroma of warm comfort. A Coleman lantern hung from the metal frame of the canvas awning. Ida Mae held a bowl of steaming soup beneath Ginger's nose.

"It ain't much, but it will warm your belly. I suspect you could use some belly warming."

She scraped the spoon through the bowl

and touched it to Ginger's mouth. The spoon shook in Ida Mae's hand. Ginger opened her mouth like a bird waiting to be fed. The warm spicy liquid was the most marvelous thing she had ever tasted. A seafood dinner could not top the soup that was more spice than noodles and vegetables. But even lifting her head slightly caused it to throb.

Ida Mae stroked Ginger's face from the forehead down to the temple. "You sleep. Won't be long. Won't be long now." Ida Mae broke into song again. "Won't be long now before my Savior comes to get me. And carries me, carries me home on His golden chariot. Carry me, carry me home . . ."

Ginger closed her eyes and focused on the hypnotic sound of the river rushing by and the gentle comfort of Ida Mae's humming.

FOURTEEN

Mallory paused to read the sign on the restaurant door in the Wind-Up Hotel. "Shopping Channel auditions to be held here at eight p.m. We will be closing at seven." She pushed the swinging doors open. Half the tables had been scooted against one wall. The other half provided a sitting area for the hopeful inventors. Inventions rested on or beside tables. Some had sheets draped over them. Others were visible in all their creative glory. Some of the hopefuls had brought banners with logos and sales pitches printed on them.

Mallory recognized Fiona Truman from the Shopping Channel standing in an area by the kitchen that had been cleared of tables. Yeah, her life had entered such a sad state that she knew the names of Shopping Channel hosts. She usually had the Shopping Channel on for noise when she got ready for work. At least that was what she told herself. It was all she could stand to watch beside her Mayberry reruns. From news to sitcoms, everyone on TV was selling an agenda. At least the Shopping Channel people were up front that they wanted you to buy what they sat in front of the camera.

Cameras and monitors were positioned at one end of the restaurant. Fiona stood by a counter interviewing each contestant. The line of on-deck inventors holding possible future products took up one wall.

Mallory scanned the room, looking for Earl and Ginger Salinski. She'd sent Jacobson home to her hubby and kids. This was the last thing she had to do before she went home to a carefully measured quarter cup of ice cream and a dog that liked the neighbor better than she liked Mallory. She couldn't blame Roxy for being disloyal. Mallory worked erratic hours; sometimes the poodle got walked at five in the evening, and sometimes it was two in the morning. Mrs. Tribecca, a retired schoolteacher, was home all the time.

No chance of spotting Mr. Salinski. The room was filled with way too many sixty-something balding men. Mrs. Salinski had a fairly distinctive hairstyle. You didn't see ringlets on a fifty-year-old woman that often. Mallory paced the perimeter, reading the various logos for the inventions and hoping that the Salinskis would recognize her and look her way.

A man with the same build as Earl Salinski slipped through a side door. Mallory trotted after him. She opened the door just as she heard Fiona ask for a five-minute break.

"Mr. Salinski?" Warm air hit Mallory when she stepped into the alley between the hotel and the discount bait shop. A twilight gray sky arched over the lake.

The man turned.

Mallory paced down the alley. "Remember me? Detective Mallory. I've been leaving messages on your cell all day."

Earl Salinski's shoulders slumped. He anchored a cardboard box under his arm. In his other hand, he held the banner with the logo for the Pepper Light. "Sorry, I haven't checked messages. Been kind of busy."

"I need to talk to you and your wife again."

"She didn't show up to help me with my audition." His forehead crinkled as he shook his head. "I've been asking everyone. Her friends haven't seen her since this afternoon."

This did not look good. "Has your wife left the hotel?"

Earl placed his box on the top of a closed Dumpster. "I don't know where she is." He rubbed his thinning hair.

"I just need to get some clarification from you two. Your wife threatened Mr. Clydell. He gave your booth to somebody else." She tapped the cardboard box. "How bad did you want to see this invention succeed?"

Earl took a step back and held up his hands. "I didn't know I had lost my booth until the Expo closed down." Earl turned slightly. "I want this invention to succeed pretty badly, but I am not going to kill for it."

The side door swung open. Fiona Truman stepped out, wobbling precariously on four-inch heels. "Mr. Salinski. I wanted to catch you before you left."

Earl perked up. "Really?"

Mallory had never seen a television personality this close up. Fiona had freckles and splotchy skin just like everyone else. Her dark hair was twirled up into a bun and glued in place with a metal doodad.

After making sure the alley wasn't a high-heel land mine, Fiona stepped toward Earl. "Salinski is an unusual last name."

"It's Italian," Earl said.

"I know the producer said that you didn't make the cut. But I just wanted you to know that I like your product."

Earl stood up a little straighter.

"Your stage presence was a little lacking. Maybe if you had a spokesperson, the producer would see the product in a new light."

"My wife, Ginger, knows about the product, and she might be good in front of the camera. She can talk. She knows a lot about selling things." His gaze rested on Mallory. "If I can track her down."

"Our hotel room is booked through the end of the convention, so I'll be around." She pulled a business card out of her pocket. "It's got my cell and my e-mail."

Earl's expression brightened. He lifted his chin and squared his shoulders.

Fiona tilted her head. "I've got to get back to work. Make sure you bring your wife. You said her name is Ginger?"

Earl nodded.

"That's an unusual first name too." She headed back toward the side door. "Hope she shows up."

Mallory listened for the sound of the door closing. She moved in on Earl. "Let's hope for both your sakes your wife shows up pretty soon."

Mallory hated this part of her job. Earl and his wife had seemed like nice people. But the evidence suggested she at least had to question them a second time. The missing wife was a red flag. She had to put a little pressure on them.

Earl gathered his box off the top of the Dumpster. "You can question me if you want to. I don't have anything to hide."

"I want to believe you, Mr. Salinski."

"I won't leave the hotel. I promise." He pressed his lips together. "Unless . . . well, unless Ginger needs me. I don't know what's become of her. It's not like her not to at least call."

"We wanted to talk to both you and your wife," Mallory said. She shifted her weight and studied Earl. There was one thing she needed to ask without the wife around. "In the course of the last interview, your wife gave you a look."

"A look? What kind of look?"

"Like what you were saying was news to her. Or you weren't telling the truth."

Earl shook his head. "My wife and I don't keep secrets from each other. What was it I said?"

"That you had just gotten into town right before you found the body."

Earl's jaw went slack. He shook his head.

"I'm not sure why she would think I had lied about that."

"As soon as your wife surfaces, I would like to talk to the both of you again."

"Yeah, sure." The faintness of his voice suggested he was lost in thought. "I'm worried about her." Earl wandered away, shaking his head.

Besides Ida Mae, only one other person in the cramped car spoke English, and she had fallen asleep against the window. From her place in the backseat, Ginger could see the lights of the Las Vegas Strip as they neared the city across the vast desert flatness.

Though the pain was subsiding, her head still hurt, and the warm washcloth Ida Mae had given her had long since grown cold. After the ride in the van fell through, they had managed to get Ida's Kirby wedged in the trunk of a Volkswagen. Her bucket of cleaning supplies rested on her lap.

The car rambled and sputtered toward the city.

"How old are you, Ida?"

"I'll be eighty-one next year." The older woman lifted her chin in a show of pride.

Ginger turned away and watched the yellow lines on the highway click by. She looked at her folded hands where her purse should be. Empty hands. Nothing. But she was still breathing. Pushing air in and out. That was something.

Ida Mae's warm voice broke through her thoughts. "Are you wondering how a woman my age ends up living in a tent and working as a cleaning lady?"

"It can't be where you planned on being at your age."

"Plans? What do they count for?" Ida Mae shook her head. "My husband was sick for many years before he died. We never had insurance, barely had enough to pay the bills and raise our two girls. I sold the house to pay off some of the debt. I get a little from social security."

It is possible to lose everything. She opened and closed her hands. The other woman in the backseat stirred but continued to rest her head against the window. She wore what looked like a maid's smock.

Ida Mae patted the woman's leg. "Jodi's been doing double shifts. God bless her. She's a twelve stepper. Sober for eight months. Trying to pay off some debts." Ida leaned toward the window and dug into the pocket of her apron. She produced a jeweled coin purse. She clicked it open and pulled out a wrinkled bill, which she slipped into Jodi's smock pocket. Then she leaned close to Ginger and whispered, "Aren't surprises fun?"

Ginger nodded.

"Please don't feel sorry for me, Ginger. I got a house by the river. Always wanted a house by the river. My youngest daughter helps out when she can. She's a single mom, so she's got her hands full. Got two precious grandchildren. One is getting ready for college."

"You said you had two children."

Ida Mae stared into her cleaning bucket. She fingered a scrubbing pad. "Last time I saw my Linda was when we took her to rehab." She pressed her fingers into the pad and tossed it back into the bucket. "She ran away from that place."

Traffic increased as they neared the city. They passed a truck stop and a trailer park. The highway morphed to city streets. The buildings grew closer together. The driver stopped, and the passenger in the front seat got out, making her way toward a lighted doughnut shop. The driver edged his way deeper into the city. At first, they passed minimarts and single-story office buildings. He stopped on a corner by a hotel with a neon bucking horse and a matching sign that said Cowboy Cottages. Jodi, the sleeping woman, roused. "This is my stop." She pushed open her door.

"You take care now." Ida Mae gripped her bucket and smiled.

"Thanks, Ida Mae." Jodi stretched and yawned.

The hotels became bigger and fancier. Several blocks of bright flashing lights whizzed past her peripheral vision. They veered away from the neon brightness of the Strip. The street curved, and they entered what looked like a downtown office district. "My stop's coming up. Why don't you get out with me? I'll help you find a phone."

Ginger tensed. She didn't have even two quarters to make a phone call. She took an assessment of what she did have. Her wedding ring and her engagement ring. She was pretty sure she had some twenty-five percent off coupons for renting a fishing boat in Calamity. Oh yeah, and she was breathing.

The car stopped, and Ida pushed the door open. The driver, a Vietnamese man with slender hands and an expressionless face, popped the trunk and hefted Ida's vacuum onto the sidewalk.

"Thanks, Anh."

The man smiled, revealing crooked teeth. He waved at Ida. Ida dug through the tiny coin purse she had stuffed in her apron and pulled out two dollar bills. Anh shook his head, but Ida grabbed his hand, placed the money in it, and folded his fingers over it.

The man thanked her in broken English.

The car drove away, the only one on the road. Red taillights glared at the two women standing alone by the high-rise. Panic invaded Ginger's senses. Her throat constricted, and her rib cage felt like it had been wrapped tightly in bandages. She had no plan. No money. She cleared her throat. "How about I help you haul your vacuum in?"

"Much obliged," Ida Mae said. "I clean a dentist office on the third floor. The man is real nice, always pays me on time. He goes to my church. It's not easy for an eighty-year-old to get hired on. I do so appreciate his kindness."

They stood in front of the glowing doors. A young woman walked by holding a cleaning canister.

"I can't let you use the office phone. That wouldn't be fair to Mr. Fredricks. There's a cleaning crew on almost every floor. I bet we can find someone with a cell phone who has some free minutes at this hour."

They tracked down a young man with bleached hair who said, "No prob," when they asked to borrow his phone. Ginger left messages with Kindra and Suzanne. Arleta didn't own a cell. She pressed in Earl's number. He wasn't answering, either. "Hi, Earl." Saying his name felt strange, like trying to remember the name of a distant relative. "I'm okay, I guess. Long story. There's no way you can get hold of me. I'm in Las Vegas. I'm going to get back to the hotel, and I'll try to call back." She pushed the End button. Unable to formulate the next step she needed to take, she looked at Ida Mae. "Maybe I could help you clean."

Ida waved the idea away with her hand. "I work better alone. There's a little all-night wedding chapel about three blocks up. The owner is real nice. She lets me sleep on her couch when my ride can't pick me up right away." Ida touched the side of Ginger's head. "You get some sleep, and then you can try calling again. You can always find someone with a cell."

"Thank you. For all you've done for me."

Ida pulled her into a hug and whispered in her ear. "You're going to be all right."

She left Ida on the third floor stacking magazines and humming another made-up tune. Ginger took the stairs down to the first floor and wandered out into the empty street.

Kindra didn't like the way the old man cut his gaze in her direction. His eyes held a lusty smolder that made her uncomfortable. She stared down at her silverware and reread the note that had been left for her at the hotel desk. "Meet me at Little Italy restaurant at 10:30. Ask for a table on the balcony. Xabier."

Kindra arranged her sweater around her shoulders and took a sip of her Diet Coke. She'd been waiting for nearly fifteen minutes. Maybe Xabier wasn't going to show . . . again.

The old man rose from the table where he had been seated and sat down at an empty bistro table closer to her. Being at the restaurant alone at this hour was maybe not such a good idea. She'd been so excited to hear from Xabier that she hadn't even told anyone about the note.

With all the people checking out and leaving, they had managed to get another room. Suzanne and Arleta had crashed. She hadn't seen Ginger since they'd gone looking for Phoebe. She touched the note, tracing the outline of his rounded signature. *This is what warm gazes from good-looking guys make you do.* She should have exercised more caution. The police were looking for Xabier. She didn't think he was guilty of anything. Then again, feelings of attraction messed with your ability to think clearly.

The old man got up a second time and positioned himself two tables away from her. Kindra pushed her chair back. They were the only two people on the veranda at this hour. Inside, a single male waiter dealt with the smattering of customers. He was the same waiter who had brought her Diet Coke fifteen minutes ago. Kindra checked her watch. Now she'd been waiting twenty minutes.

Lots of foliage surrounded two sides of the veranda. The side that looked out on the water was kept greenery free to provide a better view of the lake. Strings of white Christmas lights hung from the veranda canopy, contrasting with the night sky.

The old man slipped into the table next to her and leaned toward her. She pushed her chair back and jumped to her feet. Her sweater fell off her shoulders.

"Had enough of the view?" said the old man.

Kindra's heart pounded. She could deal with the likes of him. "Why don't you just pick a table and stay there?" *Creep.*

" 'Cause I wanted to sit by the pretty lady." His voice had a vague familiarity to it. "Why don't you have a seat?" He patted the chair she'd been sitting in.

Ooh, this guy was forward. "I know some people come to places like this, at this hour, for that kind of thing." She leaned over and snatched up her sweater. "But I am not one of those women."

The old man chuckled. "I know you're not one of those women. That's why I like you." He shifted in his chair and then spoke out of the side of his mouth in a low whisper. "Kindra, it's me."

She leaned toward him. "Xabier?"

He pulled her down with a swiftness that took her breath away. She clattered into the chair.

"Don't say my name."

"Have you gone off the deep end? What's with the disguise?"

He leaned close so he was only inches from her ear. "People are after me. Two guys in suits with guns."

She clasped a hand onto his arm. "We saw them in the outlet corridor. They were chasing you in your bear costume."

"That wasn't me," he whispered. "It was Dustin, my dad."

"Why didn't you tell me he was your

father?" He did have a lot to explain.

"Because sometimes I don't want to believe that he is . . . was my father."

"What was he doing in *your* bear costume?" Kindra stirred her soda with the straw.

"After I saw you down in the outlet place, I went to Dustin, and we had a big fight. Dressing up in the stupid costume was humiliating. It wasn't what he promised. I told him I wasn't going to do it anymore. So he ran out onto the floor as the bear and then was going to slip out of the costume backstage and come out to do the speech. He cut out the elevator entrance. I watched the convention floor. He never came back out to give his big speech. I think those guys caught up with him and he was on the run."

"Why are the men after you now? Who are they?"

"I don't know. After my big blowup with Dad, I just needed to be alone. I took a long drive out to the desert. I'm sorry I missed our date. I was just upset and needed to clear my head."

"It's okay . . . I guess." The disguise was convincing even close up. He must have put some sort of fake skin on.

"When I got back to the hotel, all you-know-what had broken lose." He gathered a

202

section of tablecloth into his hand. His knuckles paled. "Dad was dead," he whispered. He stared at the table for a long moment. "I guess I inherited the hotel. The two guys started chasing me down, saying Dad owed them money, lots of it, and that I'd better pay up."

"Who are they?"

"I don't know. They showed me this agreement that Dad had signed."

"What was the agreement for?"

He rubbed the fake skin on his cheek. "I just glanced at it. I can't remember."

"Sometimes if you close your eyes and picture the moment, details will come back to you. That's how I study for a test. I try to visualize the information on the page."

"I'll have to try that." He took a sip of her drink then tapped the side of the glass with his fingers. "Their threats scared me. They have guns."

Men with guns. "You need to go to the police. They'll help you."

Xabier's eyes iced over. He moved away from her. "I don't like the police." He jerked as though he had been poked at the base of his spine. "It's a long story. But I don't trust them." His voice etched with bitterness.

Kindra chewed on her straw, uncertain of how to respond to such strong emotion.

Xabier cocked his head and slumped down in his chair. "Besides, I'm afraid if I surface, those guys will come after me again." The hard edge had left his voice.

Maybe someday she would hear the story of why he didn't like the police. For now, she chose to follow his lead and keep the conversation light. "So dressing up like a creepy old man keeps them from finding you?"

Xabier sat up a little straighter and turned side to side. "It's a pretty good disguise, don't you think? I fooled you."

"You changed your voice and everything, even the way you moved."

"Four years of theater school." Xabier patted his cheek. "Who would have thought it would have practical application?"

"So why did you get in touch with me?"

" 'Cause I missed you." He leaned even closer so their shoulders were touching. "I knew I could trust you. You remind me of my mom that way."

His words made her stomach warm and her skin tingle. "You got to go to the police, Xabier."

Xabier made a shushing sound, putting his fingers to his lips. "Don't say my name."

In the main part of the restaurant, a man sitting close to the veranda shifted, causing the chair legs to scrape across the floor. The man rose to his feet. Her memory was dimmed by time, but the guy didn't look like one of the men she'd seen chasing Dustin, a.k.a. Cute Teddy Bear, in the underground mall.

Xabier's attention was drawn to the interior of the restaurant as well. He slammed his back against the chair, eyes widening. "Gotta go." He kissed her cheek, leaped over the railing of the veranda, and then disappeared into foliage.

FIFTEEN

The Southern Belle wedding chapel stood on a corner next to a convenience store. Pink and yellow neon twisted around the Roman columns on either side of the doors, which were wide open. A warm glow spilled out from within. Ginger stepped into a lobby that featured a mannequin in a dress that was a flourish of lace and taffeta. Baskets of silk flowers rested on columns and were hung on the wall. Lilting instrumental music played somewhere deeper in the chapel.

When she stepped across the threshold, a bell chimed. A woman came through a side door, holding a manila folder in one hand. Her half glasses hung from the neckline of her blue T-shirt.

"Yes, may I help you?"

Nothing in her tone of voice indicated that this late hour was an inconvenient time. The woman didn't even have the hint of a southern accent. She had achieved four shades of blond, from light brown, to golden, to blond, to almost white, in her long, wavy hair. Narrow face, high cheek bones, and crow's feet gave the impression of an aging beauty queen.

Ginger shuffled her feet. Asking for help was harder than giving it. "Ida Mae sent me."

Shifting the folder to under her arm, the woman grabbed Ginger's hand and shook it. "You're a friend of Ida's. Come on in."

Despite the warm welcome, Ginger's feet remain planted. "I just need to use your phone in a bit. My friends and husband aren't answering their phones at this hour. If I can get hold of someone, they can come and get me."

"Are you from the tent city?"

"Actually, I am staying at a hotel in Calamity." Ginger touched the back of her head, still feeling some pain there. "It's a long story. I don't want to be any trouble. Ida just said that I should come here."

"A friend of Ida's is not a burden." The woman held out her hand. "My name is Ann Jannette Williams. I run the Southern Belle even though I'm from Eugene, Oregon. Las Vegas is all about themes. Southern was the one my husband and I could live with. Follow me, I'll show you the room where you can wait to make your phone call." She inclined her head to one side, probably assessing Ginger's appearance. "Maybe you can catch a nap."

"How do you know Ida?"

"We go to the same church."

Ginger slowed. "Oh."

"I know what you're thinking." Ann Jannette walked down a hallway, talking over her shoulder. "Why would a Christian lady be doing quickie weddings?"

"It's not the profession you would expect a believer to gravitate towards."

"My husband has been to seminary. He does the ceremonies. A lot of these chapels turn matrimony into a joke or a costume party." She stopped outside a closed door and turned to face Ginger. "Do you want to know a secret? You can take the most hard-hearted dancer off the Strip and when you push her to an honest place, you know what she wants more than anything? To wear a pretty dress and to be made to feel special." Ann rested her hand on the doorknob.

"Guess I hadn't ever thought of it that way." She didn't know any women who were exotic dancers. Everyone she knew was pretty much like her, middle-class suburbanites. Until tonight, she had never met people like Ann or Ida Mae. *I need to leave my hometown more often.*

"My husband finds a way to get the gospel into the ceremony." Ann pushed the door open, revealing a long, narrow room with a couch, coffee table, and television. "I find a way to let the bride know she is beautiful and valued by God while she picks from our wedding dresses. After the ceremony, we eat with them. People from the church sometimes join us for the ceremony and reception. They bring gifts and casseroles." Ann cupped Ginger's shoulder. "In Vegas, you got to live outside the box if you want to reach people."

"It sounds like a good thing that you do."

Ann nodded, stepped inside the room, and clicked on the light. A portable clothing rack with wedding dresses hung on it stood in a corner of the room.

"Some of them have had too much to drink." Ann laughed and shook her head. The laugh was more to herself, and she stared at the carpet while she talked, probably seeing some memory playing in her mind. "You can speak a lot of the gospel into a drunk woman's ear without meeting much resistance. You never know when your seeds will sprout. The reason why some of these people are here is because no one has ever made them feel valued. They want a special day, but they don't think they deserve it. Not all of them, some just want to get married without all the fuss and money. They sure aren't the people who would come into a church, so church has to come to them."

Ginger followed Ann into the room.

A box heaping with mesh and satin rested by the wedding dresses. The coffee table contained brides magazines, a candy dish, and two devotional books.

"This room is sort of extra storage and a place for people to wait; the fitting room is through that door. The couch is pretty comfortable. I'll wake you in a couple hours, and you can make your phone call."

"Thank you, thank you for everything." She had been saying that a lot tonight. Help had come from such unexpected places and unexpected people. All her assumptions about what a Christian was had been turned on their heads. Life outside of suburbia sure wasn't boring.

Ann Jannette nodded. "Should be pretty quiet for the next couple of hours. Since they changed the law about us not marrying between midnight and eight, business has slowed a bit. I'm just doing the books. Jon, that's my husband, is praying."

"I'm not usually the person who has to ask for help." Ginger plunked down on the couch and picked up one of the devotional magazines. "I'm usually the person giving it."

"Sometimes God does that." Ann leaned against the doorway, crossing her legs at the ankle. "He turns things upside down, so we can see them better. Have a good rest."

Ann Jannette closed the door. Ginger curled up on the couch. Her sense of urgency, of needing to get back to Calamity and tell the detectives what she had found had been replaced by a peace that everything would work out okay. She'd call in a few hours, and someone would come and get her. Worrying about it wouldn't make it happen any faster. She closed her eyes and drifted off . . .

The buzz of a television jerked Ginger awake. The male commentator said, "I am standing here outside of the Wind-Up Hotel on this Saturday morning . . ."

She sat up. *Not another murder.* The television commentator stood beside a hand-painted sign that said Garage Sale. An aerial-camera shot showed several parking lots and fields filled with garage sales. They cut back to the news commentator. ". . . where the World's Biggest Garage Sale is about to be kicked off with a ribbon-cutting ceremony. We have two celebrities who are going to do the ribbon cutting and the countdown to 7:00 a.m.: Fiona Truman from the Shopping Channel and Victoria Stone, child star well-known for the song 'My Heart Belongs to You.' Fiona, how does it feel to be here?"

Ginger watched the festivities feeling far removed from the excitement. She had forgotten about the garage sales starting today.

Fiona looked very pulled together in her navy shirt and brown slacks despite her hair being tossed by the wind. She leaned toward the microphone. "I'm used to buying stuff new and at full price, so this hunting-for-treasure thing should be fun. I'm delighted to be here."

The door opened, and Ann Jannette's eyes went to the television. "Sorry, one of my kids must have come in and turned that on. Oh hey, that's Little Vicky."

"You remember her?"

"Vaguely. Jon performed the ceremony for her and her third husband a few years back."

Hadn't Vicky said she never had a husband? "Do you get that many celebrities in here?"

"We get a few. Las Vegas is a place where

former celebrities come to live out their last days quietly. It keeps them close enough to the spotlight for the occasional photo op." Ann clicked off the television.

Ginger stretched. "Someone should be up and answering their phone by now."

"Listen, the reason I came in here is that we have a couple who are on their way back to Calamity. They're not flaky. It would save you having to wait for someone to come and get you. You can still call and let them know you're coming home."

Ginger wasn't so sure about getting a ride from strangers. Then again, she'd been relying on strangers for the whole night.

Ann read her mind or picked up on some signal in her expression or body language. "Why don't you meet this couple and then decide?"

"Okay."

Candace and Barry Sheldon turned out to be a very normal twosome. She was a nurse and he was an insurance salesman. They had done the quick wedding so they could put the money toward a honeymoon. Smart and practical.

Ginger tried calling Earl from Ann's office where the sun shone in from a high window, washing the office in an early-morning golden glow. Earl still wasn't answering. She tried Kindra.

"Hello?"

"Hey."

"Ginger, where are you?"

The sound of Kindra's voice made Ginger want to cry.

"It's a long story, kiddo. But I'll be back soon."

"So much has happened here."

"Did those detectives find the bear suit with jewels?"

"Ah . . . no. Xabier found me." She said Xabier's name with nuances of affection. "Some guys are after him. I haven't talked to the detectives."

"I need to talk to them." Ginger flipped through a magazine while she talked. "We'll get this straightened out when I get back. Kindra, it sure is good to hear your voice."

"You sound different."

Her eyes rested on a picture in the magazine of a meadow of wildflowers. The detail in the photograph, the separation of each petal on the flowers, the greenness of the grass made her chest feel tight. "I feel different." Something had changed. She flipped the page to a picture of an older couple standing at an altar. "Have you seen Earl?"

There was a long pause. "Oh sorry, I was

shaking my head," Kindra laughed. "Like you could see that. I haven't seen Earl. Do you want me to meet you when you get back?"

"Sure, kid, it should take me an hour to get to the hotel. I'll meet you in the lobby."

"Sounds good. See ya."

Ginger held the phone to her ear for a long moment after Kindra hung up.

A few minutes later, she stepped out of the chapel. Sun warmed her face. Ann hugged her good-bye. Barry and Candace waited in their Honda Accord. When she crawled into the backseat, Barry turned around and asked, "Would you like us to stop for a coffee or anything before we hit the highway?"

Ginger relaxed into the plush backseat. "Whatever you want to do is fine with me."

Candace craned her neck and smiled.

An hour later, after fighting the traffic created by the World's Biggest Garage Sale, the newly married couple dropped Ginger off several blocks from the Wind-Up.

"Ever notice how roses don't have a smell anymore, Jacobson?" Detective Mallory pressed her back against the wooden bench. The rooftop gardens of the Little Italy Hotel were nearly vacant in the morning. In the cool postdinner hours, couples looking for that just-right romantic spot took to this place like a rookie on night shift took to espresso. At this time of day, though, it was the perfect place to have a private conference.

"They die so fast too." Jacobson opened her foam container. "Nathan got me some for our anniversary. Two days later, they were dead."

The swirl of oregano, basil, and pepper that rose up from Jacobson's takeout overwhelmed Detective Mallory. How could she eat Italian this early? Deep inside her, the voice of a plus-size gal, the one that didn't care about silly things like heart attacks and diabetes and fitting into a size ten screamed, "Oh baby, get me some pasta now."

Jacobson brought the plastic fork to her mouth. "Are you all right? You look a little pale."

Mallory pictured a steak fried in butter and a salad with vinegar and oil dressing. On the protein diet, she could be bad in her own special way. "I'm fine. Let's make our list and check it twice." Mallory pulled a laptop out of her briefcase.

Jacobson shoveled the lasagna into her mouth, in a delicate ladylike way, with one hand. With the other, she flipped open her notebook. She spoke between bites. "We have a missing squirrel who winds up being part of a crime. Do we know for sure if the squirrel is what killed Mr. Clydell?

"They x-rayed the squirrel. Lot of broken bones." Mallory tapped under her eye. "Remember Clydell had some petechial hemorrhaging and bruises on his neck."

"So our murderer strangles the victim." Setting the takeout on the bench, Jacobson rose to her feet and paced. "Binky has the misfortune of being in the wrong place at the wrong time, gets crushed when Dustin falls. Our murderer stuffs the squirrel in Dustin's mouth, out of anger or to throw us off. Then he seals the bear head on Dustin and hauls the bear and the squirrel to the boat."

"Mr. Simpson seemed genuinely upset about the loss of his squirrel. The one anomaly in his room was an excessive amount of ice. Maybe the squirrel was at the scene by accident." Mallory typed. "What's your take on the woman who was with him, Martha Hillstrong?"

Jacobson shrugged. "If we get desperate, I suppose we can question her. We have jewelry thefts, mostly diamonds, according to Officer Spurgen's report. The thefts stop after Dustin Clydell dies." She sat back down on the bench. "His missing kid, Xabier Knight, will probably inherit the hotel. He's got motive if he knew that. Father and son are seen fighting shortly before Dustin's death. We have a second ex-wife who was told she was going to inherit. We have a ransacked room and a stolen bear suit." Jacobson picked up her takeout box and fork.

"Dustin had appointments with Victoria Stone and somebody named Edward Mastive who nobody else seems to know. Victoria told us Dustin never showed. Gloria said Dustin never met her on the boardwalk. I wonder if he kept the appointment with this Mastive guy? We still don't have a lead on who he is." Mallory glanced up from her laptop. "Don't forget the note 'Walt Disney did it.' "

Jacobson pressed her lips together, then looked down, pushing the lasagna around in its container.

"You don't think that should be on the list?"

"It just doesn't seem important."

"I don't know if this makes any sense to you, but I just got a feeling when I saw that note."

Jacobson scraped tomato sauce off a noodle. "Okay, we'll leave it on the list."

"But you don't think it's evidence?"

"You're the senior detective." Jacobson scratched foam with her fork.

Her partner thought she had gone off the deep end. Mallory decided to let it go. She had been able to solve more than one case by following up on a feeling. Jacobson could be a little too textbook and procedure sometimes.

"Forensics confirms your theory that the body was moved." Jacobson closed her takeout container. "Whoever took him out to the boat was probably planning on dumping him in the middle of the lake. Maybe that's why they put the head back on. For weight."

"And the perpetrator got interrupted?"

"The convention floor and the connecting hallway were cleaned that night, but they don't think it took place there." Jacobson paused. "We combed the pier and didn't find anything. It makes sense, though, that the murderer wouldn't want to haul the body too far. Trying to find forensic evidence in an outdoor location can be tricky. Let's assume he was killed somewhere outside."

Mallory continued to type as she spoke. "People were milling around at that time of night, but maybe there was enough darkness to get to the boat undetected."

"What do you have to do to make some-one want to kill you in such a violent way? What fear, what threat would drive such an impulse?"

Mallory shrugged. "Loss of identity or fortune or both, revenge. I agree that this had to have been an impulse murder." Mallory lifted her fingers from the keyboard. "So what's next for us?"

"We still have to get the Salinskis in for questioning. If the Mrs. doesn't surface soon we can press Earl Salinski. What if they're jewel thieves? He stayed here to play the innocent while she takes off to find a fence for the stuff."

"According to Tiffany, the thefts started before the Salinskis showed up. They would have to have an accomplice."

A faint meow sounded in the garden, and a gray cat with white toes emerged from some rosebushes. The cat swept past Jacobson and rubbed against Mallory.

"She likes you."

Mallory gathered the ball of fur into her arms. The cat purred and nestled against her. "I didn't know they allowed cats up here."

"I bet you she sneaked up."

"No tag on her. She's probably one of those alley cats down by the Dumpster that live on pizza and pasta."

"Didn't you say your dog ran away?"

"Just to the neighbor's house. I thought dogs were supposed to be loyal." The cat purred so intensely she was vibrating. It was nice to be liked and appreciated. The cat was well nourished. "Maybe I'll take her home." She nuzzled close to the cat's face. "You deserve better than the alley, don't you?"

"What are you going to call her?"

"I think I'll call her Aunt Bee after my favorite Mayberry character. Just call her Beebe for short." She stroked her new pet under the chin. "You'd like that, wouldn't you?"

Jacobson's cell rang. She answered the call with a series of yeses and okays and a "How soon can you get it over to forensics?"

"I take it that wasn't a personal call?"

"A little bit of a lead. An officer found the squirrel's rolling ball tossed down a laundry chute. They're going to see if there are any fingerprints on it. We need to figure out if the jewelry theft, the squirrel abduction, and Clydell's death are connected or separate crimes."

Mallory nodded. "True, we could be working this thing all wrong. Why don't we break for a couple hours? You can go home so your kids and hubby don't forget what you look like, and I'll take my new friend home."

Ginger stepped into the lobby of the Wind-Up Hotel. A cool and constant artificial breeze swirled around her. She scanned the lobby couches for Kindra's blond head and then searched the area by the elevators and the slot machines. Tiffany stood behind the counter handing a key to a young couple. She would know if Kindra had been here.

Tiffany looked fresh and professional in her off-white sleeveless blouse. Her makeup was subdued. But the hair was as big as ever.

"Are you running the place now?"

Tiffany drew her eyebrows together, an instant darkening of mood. "I'm running it because nobody else seems to care about running it. Even the new owner, Dustin's one and only child, hasn't bothered to show up and claim his inheritance."

Xabier inherited the hotel. That was news. "What did Dustin leave you?"

Tiffany held up her hand, forming a big *O* with her fingers. "None of it is official; the lawyer's secretary let it slip when I talked to her. Everything is stalled because of the investigation." She blew a strand of curly hair out of her eyes. "I suppose I can still hope I'll get something, but then I'd be thinking the same way I did when Dustin was alive."

"So why are you still here?"

Tiffany stopped flipping the papers she had been sorting through. " 'Cause I'm good at this, running the hotel. A murder could be a PR disaster. Yes, the Inventors Expo fell apart, but the hotel is almost totally full again because of the World's Largest Garage Sale. The staff likes me. People are depending on this hotel continuing to run." She shook her head and lowered her voice. "It should have been mine."

"Have you seen Kindra? You know, the young blond who came in with me on Thursday."

Tiffany shook her head. "She picked up a message just when I was getting on shift, read her message, and left."

"Hmm." It wasn't like Kindra to miss a meeting. "Did my friends get another hotel room?"

"Let me check, sweetie." Tiffany turned her attention to the computer.

On the other side of the lobby, the elevator doors opened. Victoria Stone stepped out.

Earl was behind her.

223

Ginger stared at her husband of thirty-nine years with the same mixture of anxiety and excitement she used to feel on a first date.

Sixteen

Like an approaching train, the ringing of the phone grew louder, slowly penetrating the deep sleep Cynthia Mallory had fallen into. Beebe purred on her chest. She had never slept so well and so deeply in her life. Beebe was an all-natural sleeping pill, a narcotic. Mallory opened her eyes. She turned her head slightly, absorbing her surroundings. She'd fallen asleep on her couch. What else? The phone rang again. It was a normal ring, not her cell, which chimed the whistling theme from *Andy Griffith.*

Mallory twisted slightly and grabbed the cordless off the coffee table.

" 'Lo." Mallory swallowed to produce some moisture in her mouth. Her voice creaked.

"I'm down at the lab." Jacobson sounded downright chirpy.

"Weren't you supposed to go home and reconnect with your family?"

"I did that, and then I came down to the lab to see what the results were on the squirrel ball. What did you do?"

The question implied that Mallory had made some brilliant leap forward with the case. She had in fact consumed half a bag of Famous Amos cookies, felt guilty about that for about ten minutes, and then fallen into a deep sleep thanks to her new pet. "I got a few things done around the house and then took a little nap. Anything good with the lab results?"

"Simpson's prints are on it, no surprise there. And Martha Hillstrong's are on it too."

"Hillstrong and Simpson are acquaintances. It is entirely possible that Martha had a good reason to pick up the Binky ball." Mallory planted her feet on the carpet. The half empty bag of store-bought cookies rested on the coffee table. Maybe they were placing too much importance on the squirrel-napping. Chances are it was just one of those weird, unconnected crimes. "Was Hillstrong in the system?"

"A minor assault a few years ago. A teenager was shooting a pellet gun at squirrels in the park. Hillstrong took offense."

"From protecting squirrels to murder. That's a leap. Plus, I really doubt a squirrel lover would use one as a weapon, even postmortem." She pushed the bag of cookies to one side. So much of police work was finding answers for questions. That squirrel got out of the room somehow and for some reason. "For lack of a better lead, we might want to talk to her." That was the problem. Until Xabier Knight and Mrs. Salinski surfaced, they didn't have any strong leads. So they were killing time with this squirrel thing. "Mr. Salinski hasn't checked out of the hotel, is that correct?"

"Last time I asked the front desk, he was still checked in."

Mallory massaged the back of her neck. Beebe had made herself comfortable on her thigh. "Why don't you meet me in the hotel lobby, say in an hour? I got to go down to the corner market and get some cat food."

"Things are working out pretty good for you two?"

"Yeah, it's nice to have somebody who actually likes me around. I went by the Dumpster to see if she wanted to stay there. She chose me over a lifetime supply of pasta and pizza. That made me feel good." Mallory lifted the bag of cookies and sniffed, absorbing the lingering aroma. Her mouth watered. "Our missing bear suit was in the garbage." She had forgotten about accidentally accomplishing that bit of police work.

"That might give us a lead," said Jacobson.

"Maybe. I turned it into the lab. It was shredded with a scissors or knife and pretty contaminated."

"Sounds like somebody was looking for something."

A strong hand squeezed Ginger's upper arm. Victoria had rushed over to greet her.

Ginger turned her attention away from Earl, who was doing his statue impersonation by the elevator. She'd been gone for a day and a night. Why didn't he come over and give her a hug?

Victoria gripped her upper arm, smiling placidly. She was decked out in a lavender exercise suit. Except for the penciled brows, she wore no makeup.

"I'm on my way to do my workout and then spa. Fiona Truman and I have paid extra for privacy in the spa." Victoria lifted her chin. "You can do that when you have celebrity status. I'll wait for you, if you want to change into workout gear."

"Thanks for the invitation." Ginger veered her eyes toward Earl. "It's not a good time." Her husband still hadn't moved. "How about a rain check? Tomorrow?"

"Sounds good." Victoria performed a stretch that involved clasping her arms behind her back and swinging side to side. "What's your room number?"

"I'm in 517."

Earl took a single step in her direction.

"Are you feeling okay?" Victoria placed a hand on her hip and bent sideways, stretching her arm toward the ceiling. "You seem a bit distracted."

She looked at the aging starlet. Victoria's eyes were clear, her cheeks had a natural blush to them that suggested a high level of health. She'd been so fixated on Earl she'd almost missed the open door God had provided for her to share with a stranger. "I've just been through a life-changing event. I —"

Victoria squeezed Ginger's shoulder. "How about I just meet you in the gym tomorrow, say eleven o'clock?"

That door slammed pretty fast. Apparently, life-changing events weren't Victoria's thing. "Okay, that sounds good." Again, Ginger turned her attention to her husband.

Earl shook his head.

Victoria sauntered around the corner and out of view.

Husband and wife performed a strange

choreography. She took a step toward him, and then he took a step toward her, until finally she was close enough to see the level of sadness in his eyes, the droopiness of his expression. What was going on here? Wasn't he glad to see her?

He lifted and lowered his hands as if he didn't quite know what to do with them. "I missed you. I was so . . . where did you go?"

I missed you too, my sweet man. "So much has happened in such a short time."

He stroked his widow's peak. "A lot went on here too." The pace of his head rubbing slowed, and he looked directly at her. "The detective said . . ." He stepped toward her. "Don't you trust me?"

That was the last thing she had expected to come out of his mouth. "What are you talking about?"

"When we were being interviewed by that detective, she said you gave me a look."

This was not how she imagined their conversation going. Disappointment pressed down on her like a lead shawl. "Earl, I saw you on the convention floor hours before Dustin was killed."

"Do you think I had something to do with the murder?" His voice was almost a whisper. He leaned over, looking like he was about to crumple into a fetal position.

"Of course not. It's just that . . ." She hadn't meant to torment him, to plant such doubt, but she couldn't deny what she had seen.

"Why didn't you show up to the Shopping Channel audition? I needed you." He bent his head and lowered his voice. "Have you lost faith in me?"

"No, Earl, that's not it." While her world had been coming together, his had been falling apart. "I've been worrying too much about money. I lost everything, and God took care of me —"

"I don't know what I would do if you didn't believe in me."

"It's just that you've become this different person. This goal of becoming a great inventor is consuming you, Earl, and it scares me." She touched his upper arm. "Where's the sweet man I married?"

"He's still here, Ginger." He held out his arms.

She stepped toward him, let his arms envelop her as she rested her cheek against his warm chest, melting into him. Yes, that was what she had missed.

He patted her back. "We just need to find a distributor, and then things will get back to normal."

Ginger stiffened in his embrace. "You say

231

that, Earl, but after that it will be some other thing connected with the invention." She lifted her head off his chest. "I want to be supportive of you, I do, but something is out of whack."

"Just help me out with this one thing, and then I promise. Fiona Truman from the Shopping Channel might have us on. I'm no good on TV, but you are; you're a great salesperson."

Ginger leaned back. "You haven't heard a single word I said."

Earl dug into his wallet. "She gave me her card and everything." He waved the business card like a little boy with a new action figure.

They were two trains headed in opposite directions on different tracks. "It's just that it seems like you don't see people anymore."

"We've staked so much financially on this." He leaned a little closer to her. "I'm working hard. Isn't that a good thing? Doesn't God call us to excellence?"

"Not at the expense of everything else. There's a fine line between striving for excellence and becoming a workaholic."

His mouth opened slightly, and he shook his head.

She couldn't make him understand. She stepped away from him. "I'm going to go find that Detective Mallory. I have important things to tell her."

Hanging out in a discount bait shop wasn't Kindra's idea of a good time. But, at least, the place didn't smell like fish as she had expected. It was more like the scent of fresh-cut wood.

While she had waited in the lobby for Ginger, she had checked the front desk for messages. Xabier wanted to see her again next door at the bait shop ASAP. The guy really needed to invest in a cell phone. She'd made a spur of the moment decision, something she rarely did. Xabier needed her more than Ginger.

Kindra scanned the shop. No Xabier. Fishing flies held her interest for about ten seconds. She sauntered in the direction of attire, where she could watch the door in case Xabier came in. What did the well-dressed fisherman wear these days? Waders and flannel shirts were all the rage. Several patrons perused the store. One of them, an older man, engaged the clerk in a conversation about bobbers.

She stopped to examine an odd contraption, waders with a sort of inner tube around the top. What would a fashion show for fishermen be like? Half-starved models stalking down the runway in flotation devices complete with feet. The image made her smile.

A hand warmed her shoulder. She turned slowly and gazed at a man in a baseball hat and dirty T-shirt. Xabier was good at this disguise thing. She had looked at this man several times and dismissed him as a possibility. He had a potbelly and five o'clock shadow. Only the eyes gave him away this time. He'd opted not to use the colored contacts. Looking in those brown eyes was kind of nice.

"I like your smile." Xabier pulled the cap down so it covered more of his face. "Are you having any luck finding what you need there, pretty lady?"

He had changed his voice, making it more gravelly with just a hint of redneck. Kindra leaned a little closer. "You're really getting into this, aren't you?"

"Yeah, I guess, but this isn't how I planned to use my theater degree." He pushed up the volume on his voice. "I'm partial to this green flannel myself."

She caught herself about to say his name and glanced around the store again.

He leaned closer to her and whispered, "I need you to find my mom. I can't risk them connecting her with me. They might put pressure on her. But I got to take some action, get this thing to move forward. She's not strong . . . physically. Her name is Gloria."

"I know who she is. My friends have met her."

"Tell her I'm okay." He turned slightly, pulling on the sleeve of a flannel shirt. He pressed his lips together. "Tell her not to worry."

It was nice to meet a guy who cared about his mother's feelings. She touched his hand. "We'll get this worked out."

"One more thing. You said that I should do that visualization thing. The agreement they showed me had the name at the top. It was Eternal something or Infinite something."

"Something to do with things going on forever?"

"Yeah. Maybe Dustin had some record of it in his files. I was thinking maybe you and my mom could look for it together. That would help us figure out who these guys are."

"We have to go to the police at some point."

Xabier arched his back. "I told you. I don't trust cops."

She tried a different tactic. "Where are

you staying?" Maybe if she hit him with the reality of how being a fugitive forced him to live, he'd be more inclined to go to the police.

"I'm moving around a lot. I haven't been back to the room Dustin gave me to live in except to grab a few things real quick. I know they're watching that. There are storage closets on almost every floor; most of them have one of those fold-down beds in them."

"That can't be fun."

"Hopefully, it won't last much longer. Find my mom and tell her what is going on. She'll know how to handle it."

"Take care of yourself." She swallowed to keep from saying his name. His gaze made her heart beat faster than the prospect of a half price sale on shoes.

His hand grazed over hers, sending tingles up her arm. She leaned close and kissed him on his fake stubble. "You go out now and catch some big fish."

He whispered in her ear, "Turn your back and I'll be gone."

She pivoted pretending to be fascinated by fly fishing poles. His hand brushed over her hair, with a gossamer touch. When she turned back around, there was no sign of him.

Stay safe, Xabier, stay safe.

Ginger stared at the hotel room phone.

"That won't make it ring sooner." Arleta played with the zipper on her purple, sequined, satin jacket, turning side to side in front of the mirror.

Suzanne rested on the bed, legs crossed at the ankles, flipping through a magazine. "It's only been like twenty minutes since you called the station house."

Half an hour ago, Ginger had walked into her hotel room to find two members of the BHN. They had greeted her with long hugs, and she had shared the ordeal of the night before. Something Earl hadn't even asked her about.

Suzanne tossed her magazine on the bed. "You left your cell number with the police, didn't you?"

"I lost my cell when I lost my purse. I gave him your number."

"Why don't we go out and do something fun to get your mind off of this?" Suzanne swung her feet to the floor. "Detective Mallory can just get hold of me."

"I want to get this resolved, so they can find who hit me in the head." Ginger rose to her feet, crossing and uncrossing her arms. "The stolen jewelry might have something to do with Dustin's death. I'm sure that was the bear costume he was killed in. How many bear costumes can there be?"

A phone buzzed. Ginger jumped. Hope that the call was for her vaporized when Suzanne flipped it open and checked the screen. Her face brightened. "My kids." She chimed into the phone, "Hey, sweet baby. How's Mama's girl?" She meandered toward the bathroom.

"Maybe I should just go down to the station house." Ginger's finger tapped the table.

"That sounds like a time waster. You would just be waiting at the station house instead of waiting here. What if she's here at the hotel investigating?" Arleta plunked down on the bed. "I'm sure she checks in for messages, and the station probably can reach her on her cell."

She hated not being able to do anything. Waiting was the worst. What to do? Her feet sunk into the plush carpet as she paced.

Arleta propped a pillow against the wall, leaned back against it, and closed her eyes. Her hand fluttered to her forehead. Skin, tissue-paper thin, revealed blue veins. Age spots occupied more territory than clear skin.

She'd never thought of Arleta as old, but

now . . . She noticed the slight shaking when she held her hands up. "That jacket suits you." Ginger sat back down in the chair. "It brightens you up. Brings out the color in your eyes."

"I need brightening, do I?" The older woman opened her eyes and smoothed the jacket over her flat stomach. "I think I'm dressing in these flashy things because I want to feel less close to dying."

Ginger blinked several times. What a shocking thing to hear her robust friend say. "Arleta, you're in great health. You've got twenty years ahead of you."

"It's just that I met that Gloria Clydell the night her ex-husband was killed. She could die anytime. Yet, she was happy. I suddenly saw my own life in perspective." She patted her chest. "This old ticker is going to stop sooner or later."

Ginger leaned back in the hotel chair, allowing herself one more glance at the phone. "We're all going to die . . . sooner or later."

"But you're going to go to heaven." Arleta picked microscopic fuzz off her jacket.

Ginger stared at the senior member of the Bargain Hunters. She sat up a little straighter. They didn't talk that much about their faith. But something they did or said had impacted Arleta. Ginger opened her mouth to speak. The important moment was interrupted by Suzanne yelping from the bathroom and emerging holding her phone.

Ginger squeezed Arleta's hand. "We need to finish this conversation. It's important."

Suzanne trotted back into the room waving her phone. "Ginger, your cyber stalker is getting quite hostile. You've got like ten e-mails forwarded from the address we set up for the blog." Suzanne read: " 'Where are you? You are the only one who can help me. My spending is out of control. Please help me. Why aren't you posting? I live for those blog entries.' She or he signs it Crazy in Calamity."

Ginger's thoughts tangled. She rested her head on the table. "I'm not going to post, and I'm not going to respond to that terrible person. I have bigger fish to fry. My cat is still missing. I need to clear mine and Earl's name." *And . . . my husband and I are on two separate planets.* Ginger rose to her feet.

Suzanne shut her phone. "We will think of Crazy in Calamity no more."

Arleta threw her hands up. "We can't just sit here. Ginger will go insane. We have to do something. I'm with Suzanne. Why don't we go out and visit the garage sales? That's one of the reasons we came to this town anyway."

Suzanne bumped Ginger's shoulder. "Come on, you love garage sales, and this is the world's largest. It'll get your mind off of things, and then before you know it, that detective will call you back."

Ginger nodded, taking note that maybe God would open up an opportunity to talk more to Arleta about heaven while they were shopping. "Okay, let's go bargain hunting."

"Mr. Salinski, I thought you said you were bringing your wife with you." Fiona Truman, Shopping Channel sweetheart, wore no makeup. The dark circles under her eyes and the sagginess of her skin were no longer hidden. Even the bright pink of her workout suit didn't hide her fatigue as they stood outside the door that led to the Wind-Up's spa and gym.

Earl hung his head. "She doesn't want to come . . . yet. If you'll just give me another chance to audition, I promise I will have better stage presence this time." His chances were slipping away. He had to make this happen.

"Stage presence isn't something you acquire like life insurance. It's something you either have or don't have. You said your wife, what was her name, Ginger, would be here."

Why was Fiona constantly reminding him of his failure to get Ginger to rally for him? *I'm such a loser.* "Why does it have to be my wife?" He grabbed her arm and squeezed it. "I can do this." He pounded out each word.

Fiona pulled away and stepped back. "Mr. Salinski, please don't pull on my arm like that." She massaged the spot on her bicep where he had pressed.

The shock on Fiona's face mortified him. He hadn't meant to be so forceful. He just wanted her to see how badly he wanted this. "I'm . . . I'm so sorry." He reached toward her and then let his arms fall at his side when she jerked away. "I have two daughters your age. I would never hurt a woman." He shook his hands. There was no excuse for what he had just done.

"I was trying to help you." She opened the spa door and stepped behind it so it functioned as a shield between her and Earl.

"At least take one of the Pepper Lights. Maybe you can show it to your producers and they'll have some marketing ideas." His need to push for the success of the Pepper Light was almost involuntary. He couldn't stop. *I don't like myself right now.*

She took the Pepper Light, unzipped her gym bag, and dropped it in. "Sure, okay."

Her hand shook when she unzipped her bag. He'd really scared her. He had never felt so ashamed in his life.

"Maybe I can still talk Ginger into it." He didn't want to believe that his wife had lost faith in him. What was the point in going on if that were true? Then again, look at what his need to make the dream happen had done. He had lost his wife and scared a stranger.

Fiona spoke rapidly, slipping behind the door even more. She was trying to be polite, but she didn't want to talk to him. "I have to leave for the airport on Sunday around five. I would really love to meet your wife, see how she is on camera." Fiona pushed the spa door open wider. A cacophony of banging weight machines and groans spilled into the hallway. "But no promises." She stepped inside, door easing shut behind her.

Earl wandered out of the hotel to the boardwalk by the lake. He gazed out at the rippling water. Boats buzzed and sputtered in the distance. Chatter and laughter spilled out from the Little Italy terrace. A crew blew up an inflatable pool on the dock. According to the sign, Binky would be water-skiing in less than an hour.

Everything, everyone seemed distant. At the periphery of his understanding, a faint prayer formed. *Oh, God, I'm so sorry.*

Ginger's words came back to him. This dream was consuming him. He had been so focused on getting the next thing done for the invention, he hadn't been able to hear what she said to him. He slumped down onto the bench. *If I ever stop listening to my wife, I am doomed. She's the smart one.*

He placed his face in his hands. He hadn't meant to hurt his wife and her friends, sure hadn't meant to scare Fiona like that. All this time, he had thought he was working so hard, striving toward excellence, thinking God would smile on that. Really, he was just being selfish.

On the other side of the hotel, the noisy buzz of traffic and garage salers carried to the lake side of the hotel. He'd never cared much for garage sales. That was Ginger's thing. Maybe, though, he could just wander around and think things through . . . be with people again and see them, really see them.

He walked on the path that separated the Wind-Up from Little Italy and out into the revelry of the garage salers. From a distance, he thought he saw Ginger's distinctive hair.

SEVENTEEN

"I know you think it's silly." Martha Hillstrong stood on the edge of the crowd watching the new Binky be pulled by his little remote-control boat. An inflatable pool with a depth of two or three feet had been set up on the dock.

Mallory crossed her arms. The sun beat down from a cloudless sky. She could feel her skin turning red and crispy as she spoke. "Think what is silly?"

Martha Hillstrong pushed her plastic-frame glasses up on her face. "Squirrel lovers, getting together, having a convention."

"I don't think it's a good idea for me to pass judgment on people." It hadn't been a planned interview. She didn't think Hillstrong had anything to hide with the fingerprints. She had run out of people to talk to in an official capacity when the roar of the crowd had lured her out to the lake.

"They're special creatures. I can be having a bad day at the lab and go to the park for lunch with a bag of peanuts. Just feeding them makes me feel better."

"I don't have anything against squirrels or squirrel lovers, Miss Hillstrong."

"It's Mrs. I am married, and I have two kids." Martha tucked a strand of stringy hair behind her ear. "You just assumed that I was some recluse weirdo."

"That's not at all what I meant." She had to give Hillstrong credit. The woman was pretty good at reading people. Mallory had mastered the art of hiding her feelings as part of her police training, but Martha had picked up on some subtle clue and determined her prejudice. "I spoke without thinking." If Martha ever quit her job at the lab, she had a bright future in police work.

The crowd erupted in applause as the new Binky made another round in the pool.

"There are some people who can't even handle the responsibility of a pet, but they can go to the park and hang out with the squirrels."

Mallory shaded her eyes from the sun. "Mrs. Hillstrong, I am not here to indict your love for squirrels."

"Then why did you track me down?"

Hillstrong didn't need to know that after two days, she was the strongest lead they had and that the interview was accidental. "We found the ball Binky was in when he was abducted."

Hillstrong shifted her weight, tugged on a strand of hair, and crossed her arms. "How do you know it was Binky's ball? This place has tons of squirrels and tons of balls."

The flash of guilt in Hillstrong's eyes, that furtive glance, surprised Mallory. Maybe she was onto something. "This one had Binky's name on it. Mr. Simpson identified it."

"So what does that have to do with me?"

"Your prints were on it."

"Mr. Simpson and I know each other." Martha stared out at the water. "I can't remember when, but it is entirely possible that I touched that ball. I was fond of Binky. He was a smart squirrel."

Mallory would have taken Hillstrong at her word except for the signals she was sending up like bottle rockets: nervous gestures, no eye contact, precise enunciation. No doubt about it, she was lying.

"Why don't you tell me why your prints are really on that ball?" Mallory infused her voice with sympathy. Where interviews were concerned, overt hostility only worked in detective movies.

Hillstrong breathed Lamaze style, exhaling audibly. Mallory feared the woman would hyperventilate. "I just feel . . . so guilty."

Mallory closed the distance between her and Hillstrong. "And why is that?" she asked gently, barely letting her voice get above a whisper.

Hillstrong rubbed her forehead with the heels of her hands. "I think I am responsible for Binky's death."

Mallory didn't say anything. She waited. A confession comes easiest in silence. *No pressure here, Martha; just tell me what you know.*

"I wanted to help him, Binky. To get him free from the life Mr. Simpson had set up for him."

"You mean . . . the water-skiing."

"No, Binky loved to water-ski. His show was good PR for all squirrels." Hillstrong wet her lips. "I'm pretty sure Mr. Simpson was stealing jewelry and he was using Binky to help him."

Ginger bent down to study a hand-woven welcome mat that looked like new. When she stood up, she'd lost sight of Arleta and Suzanne. Those two! The lure of a good sale made them lose track of where they were. They couldn't have gotten far. People milled around her.

No matter, she had plenty of good deals to look at. If she worked her way down the long, somewhat crooked line of sales, she'd run into them sooner or later. The girls had been right. Staring at the phone wouldn't make the detective get back to her any sooner. The peace she had felt when she was with Ida Mae returned. There was very little she could control. She'd done her part. Things would happen when they needed to happen.

"You," a voice croaked out.

Ginger's looked up. Binky's owner — she couldn't remember his name — stared at her, shaking his head. The expression on his face confused her. His eyebrows were all knit together, like this was his personal garage sale and she shouldn't be here.

Maybe a sympathetic word would get rid of the scowl. "You're the owner of that squirrel who died. I'm so sorry for your loss."

The man nodded. Even in the hot sun his face paled. Was he coming down with the flu?

"I'm sorry, I don't remember your name."

"Simpson. Alex Simpson."

People pushed past Ginger. Mr. Simpson continued to stand close to her, to stare.

Might as well try to make conversation. "Are you finding any good deals out here?"

"What?" he snapped.

"At the garage sales." Maybe she shouldn't have brought up the dead squirrel. His grief was coming out in hostility. "Have you found any treasures?"

"I . . . no."

"I'm really not here to shop either." She picked up a bronze statue and turned it over in her hand. "Just killing some time."

Without breaking eye contact, he brushed his hand up and down his thin, freckled arm. "What did you say your name was?"

"I didn't say, but it's Ginger." She stepped free of the force field of his gaze. Maybe he was just broken up about his squirrel, but Mr. Simpson was acting peculiar.

His arm shot up, clamping onto her forearm. "Do you know anything about antiques? Because I saw some pottery." He pointed with his free hand several garage sales over. "It had a signature on the bottom. Does that mean it's worth something?"

"I know a little about pottery, and a signature is an indication that it might be valuable."

He leaned toward her. "Would you mind coming with me?"

"I'm kind of looking for my friends —"

She turned slightly, and his grip tightened.

"It's just a few tables over. I could use your expertise."

His eyes held a desperate, pleading quality. She did like helping people get a good deal. "I suppose I can keep an eye out for my friends while we walk."

The crowd on the boardwalk and pier had dispersed. A lady in a leotard gathered up the new Binky and turned a half circle while the audience applauded. His trainer gave the audience a final wave.

Mallory moved closer to an awning to get out of the sun. Hillstrong trailed behind her. "Why didn't you tell the police of your suspicions?"

"I wasn't sure. Mr. Simpson and I do a lot of shows and conventions together. At a different convention, I saw him working with Binky, teaching him to retrieve a piece of plastic the size of a card key. I didn't think anything of it at the time. Then at the start-up of this convention, I was in his room going over an itinerary. I spilled one of his buckets of ice while he was in the bathroom. There was a diamond tennis bracelet in it."

In the little patio that separated the two hotels, Mallory spotted a vacant table with an umbrella. She spoke over her shoulder as she made her way to the table. "Why didn't you speak up when my partner and I were talking to Mr. Simpson?" Once the confession spilled out, Mallory had no doubt that Hillstrong would be an easy interview. The need to tell someone in authority must have been building for some time.

Hillstrong plunked down in the chair opposite Mallory. "Mr. Simpson scares me. He has a temper. I don't know if he could be violent, but" — she pulled her glasses off — "I just wanted to get Binky to a safe place, a good home and away from his life of crime." She opened and closed the stems on her glasses. "I was thinking of the squirrel. Nobody thinks about the squirrels."

"Something must have gone wrong. Binky ended up out on the pier . . . dead."

"There was a large cat in the hallway. Who expects to see that? I dropped the ball; it broke open. Binky ran away with the cat after him." She closed her glistening eyes. "I tried to find him; I did."

"Do you know where Mr. Simpson is now?"

Ginger didn't like the way Mr. Simpson's fingers dug into her arm. "I thought you said it was just a few tables over?" She stepped around two four-foot stacks of encyclopedias. The crowd was thinner on this side of the parking lot.

"I must have been mistaken. I've looked at so many things today." He dragged her toward the edge of the lot. "If you would just please come and help me."

He hadn't overtly said or done anything to make her suspicious. It was just that the urgency in his voice caused a prickling, tingling sensation at the back of her neck and his fingers pressed hard into her flesh. "I'm sorry, Mr. Simpson, but I have to go." She pulled herself from his grip. Best to be as polite as possible. Her instincts could be wrong.

He grabbed her again and squeezed, igniting the nerve endings in her arm muscles. "Please, I really need your help."

Ginger's fear calibrator moved up the scale. "We'll talk pottery some other time." She wrenched away from him.

He stood, hands at his sides. She waited for him to lurch toward her. He didn't move. Okay, so he wasn't dangerous. She'd let her imagination go into overdrive again.

"You have a good day, Mr. Simpson." She turned to leave, her back to him. She'd taken two steps when a tug on the shoulder of her shirt stopped her. Fabric ripped. He twisted her around to face him.

She clamped a hand on the torn shoulder seam. "Why are you doing this?"

He latched on to her shirt collar with both hands and pulled her face very close to his. "You haven't gone to the police yet, have you?"

Though she tilted her head back, she could feel his breath on her face. What was he talking about? It took only a second of staring into his wide eyes for her to process what he was saying. "It was you. You hit me on the head." No wonder he was surprised when he saw her. He thought he had gotten rid of her.

Like a searchlight moving across a landscape, a flicker in Mr. Simpson's expression, a momentary illumination, told Ginger she was right. She opened her mouth to protest.

He grabbed her by both arms, spun her around, and pushed her toward the open door of a trailer.

Kindra stared at the stack of papers Gloria Clydell had pulled out of her dead ex-husband's desk drawer. The task before her suddenly seemed daunting. "Maybe this isn't the best way to go about things."

"You said yourself figuring out who is

chasing Xabier would be the fastest way to make it safe for him to come out into the open." Gloria patted Kindra's back. "Come on, Tiffany has been nice enough to let us in here. We'll work on this together, and then I can see my son again."

"He would have gone straight to you, Gloria. He was afraid the men might hurt you if they found out you were at the hotel."

The older woman divided the stack of papers. "Here, you take half, and I'll take half. You said he thought it had the word *eternal* or *infinite* on it?"

Kindra nodded. She flipped through the first six pieces of paper, all repair bills for the hotel. This seemed like a lot of work that the police could be doing. "What's his problem with the police, anyway?"

The stack of papers Gloria held fell to floor. She kneeled to pick them up. Kindra situated herself on the carpet. "Let me help you."

Gloria gathered a stack of papers into her hands, then let them slip to the floor again. She touched Kindra's knee and studied her for a moment. "Sorry, mother's guilt is getting the best of me." She sat cross-legged on the carpet. "I got sick shortly after Dustin left us. The scleroderma had spread to my lungs. I had to go to the emergency room. Xabier had gone to a park to play." Gloria shook her head. "It was a new town. He didn't know his way around, couldn't remember our phone number. He found a policeman like I had taught him. The policeman told him to wait on the bench and that he would be back with help. He never came back. The next morning when I got out of the hospital, I found my little boy sitting at our kitchen table. He'd had to find his own way home." She put her hand over her mouth. "He looked so vulnerable. He had on this little red jacket he always wore, and his hands were folded in his lap."

"He must have been afraid when he got home and you weren't there."

"Xabier tried so hard to be a good boy. I don't know why the policeman didn't come back. Maybe he got caught up in some crime, maybe he sent someone and they never went. I'll never know."

"I guess I understand why he doesn't trust the police . . . but that was so long ago."

"He was only nine years old. Everyone he trusted abandoned him. I tried, but I was so sick and so torn up about the divorce." Her voice trembled. "I abandoned him too." She shuffled through the stack of papers, moving them from one pile to the next so quickly that she couldn't be reading them.

Kindra had opened an old wound. Time to change the subject. "You don't seem to be angry at Tiffany. When she let us in, you were kind to her."

"I was married to Dustin. I feel sorry for her."

"She's still mad at him, and he's dead." Kindra propped herself on the huge wooden desk.

Gloria laughed and shook her head. "Anger is the flip side of love."

"You don't think she, you know . . ."

"I understand the rage she must have felt." She rose to her feet with the papers in her hand. "He was still playing her when he died."

"She told me she thought she was going to get the hotel."

Gloria turned over another piece of paper. "I'm not seeing anything here with the words *eternal* or *infinite*. Do you think Xabier was mistaken?"

"Your voice gets all warm when you say his name."

"Yours does too." Gloria tapped the stack of papers on the desk to straighten them. "You like my son."

Kindra's cheeks warmed. "He seems nice. We haven't had much of a chance to talk. Right at the first, when they said that a guy in a bear costume died and I thought it was Xabier, I realized how much I liked him. We had this instant connection." Kindra pushed the papers aside. She leaned back, lacing her fingers around a knee. "But I have my checklist, and I have to finish college first."

"Your checklist?"

"I haven't dated much. I spend most of my life with my face in a book. Ginger and the girls helped me put it together. It's the list of things I want in a spouse. Top of the list is that he must be a Christian."

Gloria pressed her lips together. "I tried to raise my son so he would comprehend God's love, but it all got so tainted by the things that Dustin wanted to do in God's name. Then I got sick." She rubbed her thumb over a section of the desk. "I'm afraid it's left a bitter taste in Xabier's mouth."

Kindra shook her head. "What your husband did doesn't change who God is."

"When you're young and impressionable, it gets all mixed up in your head. Xabier and I sort of became props for Dustin, the supportive wife and the cute son of the businessman who was building a business for the Lord." Her tone was mocking, and then she seemed to collapse in the chair, spine bending, shoulders drooping. "He forgot that we were people who needed him."

"I'm sorry to hear that Xabier's faith is shaky." *More than sorry — devastated.* "Maybe he'll come around."

"That's the prayer I repeat every day." Gloria rolled the office chair away from the desk and stared at the ceiling. "I don't think there's anything here that's going to help us. Maybe Tiffany would let us go through his personal desk in his apartment."

Jacobson and Mallory made their way across the street to the first parking lot that contained one part of the World's Largest Garage Sale. There seemed to be no rhyme or reason to the way people had set up their booths, no clear lines or aisles. People had just squatted wherever they felt like it.

"We've been operating under a false assumption." Mallory crossed her arms over her stomach. "We assumed that because the thefts stopped the night Dustin died that he was the culprit."

"But there were two victims that night."

"And who planted the false assumption in our heads?"

"Tiffany Rosemond," Jacobson said.

"It was bad police work on my part." Mallory tugged at the placket of her size-too-small blazer, hoping the buttons would reach the buttonholes. "I'm not supposed to be swayed by the suggestions of others." The jacket had fit her fine six months ago.

"Yeah, but what detective would think 'hey, maybe the squirrel is the thief'?"

"Jacobson, you made a joke."

"Yeah, so I did. That's usually your department." Jacobson beamed from the compliment. "You don't need to beat yourself up over this. I think your police work is always really solid."

"We got this parking lot and five or six more." She scanned the lot. The booth in front of her specialized in vintage clothing and stuffed animals. It would take a million years to find Simpson in that maze. If he was even still out there like Hillstrong said. Plus, there were several more parking lots. "I say we just wait until he gets tired of shopping. We can put an officer in the lobby and one by his room door. Then we'll pick him up for questioning, get a warrant to search his room, and dump out a few ice buckets."

"So do you think Miss Rosemond planted that suggestion to distract us from the possibility that she was a suspect?"

"That's one motive; the other possibility is that she really believed that Clydell was stealing. His note to her said he was about to come into a lot of money. Say he had been stockpiling the jewelry and he had found a buyer. Simpson might have been the buyer or had lined up a buyer for a cut."

"The jewelry wasn't in Clydell's office or private residence."

"This is a big hotel. We won't know anything until we find Simpson." Mallory patted Jacobson's back. "Let's go inside and wait for Mr. Simpson to come to us."

EIGHTEEN

Mr. Simpson pushed Ginger against the table in the tiny trailer. He scanned the room and pulled a knife out of the butcher block on the counter.

Her back pressed into the table. "What . . . what are you going to do?"

"Just don't go to the police." He waved the knife like a baton.

"Why did you hit me on the head and put me in a boat?"

He touched his free hand to his chest. "Those jewels were mine."

Mentally, Ginger scanned her clue cards. The jewels had been in Dustin's bear suit. "He figured out you were stealing?" She pushed herself off the table. "So you . . . killed him."

Mr. Simpson took a step back. "No." He glanced around the room and ran his fingers through his spongy hair. The knife blade reflected glints of light as a makeshift clothesline above their heads caught his attention. "Get back over there." He sliced through the thin rope then jabbed the knife at her as an afterthought.

Ginger's heart skipped into double time, but she planted her feet. Mr. Simpson wasn't a big man, and he didn't act like he knew how to use that knife.

"I said to get back on that couch." His voice lacked conviction.

He sounded as afraid as she was. She eyed the door. Once she was tied up, there would be no chance of escaping him.

Now or never, Ginger.

She dove toward the door. Simpson groaned in protest. Cold metal grazed her skin; pain threaded up her arm. She clamped a hand over the cut. He had more gumption than she would have predicted.

Her hand touched the cold steel of the door handle. When she pushed it up, the door didn't budge. Darn. One of those tricky handles that took a second to figure out, a second she didn't have.

He yanked her by her hair. Her scalp burned. She had underestimated him. Her escape attempt seemed to fuel his anger. She twisted her body. They both fell backward with Ginger falling on top of her assailant. She rolled to one side and scrambled to her feet. Mr. Simpson stared at her, eyes wide, chest heaving. She stumbled the two steps to the door and pushed the handle up and then down. Down worked. That was the trick. The door swung open.

Ginger froze.

Earl stood at the bottom of the stairs. His hand hung in the air as though he had just reached for the door handle.

"I saw you from a ways away. Something didn't look right. Took me a minute to figure out where he had taken you."

Ginger collapsed into her husband's arms. His voice, the strength of his arms around her . . . she never wanted to lose that. She was shaking, gulping in air, and crying.

"You're okay now. You're safe." He whispered in her ear, pulling her closer, stroking her hair. "I am so sorry. You were right."

She pulled back from the hug so she could look at her husband. There was so much to say, so much to share. But now was not the time. "He's still inside, Earl. We have to call the police."

Earl pulled his cell phone out of his belt. He put one foot on the metal stairs and flipped his phone open. He glanced inside the trailer and then leaned in even farther. "Ginger, he's not in here."

"He has to be." Her heart still pounded

erratically from the adrenaline overload. She struggled for breath. "He must be hiding."

"Or he slipped out that window." Earl pointed with his phone.

A muscular man with long hair and tattoos covering his arms stalked toward them. "Hey, what are you guys doing in my trailer?"

Ginger and Earl backed away from the trailer. "We're sorry. A man pushed me in here." She pointed with trembling fingers. "We think he might still be hiding in there."

The trailer owner stepped up the metal step. "Gee whiz, it's a mess in here."

"I'm sorry." Her legs had turned into wet noodles. Her hands were almost vibrating. "I'll . . . I'll pay for the damages."

The man looked her up and down. "That's all right. It looks like you've been through enough. If he is hiding anywhere . . ." He stepped into the trailer.

Ginger poked her head through the open door. Earl's hand rested on her back.

The man lifted a seat cushion by the table and then removed the plywood lid. He shook his head.

Ginger stepped back into the trailer. "Could he get out some way other than the door?"

"Was he a big guy?"

"No," said Ginger.

The man made the entire trailer shake as he sauntered across the floor. "Looks like my screen has been pushed off."

Ginger bolted out of the camper. Simpson couldn't have gotten far in such a short time. She scanned the crowd, the salespeople, the displays, racks of clothes, and piles of boxes. About forty yards from her, Mr. Simpson grabbed a bicycle with a *For Sale* sign on it. This guy was not going to get away. Not on her watch. Ginger ran toward the bicycles. Her cross-trainers pounded the pavement.

She grabbed a bike and checked the sign in front. Twenty-five dollars. A little pricey for a garage sale. Up ahead, Mr. Simpson navigated through the clutter of the garage sales toward the open street. An older man with a brown apron tied around his waist walked toward her, increasing his pace.

Ginger swung her leg over the bike and yelled back at Earl. "Pay the man." Rather than follow Mr. Simpson's poorly planned path, she assessed the quickest way through the maze of merchandise, riding in a somewhat parallel path to Mr. Simpson, about twenty yards behind him.

Earl had just shaken the hand of the bicycle salesman when Ginger pressed hard on the pedal. She sped forward twenty yards, swerved around an antique lamp, and pumped her legs. Mr. Simpson had been slowed by a labyrinth of blankets containing china and other kitchen items.

He glanced over at her.

She slammed into an old couch. The impact jarred her; her teeth clacked. She hadn't been going fast enough for it to throw her off. With this level of inert traffic she had to navigate around, it would just be easier to push the thing until she got out into the open street.

She leapt off and wrapped her hands around the handlebars. A crowd swarmed toward her, gravitating in the direction of a table with Christmas items. She angled away. Metal clanged on the old bike.

Mr. Simpson had moved some twenty yards from her but had stalled out as he searched for a way through a series of tables. She couldn't get a straight path to him, too many people were in the way.

At best, the paths between merchandise were short and disconnected. She focused on getting to the street. If she got there first, she could simply ride up and down the edge of the parking lot until he emerged. That is, if he didn't see her out there. If he did see her, he might plunge back into the muddle of the garage sales and slip out somewhere else on a different side of the lot or simply melt into the jungle of people and merchandise.

She pushed past a group of people who had become fascinated by stuffed animals and posters of Scott Baio and the A-Team. A fairly long display of clothes hung on racks; two rusting antique car bodies provided shelter from view. She could peek through the clothes, lift her head up over the cars, and keep a bead on Simpson.

Sweat trickled down her back. The air smelled of cotton candy and popcorn as she neared the edge of the lots where the food venders had set up shop. Her mouth went dry. She had maybe ten yards until she would be back in view. Right before the last clothing rack, she slowed. A woman running with a bike would call attention to herself. If she went slow enough, she was more likely to blend in. Just a sweet senior citizen pushing the bike she bought. A crowd gathered around the pizza by the slice stand.

" 'Scuse me." She pushed her way through. She veered toward a cluster of people, then stood on tiptoe, scanning the lot. Glints of metal. His fuzzy hair. Rapid movement. Something that would distinguish him. No Mr. Simpson.

The crowd around her flowed in different directions leaving her exposed. She pushed the bike the last ten yards to the curb and hopped on, ready to take off. This side of the lot ran parallel to the hotels and stretched for a good three hundred yards. She had a clear view of the entire length of the lot, the empty street, and a portion of the other side of the lot.

She waited, rocking her bike. She should have told Earl to call the police. Maybe he would think of it on his own. No sign of Mr. Simpson. No sign of Earl.

Ginger pedaled twenty yards and stopped.

"Little hot for a bike ride, isn't it?" The ice cream vendor was a skinny man with a gift for stating the obvious. His red hair curved up like wings on either side of his paper hat. "You look like you could use a refreshingly cool treat."

Ginger read the man's price board. An expensive refreshingly cool treat. She swallowed to produce some moisture in her mouth. No luck there. Her throat was drier than Death Valley. "Do you have any water?"

The man shook his head.

Sometimes overpriced things were worth the money. She fingered the two dollars in her pants pocket while she glanced up and down the street. She didn't have a purse. "How about one of those lemon-lime ICEE things, small?"

She slapped her two bucks on the counter while he poured the slushy ice from the dispenser into the paper cup. She watched the road the whole time.

Ginger relished the coolness of the cup and brushed it over her forehead before she took a drink. She sucked the liquid through the straw. *That hit the spot.* Her straw had just made that slurping, desperately-seeking-some-liquids sound when Mr. Simpson emerged from the fray of the garage sale mania and pedaled down the road.

NINETEEN

Xabier was Xabier. He had called her from a pay phone and said he wanted to meet her in the park two blocks from the Wind-Up. He stood by the swings, dressed in sweatpants and a baggy shirt. No wig, no colored contacts. Just handsome, dark-haired Xabier.

She walked toward him. He grabbed a swing and pushed off.

She rested a hand on the metal leg of the swing set. "No disguise?" The park bordered the lake. Beyond the park, a golf course hummed with late-afternoon activity.

"Kind of out of ideas. All I got is my portable makeup kit. I think I'm safe here. They seem to hang around the hotels mostly." He slowed his pumping. "Did you find out the name of the business?"

"We couldn't find anything. Your mom is looking through his private office. I gave her my cell number." She gripped the chain of

271

the swing next to Xabier. "Your mom really wants to see you."

He skidded to a stop. "Whatever for? I'm just starting to get good at this hiding out." He gazed at some unseen object in the distance while he dug a foot through the wood chips, making deep furrows.

Kindra plopped into the swing beside him. He needed cheering up. "There's got to be a bright side." She stepped sideways toward him, resting her cheek on the chain. "You like coming up with the costumes and disguises."

"Okay, that part was fun." He slipped out of his own swing and stood behind her.

"How much money did Dustin owe the Eternal or Infinite guys, whatever they were called?" She duck-walked backward, gripping the chains of the swing. His palms pressed against her back, and he pushed. She arced upward, enjoying the dizzy sensation.

"I just glanced at it. There were either six or seven numbers in front of the decimal point."

"What would cost that much? It can't be a legitimate business." She swung back, closing her eyes and concentrating on the rush of wind around her. "Otherwise, wouldn't they go to Dustin's lawyer and

272

make him pay up through the estate?"

"I guess." His hands pushed against her back. "All Dad's assets are tied up. Maybe they need the money right away."

"Speaking of estates, what are you going to do about the hotel if it is yours?"

"Ever the practical one, aren't you?" He grabbed the swing and stopped it with a jerk. He fingered the chain and leaned toward her. "I don't know. I don't know anything about running a hotel. I know theater. Maybe I'll sell it and start my own theater company."

Xabier didn't have a plan. What a foreign concept. How could he operate that way? "You can't remember anything else about these guys?" She liked looking into his dark chocolate eyes.

He yanked on the chain until she laughed. "One is bald and overweight, and he smells like a smoker. The other is tall with square shoulders."

"Definitely the same guys we saw chasing your dad through the underground outlet mall. One of them looks kind of like Frankenstein in a suit?"

"Yeah, exactly." He stepped away from the swing with a dance move that looked like the grapevine she did in aerobics.

"They probably didn't kill him. Can't get

money from a dead guy. Unless they were trying to get the money and their method of persuasion got out of control." She kicked at wood chips while a plan formed in her head.

Xabier twirled on the heel of his shoe. "The impression they gave me was that they were capable of murder . . . tough guys."

"You said they seem to find you when you're at the hotel?" Kindra jumped out of the swing to face Xabier.

"I don't know their names."

"We don't need to know their names. Maybe we should set some kind of trap for them. Where have they spotted you?"

"The first time was outside my hotel room." He pounded a fist on the metal leg of the swing set. "That's when they showed me the paper with Dad's signature on it. The other times it was in the lobby or one of the restaurants."

"So they're waiting for you in public places. I bet they're staking out the lobby." She touched his hand. "Xabier, what if we stalked the stalkers? We could follow them and find out where they're staying, find out the name of the business." She plumped back into the swing. "That invoice has to be in their stuff."

"It might work." He pulled back on the

swing, holding her so her feet dangled. "It would be like an acting job."

She fingered the swing chain. " 'Course, we would let the police take over once we found out the name of the business."

"Why?" he barked. He let go of her, pushing hard on her back before she swung away.

Kindra pumped her legs. She had tried. Xabier wasn't going to overcome his distrust of the police any time soon. " 'Cause it would be safer that way."

Xabier pushed her even harder, probably working out some flare of frustration. Clouds filled her vision and then grew distant. She closed her eyes and relished the sensation of speed. The sun warmed her skin. The force of his pushing decreased until he stopped altogether. She giggled, held her legs out, and leaned back. The arc of the swing decreased.

Xabier pulled her to a stop. He stood over her. "Safe, who wants to be safe?" His hand swept over her cheek.

An electric tingle enveloped her. Xabier leaned toward her, his face inches from hers. He brushed butterfly-soft fingers along her jaw and under her chin, then leaned in and kissed her.

The warmth of his touch made any

thought of her checklist fall completely from her mind.

Ginger slammed the empty drink on the counter. "Thanks for the recharge." She pushed off on the bike and placed her feet on the pedals. The street had been closed to through traffic for the garage sales, so there were no cars to block her view. Simpson rounded a curve as he rode away from the buildings that bordered the lake.

She pumped harder. The bike was old, the kind without gears. So far, the road was level. She breathed a little heavier. Pain flared in her leg muscles. What would she do if she had to climb a hill? Biking at high speeds was maybe not on the list of recommended activities for a fifty-seven-year-old woman.

She pedaled through the curve. Mr. Simpson was maybe a hundred yards in front of her and in full view.

He glanced behind, then angled the bike and slipped onto a side street. Ginger turned as well. She sped past a minimart and into a residential neighborhood where most of the lawns were brown from lack of care. Simpson zigzagged through the streets. The bad news was that she was a fifty-seven-year-old who rode like a fifty-seven-year-old. The good news was that Mr. Simpson wasn't much younger and was even more out of shape. She closed in on him. Thirty yards. Her lungs felt like they'd been scraped with an X-Acto knife. Twenty yards.

Her breathing became labored. *Push the pedal down, Ginger.* She stood up on the bike and straightened her leg.

Simpson pedaled toward a long, unpaved alley. The residential neighborhood transformed into taller buildings. She followed him, working even harder when the tires hit the rocky dirt of the alley.

He got to the end of the alley and turned left.

When she rounded the corner, Mr. Simpson's bike rested on its side, not too far from a door. The back wheel spun. She stared up at the tall brick building, probably the backside of an older hotel.

Ginger glanced up and down the street. Nothing. The street was long enough that she should have seen Simpson running if he had decided to hoof it. He'd ditched the bike. He must have gone into the hotel. She pulled the black door open.

Applause floated down the long corridor. She had stumbled onto some late-afternoon show. She walked past a door that said Drake the Magnificent. Drake's door was locked. She trotted down the hallway, peeking into the only open door, which was an empty dressing room whose central feature was a cage with a yellow and black snake having his noontime nap.

Stage noises grew louder. Circus music? Through side curtains, she had a view of the performance. The stage contained two rings. One featured two jugglers who kept dropping their bowling pins. In the other, a man in a leg cast dragged himself across the stage. A sparkling vest accentuated his chest hair and potbelly. Three feet away, a tiger lay on its side. At the snap of the tamer's whip, the tiger flipped his tail and yawned. In a box above the stage, a ringmaster announced, "See Drake the Magnificent bring the fierce tiger under his control." Two overweight trapeze artists took turns twirling on the swing and standing on the platform with the ringmaster.

Ginger placed a hand on her hip. She couldn't just walk across the stage. She pivoted and pushed another curtain aside. Ah, four stairs that led to a polished wood floor. Glasses tinkled, and low-level murmurs filled the air. This had to be the way out to the audience, the most likely place to find Mr. Simpson.

Ginger waited for her eyes to adjust to the

subdued lighting. Odd, considering the sun blazed outside. In this place, it was night all the time. Twelve to fifteen people were spread out among about thirty tables and a bar. Ginger squinted. Half the tables were empty. If Simpson was here, he would be easy enough to find.

She surveyed the room for possible exits Simpson might have taken while the circus continued behind her. Two double doors on the right side of the bar seemed likely to lead to the rest of the hotel. First, though, she would figure out if he had settled into the audience. If he had gone out into the hotel, it would be almost impossible to find him. *Please, God, let him be here.*

The doors that led to the rest of the hotel burst open, and a woman weighted down by at least six shopping bags wandered over to the bar and chose a stool.

"Give me something strong." The woman rested her forehead against her palm.

It took Ginger a moment to realize that the woman was Fiona Truman, the Shopping Channel lady. Earl had said something about her being interested in their invention. Ginger had stopped pushing for the success of the invention, and God had opened this door. Ginger offered her a smile. Fiona turned her back and slumped protectively over her drink. So much for open doors. There would be no chitchat with Fiona Truman today.

Ginger stepped toward the center of the floor, hoping that being in plain view would jar Simpson out of hiding. Talk about eye strain. The lighting was so bad, it was hard to discern if people were men or women. Near as she could tell, nobody jerked or rose from his seat. Onstage, the intensity of the music increased. A second lethargic tiger had been brought out into the ring. The jugglers had switched to dropping oranges.

No one in the audience so much as glanced in her direction. All eyes were on Drake as he fanned his blue satin cape like wings and demonstrated his ability to subdue heavily medicated tigers.

Ginger slipped up onto a vacant stool three down from where Fiona sent out her antisocial signals. The Shopping Channel hostess remained slumped over her drink and stared at the bar. Ginger scanned audience heads, eliminating them one by one.

"Can I get you anything?" The bartender wiped down the counter by Ginger.

"Oh . . . umm." The ICEE hadn't done much to quench her thirst. "I just had quite a workout. I don't suppose you have a glass of water?"

He pulled a bottled water out from underneath the counter. "That'll be two dollars."

"For water?" She patted her empty pocket.

He shrugged. "This is the desert."

Ginger turned back around. A man who had been hidden in a corner booth made his way toward the stairs that led to the dressing rooms. *Eureka.* Simpson had escaped while she had her attention on the gold-plated water. She pushed the bottled water back toward the bartender. "Think I'll pass."

She bolted toward the curtain, trying to pad softly. She had a feeling, though, that even a loud explosion wouldn't draw this audience's attention away from the insomnia-producing performance.

Ginger parted the curtains and dashed up the four stairs. She stepped into the dressing room corridor just as the outside door shut. She wasn't about to lose him after all that biking. She bolted toward the door. A woman in a leotard and wearing the yellow and black snake for an accessory stepped out of the dressing room, blocking her escape.

"There you are!" she accused.

Ginger looked behind her. No one else was in the hallway. "I'm sorry, I think you have me mistaken —"

"Where are the mice? You were supposed to be here half an hour ago."

"I'm sorry, but I —" Ginger tried to step to one side, only to be greeted with a face full of snake. She jumped back, touching a flat hand to her thudding heart.

"Jeremy will have to go on without his dinner. You know, when I signed the contract for this gig, they said that meals would be part of the deal for all of the performers. It's not like I can just go down to the buffet and get Jeremy some shrimp on a stick." The woman put the snake's head close to her face and kissed him while he flicked his tongue at her.

Ginger angled her head to stare at the door Mr. Simpson had just gone through. "Please, I am not the mouse-supply lady." She stepped to one side, careful to keep her distance from the snake.

The woman stomped her foot. "They said an older woman would be coming from the pet store with Jeremy's lunch." She checked her watch. "I have to go on in ten minutes."

Cutting a wide circle around the snake, Ginger slipped past the woman. "I'm real sorry your snake has an empty stomach, but I gotta run."

Ginger pushed the back door open. The bike and Mr. Simpson were gone. She glanced up and down the empty street. Her chest and legs ached. She'd had just about enough of playing detective. Time to make nice with the professionals.

TWENTY

"Frankenstein has entered the building."

Even through her thick fake hair, Xabier's breath tickled Kindra's ear. She smoothed the skirt of her silky dress. Who would have thought that a dark wig and red lipstick could turn her into a different person? "Are you sure?"

They'd chosen the two vinyl chairs in the lobby that provided them with a view of the front desk and elevator. Xabier tugged on his tie and nodded. He looked cute in a suit.

"Now what?"

He spoke without moving his lips. "Let's just watch him."

Frankenstein scanned the lobby, almost as if he sensed someone was watching him. Kindra's breath caught when his gaze rested on them. Xabier shifted in his chair so his face was more toward her than Frankenstein. "Remember, he's looking for a guy by himself." He tugged on his shirt cuffs. "Just don't do anything to alarm him, slow moves. We don't want him to look at us too closely."

Frankenstein stomped toward the front desk. His nickname suited him almost too well. Those clunky boots had to be at least a size fourteen. He probably put the bolts in his neck when he went to bed.

"He's talking to Tiffany."

Vinyl squeaked when Xabier swiveled slightly in his chair. "Hmm. He likes her. When you lean toward someone like that, it indicates attraction." He shifted his weight so he was closer to Kindra.

"You should know." Kindra sunk down in her chair, enjoying Xabier's proximity and the memory of the kiss. Excitement pulsed through her. Before tonight, her idea of daring was to use two colors of highlighter to mark her calculus book. "Tiffany just handed him a skeleton key."

"You were right. He is staying in the hotel." He patted her knee. "Smart girl."

Frankenstein thundered across the lobby toward the elevator.

Xabier slipped his hand in Kindra's. "Come on. Let's stalk the stalker." He placed fingers over his lips. "Just be cool."

Xabier seemed to be some kind of an adrenaline junkie. By the time they had arrived at the closed elevator doors, an older couple stood beside Frankenstein. The doors slid open. The couple stepped in, followed by Frankenstein. Xabier pulled Kindra through as the doors closed.

The older woman chimed. "Seven. Could you push seven?"

The faint scent of rose water saturated the tiny space.

Frankenstein's meaty finger trailed down the panel. He pressed the seven and then the eight. He angled his head toward Kindra and Xabier. Kindra's toes curled in her Audrey Hepburn flats. Her internal alarm system flashed bright red. *Warning. Danger. Get out.* She managed a gurgling sound.

Xabier glanced at the elevator board. "We're going up to eight too."

He sounded so casual, so in control.

Frankenstein arched a bushy brow and then turned his attention to the elevator doors. His sports jacket stretched tight against his back, threatening to rip the center seam at any moment. Xabier gave Kindra's hand a squeeze. She focused on the numbers. Two. Three. Four. *Come on, five.*

The elevator jarred to a stop.

"Huh," said Frankenstein.

"Is it broken?" The older woman stepped toward the panel.

He pushed several buttons. "I'm sure it's nuthin'."

Tension threaded through the elevator. The speed of Frankenstein's button pushing increased. "Hmm."

As if the moment had been choreographed, they all tilted their heads and stared up at the immobile numbers.

Perspiration trickled from underneath Kindra's dark wig, down her temple.

Frankenstein turned his back to the doors. "We are in a pickle."

Ginger drove through downtown Calamity until she approached the police station. Just like Detective Mallory had described it over the phone, the station resembled a miniature White House with several dome structures on either side of it.

This rental car didn't make revving motor noises like her Pontiac back in Montana. She missed her old car and her cute little blue house with the porch swing . . . and life before the police thought she was a criminal. Hopefully, she'd be able to change that last part with this conversation.

Ginger parked the car and stepped out. She took several deep breaths to calm the nerves that turned her stomach into a swelling tsunami. She strode up the stairs. After one more deep breath, she pushed the door open and stepped into the police station. She was in some kind of lobby or waiting area complete with new couches and several closed doors, one of which was designated as belonging to the county attorney. A woman in a suit that screamed *lawyer* sat on one of the couches, reading through a stack of papers. Several other people milled through, disappearing down hallways and stairs and through doors. Ginger walked over to the building directory. Mallory had told her that her office was on the third floor.

A slender, dark-haired woman approached Ginger. "Are you Ginger Salinski?"

Ginger nodded.

"Detective Mallory sent me to escort you in." She touched the ID badge around her neck. "Kind of hard to get around here unless you're official."

The woman led her toward the elevator. They rode up in silence. The number three lighted up, causing Ginger's arm muscles to tense. The doors slid open.

"Just down the hall. Hope it goes okay."

Did she look that nervous?

The dark-haired woman waved right before the elevator doors closed.

Each door was labeled with a different

detective's name. The third door belonged to Mallory.

Mallory opened the door just as Ginger's fist touched the wood. The detective must be off duty. Even in the casual gray sweats and with her auburn hair sloppily pulled up in a scrunchie, the detective came across as imposing and in control. She wasn't that much taller than Ginger. Maybe it was the perfect posture.

Mallory bent her head. "Mrs. Salinski. I'm sorry I didn't answer your first call. We got a little busy at the hotel."

Ginger tugged at the neckline of her shirt. "Thank you for seeing me on such short notice." The churning in her stomach hadn't subsided, and now her neck warmed. People would be able to fry eggs on her forehead before this conversation was over. *The Ginger Grill, open for business.*

"This case is taking a lot of my time. Just like you, I am anxious for it to be wrapped up." Mallory's eyes closed momentarily as she massaged her shoulder.

She's not the enemy. She's human just like me . . . and weary of all this.

Mallory stepped to one side so Ginger could come in. She led her into a sparse office.

No papers cluttered the desk. The pencils

in *The Andy Griffith Show* canister were all sharpened and the same length. The computer was on but turned so the screen was not visible.

A lone photo of a younger Mallory in uniform rested on the shelf, no pictures of a smiling family at a lake or in Mickey Mouse hats posing with Snow White.

Ginger rubbed the knuckle of her index finger. Seeing the human side of the detective didn't make this any easier.

"Can I get you something to drink?" Mallory tilted her head in the direction of a small refrigerator but didn't move toward it, indicating she already knew what Ginger's answer would be.

Ginger adjusted the shoulder strap of the cheap replacement purse she'd purchased. This wasn't a social visit, and they both knew it. "No, thank you." Her throat was drier than the MREs she bought for Earl's hunting trips. "Did you catch Mr. Simpson?"

"No, but we searched his hotel room. No jewels." She picked up a pencil and rolled it between her flat hands. "If he is on a bicycle, like you said, he can't get far. All the patrol officers have been alerted." Mallory set the pencil down and crossed her arms. "We're watching the hotel."

She didn't like the way Mallory punched the words *like you said.* Despite the offer of refreshments, the whole thing felt like a standoff at the O.K. Corral, two gunfighters staring at each other waiting for the other to blink. What did she have to do to win this woman over? "I'm not a criminal," Ginger blurted.

"I never said you were." Mallory stepped toward her desk. "I reserve judgment until all the evidence is in." She placed the pencil back in the canister. "When we do catch Mr. Simpson, he'll either confirm the story you told me over the phone or not."

Now her heart was racing. She tried so hard to do the right thing, to be honest. "Mr. Simpson is the jewel thief, not me."

"What is your association with Mr. Simpson?"

Let the gunfire begin. "I had never seen Mr. Simpson before I came to the Wind-Up and his squirrel went missing."

"When your husband said what time he had gotten into town, you looked at him like you didn't believe him."

That bullet went right into her heart. So that was when the suspicion seed had been planted. She paced four feet in one direction. Mallory was just doing her job. If Ginger were the detective, she probably would have drawn the same conclusion. Ginger slipped her purse off her shoulder and twisted the strap. "I know I saw Earl on the convention floor, and I know my husband is an honest man." She turned and walked back toward Mallory. "I can't answer your question."

"If you could answer that question, I might be more inclined to believe that you were hit on the head by Simpson and sent down the river. If that really is why you can't account for your whereabouts for nearly twenty-four hours."

"I can find the people who helped me." She had to admit, sent down a river and adopted by tent people ranked right up there with UFO abduction stories. Only her story was true. How was she going to convince Mallory? Ginger bent her neck and tapped her head with her fist. "I got this knot on my head. Is that evidence enough?"

Mallory's eyes grew round, and Ginger thought she saw just a flicker of a smile.

The detective straightened her spine, placed her hands on her hips. "I'm sure we'll get this all sorted out once Mr. Simpson is in custody."

Mallory was still giving the official police line, but the silliness of Ginger suggesting a bump on her head would wrap up the case must have softened the detective somewhat. "I guess there's nothing more I can say."

Mallory nodded. "I would appreciate it if you and your husband would stick around."

Ginger walked toward the door, but stopped. She needed to let Mallory know everything. *Do the right thing and God will work out the rest.* She'd driven across town to tell the whole truth. "When you do catch Mr. Simpson . . . He did hit me on the head and he is a thief, but I don't think he killed Dustin Clydell."

Mallory shook her head.

"A year ago in Montana, a dear friend of mine was murdered. I saw the eyes of her killer; I know that look. Mr. Simpson had two chances to end my life, and he didn't take them."

"We can't let a suspect go based on the look in his eyes."

"I just thought you should know. When he had me cornered in the camper, Mr. Simpson got real mad, but he acted like he didn't know how to use a knife. And he could have killed me and put me in that boat instead of just knocking me out."

Ginger couldn't quite assess what the expression on Mallory's face indicated. The detective nodded, but there wasn't so much as a lifting of a brow, very masklike. Ginger turned and walked across the carpet. It didn't matter what the detective thought. She had laid all her cards on the table, and now her stomach had calmed and the heat she'd felt in her face and neck subsided. That was all she could do. The rest was in God's hands.

She reached for the doorknob, opened the door, and stepped outside.

"Does anyone have a cell phone?" Frankenstein's gaze traveled from the old man, to his wife, and then rested on Kindra.

Her heart skipped into double time. The wig was making her sweat. She stared at the pattern in the carpet. *Please quit looking at me.*

Frankenstein leaned toward Kindra as though sharing a secret. "I think I left mine in the hotel room."

Kindra leaned back. Xabier squeezed her hand tighter. How long before Frankenstein figured out Xabier was in the elevator with him?

The older woman waved the air as if shooing mosquitoes away. "Oh, I never use those things."

Kindra turned toward Xabier, so she didn't have to look Frankenstein in the eye.

"I think — I think — I have one." She touched her purse with trembling fingers. Could he see her squirm?

Frankenstein shifted his weight. His gaze rested on Xabier. Oh no. He puckered and then flattened his lips. Time slogged forward.

Please, no, don't let him figure it out. She felt around for the cell phone. Her hand brushed over Earl's Pepper Light. That gave her a sense of security. If things got out of control, she could blast him with it . . . and run, where, to a corner of the elevator? Frankenstein tilted his head and narrowed his eyes at Xabier in disguise.

Xabier stroked his fake beard.

She pushed all the junk around in her purse. The bangs of her wig angled crookedly across her field of vision. Could her face get any hotter? She touched her head, but stopped short of adjusting the wig. That would be too much of a giveaway.

"Is it in there, dear?" The older woman reminded Kindra of her Sunday school teacher, all pink and soft. The older woman's husband tapped his foot and stared at the ceiling.

"I'm looking for it." Her hand rested on the hard plastic of the phone. Was it just her imagination or were the walls closing in?

Oh, for the controlled, cool environment of taking an advanced physics final.

Frankenstein continued to watch Xabier. The danger seemed to energize the actor. He stood up straighter, almost challenging Frankenstein to guess who he was. In contrast, she was producing enough perspiration to supply a water park. If she kept it up, they might just drown in this tiny space.

"Here it is." She lifted the phone and released a nervous giggle.

"Why don't we call the front desk and let them know we are stalled out?" Frankenstein's voice boomed, much too loud for such a small space.

Her fingers hovered over the numbers. Her vision blurred.

The older woman placed a hand over Kindra's "You okay? You're shaking like a leaf."

Xabier wrapped an arm around Kindra's back. "My wife is a just a little claustrophobic, is all. Do you want me to make the call, honey?" He squeezed her shoulder. "I can do it if you like."

He had turned slightly so Frankenstein couldn't continue his under-the-microscope examination of him. The movement was so smooth and integrated with his conversation that only she understood the reason for it. She squeezed the phone. "I can do it . . . sweetheart." *See, I can act too.*

She caught just the hint of a smile on his face.

She dialed. "Hi, Tiffany. This is Kindra Hall. Listen, the elevator is not working. I'm stuck in here with four other people . . . You can? Thank you." She clicked End and snapped her phone shut. She sought out the friendly face of the Sunday school teacher. "She says she can send someone to fix it."

Sunday School Teacher clapped her hands together. "That's a good thing."

Her husband groaned.

Silenced draped the tiny space. Kindra rocked back and forth and stared at the ceiling. She flipped her phone open and snapped it shut.

"Are you two on your honeymoon?" the older woman asked.

Kindra's neck stiffened. *What do I say?*

Xabier said, "Yes, we are. We're from Omaha. This is our first trip to Nevada."

What was Xabier doing, telling all these lies? Frankenstein was already giving them the hairy eyeball. The best thing for them to do was to be quiet and not give good old Frank too many opportunities to stare at them. He was bound to figure it out sooner or later.

Xabier worked his way to a wall of the elevator and rested his hands on the metal railing. He positioned himself so he was behind the old man, blocking Frankenstein's view.

The elevator screeched to life. Frankenstein once again turned his back to them. Kindra melted against the back wall of the elevator next to Xabier. A rock and roll drummer would have envied the rapid pounding of her heart. Might as well place her head in the mouth of a lion. She leaned into his shoulder. This was crazy. Yet, she felt safe standing next to this lion.

The older woman touched her poufy white hair. "They got to that pretty fast, didn't they?" The couple stepped out on their floor. Doors closed and the elevator rose.

The doors eased open. Frankenstein stepped out. Xabier pulled Kindra through the doors. She stopped just outside the elevator, watching the back of Frankenstein grow smaller as he made his way up the hallway.

Xabier tugged on her hand. She planted her feet. Grasping his arm, she whispered in his ear, "Don't you think we have taken enough chances today?"

"I want to get to the bottom of this. I am tired of being chased. I need to see that invoice."

Frankenstein pulled his skeleton key out of his pocket and slipped inside his hotel room.

"You said yourself you think they might be dangerous."

Three women with shopping bags emerged from the stairwell and made their way up the hall. Kindra turned away from them as though fascinated by the artwork on the wall. She spoke under her breath. "What if they did kill Dustin, by accident or on purpose?"

"This was your idea in the first place. Please help me, Kindra."

The painting on the wall was of a little girl holding a rag doll. Trains, blocks, jack-in-the-boxes, and wooden cars lined the shelves behind her. The three shoppers passed by, chattering and laughing. "We got to go to the police. You can't do everything by yourself."

"I told you; I don't like cops."

She studied him for a long moment. Even beneath the disguise, she saw the little boy sitting on the park bench, waiting for help that never came and then wandering home in the darkness. "What's your plan?"

"Thank you." Warmth laced through his voice, making her heart beat faster. He intertwined his fingers with hers. "We saw what room he went into. Let's walk by and get the number."

Their feet padded lightly on the beige carpet. Frankenstein was staying in room 812.

Xabier guided her to the end of the hallway into the room with the pop and snack machines. "Watch his door, see if he comes out. Let me borrow your cell phone."

Kindra pulled her cell out of the purse.

Xabier hit Redial. "Don't hang up, Tiffany; it's your number-one enemy." Xabier leaned a hand against the wall. "I have a favor to ask of you. Would you consider loaning me the key to room 812?"

Even filtered through the phone, Tiffany's voice nearly broke the sound barrier. Xabier used the pauses when Tiffany caught her breath to sooth her tirade with, "I understand. I totally understand." He allowed her to continue until she had exhausted herself into silence or was crying. *Xabier may not want to identify with his father, but he has some of the same charm.*

Xabier allowed the silence to go on for a moment longer before speaking. "If you give me the key, you can have half the hotel, providing Dad didn't have it in hock. It's like a gamble."

Kindra leaned a little closer to Xabier. Had he lost his mind? *Selling his birthright for a key. Hello, Esau.*

"Okay, we'll be waiting here for you amongst the ice and stale crackers."

He handed the phone back to her.

"Are you nuts? Did you just give away half your hotel?"

"It's just stuff. I don't know anything about running a hotel and Tiffany does. Half ownership would produce enough to start a little theater somewhere. There, see, I made a plan."

"But full ownership could make you financially stable, and what if Tiffany killed your dad —"

"I hadn't thought of that." He pressed his palms together. "The hotel doesn't matter to me, Kindra. I can always find a job somewhere if I need to." He ran his hand up and down the wall and shook his head. "Why are you looking at me like that?"

She wasn't sure what the expression on her face communicated, but she knew what the thought in her head was. How could two so very different people like each other so much? "It's nothing."

301

"I'm not a greedy businessman. I'm not my father." He loosened the tie that was part of his disguise. "I don't want to be like my father." Bitterness tainted his words. He studied her for a moment. "What are you thinking?"

"I have this list that my bargain hunter friends helped me come up with, for the perfect mate, which, as you know, needs to happen after I graduate."

"Let me guess, *'must dress in a suit and tie'* is on the list."

She shook her head. "But being financially stable is. I don't understand throwing away an opportunity like this."

" 'Cause it's not the opportunity I want. I wouldn't be happy running the hotel. I never cared about money, about being rich. Look what it did to my dad."

"Not the opportunity you want? I wanted to major in art. Sometimes you've just got to be practical." She rooted through her purse for change. She didn't even like soda. It was easier than looking at Xabier . . . continuing the conversation in which it became more and more obvious that they were a mismatch. What he said made no sense at all. She had been impractical and rebellious only twice in her life. In high school, she'd become a cheerleader against

302

her academically minded parents' wishes, and she had briefly taken to shoplifting in college to deal with stress.

"What else is on the list?"

She studied the drink choices. Dr Pepper or Sprite. "Just things." *Choices. Practical or spontaneous. Xabier or not Xabier.*

He grabbed her by the hand and twirled her around. " 'Must love to wear disguises and chase bad guys.' " He pulled her toward him. "Is that on your list?"

The warmth of his hand on the middle of her back relaxed her. She sighed. "No, but maybe it should be."

TWENTY-ONE

It was close to dinnertime by the time Ginger parked the rental car and walked the long distance to the hotel. The Strip had begun to gear up for a night of activity. Flashing neon invited people to lose their money at a rapid pace. Even though the street was still cut off to car traffic, throngs of people moved up and down the sidewalk. She passed the lot that ran parallel to the Wind-Up. The garage sales had closed down for the night. An orange glow emanated from some of the camper windows. A few merchants threw sheet covers over their tables.

She stood outside the big doors painted in bubblegum colors. *How quickly things change.* Two days ago, she had been a different person with very different dreams. She massaged her shoulders and neck. What a day . . . and it wasn't over yet. From a pay phone in the police station, she'd reached

Earl on his cell phone. He said he would be waiting for her in the lobby.

She pushed open the doors and stepped onto the checkerboard floor. No one was behind the counter. A young couple and a woman in a waitress uniform sat on the lobby couches . . . and there was Earl. The man in the straw cowboy hat with the peacock feather, flannel shirt, and Carhartts looked out of place leaning against a Roman column. The closed doors to the convention floor framed him. Someone had neglected to take down the poster on the easel that said Welcome Inventors. Earl lifted his chin in recognition. Her footsteps echoed as she walked across the polished floor.

"Hey."

He took his hat off and twirled it in his hands. "Hey, right back at you."

Warming up with small talk and mincing words struck her as tedious. They needed to get this thing resolved. Might as well go for the jugular. "What did you mean out there by the camper when you said I was right?"

He turned slightly toward the closed convention doors. "I wanted this thing so bad." He rubbed the brim of his hat. "I didn't mean to make you feel . . . like you didn't matter to me."

He looked cute standing there. "But you did." Cute or no cute, he still had some explaining to do.

"Don't you like me to work hard?"

"Not when you forget my name and make me feel like a prop in the *Earl Becomes Famous* show." She stepped toward him.

"I want to invent something that changes the world." He bent the brim of his hat back and forth. "I'm not getting any younger. I want my life to matter."

"Earl, you are looking at the wrong scorecard." She raised her eyes to the high ornate ceiling. "Dustin Clydell didn't get to take any of this with him. He left behind three empty people he could have poured his life into."

He studied her for a moment rubbing his razor stubble with his knuckles. "I sure don't want to end up like him."

"Me either. Death by squirrel is a horrible way to go." She waited for him to smile at her joke before grabbing his hand. "Welcome back, Earl Salinski."

"Come here." He pulled her close, swaying while he held her.

Hugs from Earl were better than half-price sales. She stopped swaying. But they needed to have a clean slate in every way. "Earl, why did you lie about what time you got to the hotel? I'll understand if you were just thinking about how questioning from the police would take you away from the convention floor."

"I didn't lie."

She searched his eyes. "But I saw you on the convention floor."

He pulled back from the hug and brushed her cheek. "I have agreed to stop being such a workaholic jerk. Now you have to do something for me."

Ginger nodded. "Okay."

"I know what your eyes told you. But I'm asking you to have a little faith in me and believe that I am telling the truth."

"Have faith in what I know about you, not in what I saw?"

"Kind of like we have to do with God sometimes."

Mallory stood at her living room window. A veil of gauzy gray stretched over the sky, signaling the coming sunset. Her conversation with Ginger Salinski had made things more confusing rather than clearer. Ginger had motive and suspicious activity after the murder.

Beebe meowed from the kitchen again. Mallory pushed open the swinging door.

"Hey, baby." She gathered the cat into her

arms. "How's my new roommate?" The cat purred. "Thanks for giving me a reason for coming home. I was getting pretty lonely." Company was nice. Maybe if she had a life other than work, she would be less inclined to make food her best friend. It had been so long since she had done anything social, she wasn't sure where to start.

Mallory placed Beebe on the floor and poured some food into the dish.

She turned the kitchen faucet on while the cat made crunching noises. Warm water flowed over her hands as thoughts cascaded in her head. Ginger Salinski could have put all the guilt at Mr. Simpson's door to detract attention from herself. Instead, she didn't want Mallory to see Simpson as a murder suspect. Mrs. Salinski could have gotten herself off the hook, but didn't.

Mallory pulled a towel off the refrigerator door handle. That could mean one of two things. Ginger was involved with Simpson, personally or professionally, and she wanted to protect him. The other option was that Ginger was an honest person who would make herself look guilty in order to speak the truth. Mallory tossed the towel on the counter.

Beebe purred against her leg.

She didn't know what to think.

Kindra slumped against the pop machine and pressed her teeth into the rubbery licorice. "I am pretty sure this licorice was put in that machine when the first Bush was president."

Xabier stood by the candy machine. "These don't look too bad. Gourmet jellybeans."

Kindra pulled her knees up to her chest. "I love gourmet jellybeans. Let's try those."

"They're my favorite too." He slipped quarters into the slot.

A door clicked open. Kindra crawled to the edge of the vending room and peered around the corner. A large woman in a red coat stepped out of the even-numbered side of rooms. "Not him. What if we wait here all night and Frankenstein never leaves?"

"I say we give it until our jellybeans are gone." He sat down beside her. "Being with me isn't that bad, is it?"

Kindra shook her head. *Not bad at all.* Her stomach growled. "Do you suppose room service would come up here?"

"This will have to be our dinner." He handed her the bag of jellybeans. "Then maybe I'll ask Tiff if she can watch the lobby and let us know when he leaves."

"You know what I like about jellybeans?" She tore open the bag and ate one; lemon-lime flavor washed over her tongue. Jellybeans were the best snack. "They're like a million desserts in one." Using her purse as a table, she spread the candy out. She picked up a yellow one and a white one and placed them in Xabier's hand. "Guess what you're eating?"

"Mixing your jellybeans. You do live dangerously." He chewed the jellybeans for a moment. "Banana coconut pie." He picked up a light brown one and white one with yellow dots on it and placed them in her hand. "Now it's your turn."

Again, her heart drummed from the heat of his touch. Kindra popped the two candies in her mouth and bit into them. "Yum, caramel popcorn."

"I don't think people are supposed to have this much fun with a bag of jellybeans," he said.

Xabier's eyes closed when he laughed. Etchings of laugh lines around his mouth appeared. The rich tones of his voice tugged at her heart. The intensity of his stare made a tingling rise up through her toes and radiate over her skin.

He smoothed his tousled hair. "Are you

going to eat the black ones?"

"I hate the black ones. Licorice is my least favorite."

"I like them best. We work well together, don't we, sweetheart?" Xabier spoke in his Humphrey Bogart voice. "Stick with me kid. You can have a bag of jellybeans anytime."

"Just finish your candy, tough guy." He was fun. Could they base a relationship on a mutual love for jellybeans?

They ate and talked and laughed until only two jellybeans were left.

Kindra stared down at the last two pieces of candy. "Well, I guess the party's over."

Xabier tilted his head. "They look kind of lonely there, don't they?"

"I'll take the blue one. You can have the burgundy one." She picked up the blue jellybean.

"Wait just a minute." He clamped onto her hand. "I think I'm getting the raw end of a deal here. Do you even know what flavor the burgundy one is?"

"No." She held the blue jellybean close to her lips.

"My point exactly. But that blueberry one. Now that is a prize jellybean."

"Oh, all right." With exaggerated pathos, she slapped the blue jellybean down on the purse.

"Now you made me feel bad. You have it." He slumped his shoulders and hung his head theatrically as he pushed the candy toward her.

"After that kind of protest, you take it." She scooted the candy across the purse.

"I insist." He picked up the blue bean and placed it in her palm, closing her fingers around it. "You take the blueberry." He held her hand in his a little longer than was necessary to make his point.

"Fine." She shoved the bean in her mouth.

Xabier opened his mouth wide, feigning shock. "You go right on ahead and have that succulent, juicy blueberry." He stuck out his lower lip in a mock pout. "I'll just have blah burgundy." He fluttered his eyelashes.

Kindra mimed playing a violin. "Oh, you poor baby." She leaned toward Xabier. Her cross necklace slipped out from where she had it tucked under her shirt.

Xabier's smile faded. He grabbed the pendant and rubbed it. "Is that thing for real or for show?"

"For real."

Xabier nodded and turned away.

"Like your mom."

"My mom's faith is my mom's faith." He still wouldn't look at her.

"But it's not yours?"

His voice sounded strained. "It's all messed up in my head."

"Sometimes when I try to understand the theological concepts, my head starts to hurt." She bounced on her knees. "Then I watch a *VeggieTales* video, and it all makes sense."

Her comment produced a grin from him. "It's not about theology."

She liked the way he could let go of a bad mood so easily. Of course it wasn't about theology. She knew that. If only his resistance could be cured with an academic explanation. "Your mom and I had a nice talk."

He crossed his arms. "You and my mom, huh? I had a feeling about you. Maybe that's why I liked you in the first place."

What did he mean by that?

Down the hallway, a door opened. Kindra peeked out. "It's Frankenstein. He's headed toward the elevator."

She'd have to get the answer to that question later.

Twenty-Two

Ginger stopped in the long hallway outside of room 515. Her hand slipped from her husband's. She whispered, "There is a light on under Mr. Simpson's door."

Earl wandered the few feet to their room. "Maybe they've checked someone else into the room." He stuck the skeleton key into the doorknob of 517. "Do you really think he would come back?"

Ginger placed her hand on her hips and stared at the band of light. "Mallory said they haven't found the jewels yet."

"But they searched the room?"

"Maybe he had a very good hiding place for the jewels. He had to leave in a hurry, so he sure didn't take them with him."

Earl relocked their door and put the key back in his pocket. "Should we call the front desk and find out if they put somebody else in?"

"I don't know if they would even tell us

that." Ginger shrugged. She knocked on the door and mustered up a tone of nonchalance. "Hello, is anyone in there?" The light went out. Electric pinpricks tingled down her neck and back, signaling danger. Ginger turned the doorknob.

Earl trotted toward her and tugged on her sleeve. "The guy tried to stab you with a knife."

"You can go with me." She gave his bicep a little squeeze. "I'll be okay as long as my big, strong husband is by my side."

"Your big, strong, *old* husband, you mean."

She laughed and snuggled up against him. "Oh, Earl." She pushed the door open and stared into the dark room. Earl slipped his hand into hers. She felt along a wall for the light switch.

The room had been cleaned and vacuumed. "I wonder what happened to his stuff." The faint impression of footprints was evident in the crosshatching created by the recent vacuuming on the carpet.

"Hello." She stepped inside. "Yoo-hoo."

Earl rested a hand on her lower back. "Maybe we should just let the police handle this."

"Let's check the bathroom." Her mouth was completely dry. Her heart pounded, yet she couldn't stop herself from going deeper into the room. It was scary . . . and exciting.

"Maybe we should call security or something."

Who was he going to call on next for help, the CIA? She swatted him lightly on the shoulder. "That'll take too long. Besides, you're the one that said we need to start having more adventures in our empty-nest years."

He put his hand in the air. "All right. All right. We'll do it your way . . . the dangerous way."

She scanned the room and then wrapped her arms in his. "We have to check the bathroom," she whispered.

" 'We?' Do you have a mouse in your pocket?"

"It's an adventure, Earl."

"A motorcycle ride is an adventure. This is dangerous."

"It's just an empty room." Of course she didn't believe that, but Earl was just being such a chicken. They stepped across the carpet. Ginger leaned against the sink outside the slightly open door that led to the toilet and tub. "Push it open."

"You push it open."

"We'll do it together, and then I'll hit the switch on three. One, two, three."

Light filled the empty bathroom. The shower curtain was pushed aside, revealing only a clean tub.

Huh. Ginger tugged on one of her curls. Somebody had been in here. She stalked back into the main part of the hotel room. The window was closed. When she peered outside, there was only wall, no way to crawl down the five floors. No ledge to hide on. Such a riddle. She turned a half circle in the room. Simpson was a small man. Where would he hide?

"Ginger," Earl walked over to a door partially hidden by the billowy curtain.

Ginger pushed the curtain aside. "The room adjoins the one next to it, 513."

Tiffany lifted her hands off the keyboard. The phone rang a fourth time. She rolled her eyes. It just never let up around here. The phone hadn't stopped ringing since she'd gotten back from giving Xabier the key. "Hello, Wind-Up Hotel, front desk." Her stomach growled. She should have eaten hours ago.

"This is Officer Smith with the Calamity police."

The possibility of being part owner in the hotel made it easier to put up with the chaos. Tiffany angled the phone slightly away. The guy sounded like he had a cold. "Yes?"

"Have you cleaned out 515?"

Tiffany sighed and stared at the ceiling. She was so over this investigation thing. "You guys said it was okay if I did that after you searched it. I need to get another person in there."

"Calm down, miss. We just need to know where you put Mr. Simpson's personal effects."

She'd been through all this with the other officer. "Why?"

"We're now thinking that some of those things need to be taken in for evidence."

Didn't these guys talk to each other? "I moved them to the old atrium that's now a storeroom on the west side of the hotel near the large boat marina. You need to come to me if you want in. I don't remember any Officer Smith, and believe me, I have met a lot of cops in the last couple of days." The sooner they were gone, the better. She didn't need them snooping around. After all, she was about to become half owner of the hotel. "Were you the tall, blond guy who didn't talk much?"

The man hung up.

Kindra's heart raced as Xabier placed the

skeleton key in the lock and turned it.

With their shoulders pressed together, they peered inside. An open suitcase on the bed came into view. Anticipation akin to holding a wrapped birthday present made her bounce three times. "I feel a little bit like Nancy Drew."

Xabier shook his head. "I don't think I have heard that reference since third grade." He tousled her fake, black hair. "I like your sweetness."

"Is that what it is?" She liked a lot about him too. "So we just go in here and find the name of the business, right?"

Xabier slipped into the room. He walked over to a desk where several papers were scattered along with a closed laptop.

Kindra stepped inside and closed the door. She scanned the room. Guilt washed over her. Maybe it wasn't right to go through someone's stuff even if he did carry a gun and threaten people's lives. Maybe it wasn't right for Tiffany to give them the key. "We should hurry, huh?"

Xabier opened a desk drawer. "There are some papers over there."

She inched toward the bed and slid the suitcase across the comforter. The papers were all brochures and Internet printouts about places to eat and visit in Calamity.

Frankenstein had combined extorting money with seeing tourist attractions, a working vacation.

"Find anything?"

Kindra shook her head. She positioned the papers the way she remembered seeing them and then scooted the suitcase back over the top of them.

Xabier wandered toward the bathroom.

Kindra glanced at the door. "Maybe the other guy has the piece of paper."

Xabier angled his head around the bathroom wall. "No, it was Frankenstein who showed it to me, and then he stuffed it in his leather jacket."

"Maybe if we find the jacket?" She trotted over to the closet by the door. Bingo. One new-looking leather coat hung in the closet. Kindra pulled it from the hanger. The jacket had at least five zippered pockets. "Which pocket was it?"

"Umm . . . I'm trying to do that visualization thing that you taught me. Just a second." It sounded like Xabier was still moving around the bathroom judging from the jumpiness in his voice. "I think it was one of the lower pockets. No, wait . . . inside pocket. Yeah, I remember seeing him stuff it like in a breast pocket."

Kindra turned the jacket toward the lining and felt for a seam. Her hand touched a piece of paper.

Three sudden and intense knocks reverberated through the room. "Hey. Hey, Fred. Freddy, are you in there?"

Kindra froze. What to do? Xabier had stopped making noise in the bathroom. *Don't let that thug open the door.* She slipped into the closet and slumped down into the dark corner, positioning the coat over her head.

The doorknob turned. The voice muttered something about the door not being locked and Fred being less than intelligent. Then the voice became loud, three feet away with no door as a barrier. "I got a lead on the kid. His mom is in the hotel . . ."

Kindra pulled the jacket away from her face. They knew about Gloria. He walked past the closet. She caught a glimpse of a sports coat, a fat guy. Frankenstein's partner.

"Come on, the door is open." The big guy muttered. "You got to be here. You haven't passed out in the bathtub again, have you?" *Stomp. Stomp. Stomp.* This guy was a bigger clod than Frankenstein.

Underneath the jacket, Kindra's breathing sounded like it had been turned up to a ten on the volume dial. She had the sensation of pressure on every inch of her skin. Footsteps pounded on carpet. The tone of the footsteps changed from carpet to the sharp click of shoes on tile. She pressed her eyes shut.

Don't hurt Xabier.

Kindra closed her eyes. Pieces of every psalm she had ever memorized floated through her head. *God is my refuge and ever present help in time of trouble, the Lord is my Shepherd, be still and know that He is God. Whatever happens, He is God. Protect Xabier, please, God. I know he doesn't fit anything on my checklist, but I really like him.*

She jumped at the sound of a shower curtain being pulled back. The back of her head hit the wall of the closet.

Silence.

She dug her fingers into the carpet. Her muscles hardened. She squeezed her eyes shut, anticipating a gunshot.

Footsteps again. The man mumbled something indiscernible, and then he thundered past the closet and out the door.

Kindra slumped forward like a rag doll, resting her face against her knees. Was there a silencer on the man's gun? After waiting a few minutes to make sure he wouldn't come back, she crawled out of the closet, rose to her feet, and willed herself to check the bathroom. Placing a hand over her churning stomach, she padded across the carpet. One step. Two steps. Three. She braced her hand on the door frame of the bathroom.

Her gaze darted from the abundance of personal grooming products on the sink to the empty, bloodless shower.

"Don't jump." A hand cupped her shoulder. She wheezed in a breath of air.

She whirled around. Xabier. "I was afraid for you."

"Dark corners work best for hiding." He turned, indicating an area by the bureau. "I heard a noise and scampered out of the well-lit bathroom."

"I found the paper." She unfolded it. "It says Eternal Nirvana at the top." She drew the paper closer. "Wow, your dad owed them a million bucks. I wonder if they have a Web site. We can figure out who they are."

"That's a good idea, but right now, we've got to go find my mom before the guys with guns do."

TWENTY-THREE

"Are there only three on this tour?" Arleta buttoned her sequined sweater to stave off the desert night chill. Even if the rest of the Bargain Hunters were busy, she and Suzanne were going to do something touristy together if it killed them. This boat tour might be fun.

The captain who bore a resemblance to Gilligan, same big nose, same silly hat, smiled. "Yep, just you three." He pushed a button on the control panel of the boat, causing it to make a noise similar to a large fan. A sign above the control panel announced that the boat provided night tours of the lake.

A third woman sat on the far corner of the bench with her back to them. She had not turned to look at Arleta and Suzanne when they boarded the boat.

Arleta scooted a little closer to Suzanne. "The night air and the sound of the water will make us feel better."

"We can still salvage this vacation." Suzanne rested her forehead against her palm. "Can't we?"

"I am determined to have a good time." Arleta had to work to sound cheerful. Who was she kidding? The whole trip had been a downer. "If it kills us."

The captain pushed another button on the panel, and the boat roared to life. He veered out of the harbor and into open water.

Clean air filled Arleta's lungs. The boat bumped over the water, headlights cutting a swath of illumination. Memories of her dear husband rose to the surface of her consciousness. She and David had taken boat rides in all parts of the world to go on archaeological digs, in all kinds of boats and under all kinds of weather conditions. Since she'd met the other Bargain Hunters, thoughts of David, that longing to be with him, had subsided. Every once in a while though . . .

The third woman turned toward them. Even though it was a cool evening, the woman seemed overdressed in her fleece coat, with matching hat and mittens. In the dusky light, Arleta recognized her. "Gloria Clydell?"

The woman jerked her head up. "Yes."

"I met you in the coffee shop, the night that Dustin . . . We're friends with Kindra and Ginger."

Gloria nodded and scooted a little closer. She studied Arleta for a moment before nodding. "Oh yes, I remember."

"This is my friend Suzanne."

"You're the ones who helped Kindra put a marriage checklist together."

"Ah, the famous list." They'd brainstormed the list over peanut butter cookies and tea at Arleta's condo.

Suzanne shifted on the wooden bench so she could stare out at the water. Nothing was going to cheer her up. The disappointment had been easier for Arleta to bear. Everyone she cared about in the world was with her on this trip.

"It's warmer than usual tonight." Gloria unbuttoned two buttons on her fleece jacket. "I'm sensitive to the cold, but I love the nighttime. Being out on the water helps me think." She lifted her chin slightly. "Usually, it's just me and Captain George."

The Gilligan look-alike waved without turning to look at them.

Gloria rested her hands on her thighs. "But tonight, there are three of us."

"The boat held but three." The increase in the wind intensity energized Arleta as the boat picked up speed. Out here on the water, it just felt like you could get a deeper breath of air. "Isn't that an Emily Dickinson poem?"

"The carriage held but three?" Gloria tapped her fingers on the metal railing of the boat. " 'Because I could not stop for death, he kindly stopped for me. The carriage held but just ourselves and Immortality.' "

"That's it." Arleta clasped her hands together. "I don't think I have heard that poem since my college days."

Water lapped against the boat, creating a hypnotizing rhythm. The Wind-Up, the Little Italy Hotel, the park, the golf course, and the businesses that surrounded the lake became a shrinking mosaic of flashing and fixed lights and shadows. People were cruising the boardwalks and terraces at this hour, but they had become only faint impressions.

The song of the water and the caress of the wind enveloped Arleta. She closed her eyes. Deep water had never frightened her. The vastness of it made her feel safe. When she had been out on the ocean with David, she had experienced an unnamed understanding that only now, this night, made sense to her. Years ago, her husband had held her while on the deck of a ship with the sun slipping below the horizon. David's arms around her and the beauty of the evening had made her think for a moment that there might be a God.

Gloria reached across Arleta's lap and touched Suzanne's hand. "Is the boat ride helping?"

Suzanne turned to face her traveling companions. "Did I look like I needed something fixed?" The wind rippled over her curly, brown hair as she tied the strings on her life jacket.

"You seem to be working through something," Gloria said.

Arleta put her arms around her friend. "Our vacation hasn't gone as we had hoped, and Suzanne is missing her kids."

"Children. How many?"

"Four. My littlest is a year old." Suzanne crossed her arms.

Gloria kicked off her shoes and tucked her feet under her on the bench. "How wonderful."

"They are wonderful. I love my kids." She tilted her face toward the night sky. "And I love this moment, here, right now."

"That's the secret, loving the gift of the moment you've been given." Gloria brushed a gloved hand over the rim of the boat.

Suzanne rose to her feet and leaned on

the boat railing. "If you ladies don't mind, I'm going to enjoy my gift."

An even deeper stillness settled around them as they got farther out on the water. Sounds from the hotel faded.

Arleta studied her own hands, blue-veined spider webs covered in translucent skin. "Death will stop for me too."

"It stops for all of us." Gloria adjusted the hat on her head. Her labored movement suggested pain in her arms. "Some sooner than others."

"At least you know where you're going."

"It's not an exclusive club." Gloria turned so she was face to face with Arleta. "Heaven is yours for the asking."

"It just seems like it should be harder than that," Arleta said.

"That's what throws most people. Gotta pay dearly for every other good thing in this world."

"Mine for the asking?" Arleta planted her feet and slapped her hands on her thighs. "Okay, I'm asking."

"You want me to pray with you?"

Arleta glanced at Suzanne, who seemed lost in some blissful moment leaning against the railing with the wind rippling around her. Captain George kept his eyes on the water. "Uh . . . okay, but not out loud. That would be just too strange."

Gloria removed her gloves, cupped a hand on Arleta's neck, and leaned toward her. They touched forehead to forehead. Arleta's neck pulsed, pushing against Gloria's cool hand. A moment later, Gloria pulled away. She held both of Arleta hands in a barely tangible grasp.

Arleta sat up a little straighter. "I don't feel any different."

"That only happens in the movies. You are different, believe me."

Suzanne sat back down on the bench with a sigh. "That was like Christmas."

Arleta tilted her head toward Suzanne, angling slightly so her face would be in the light. "Do I look different to you?"

Suzanne leaned toward her friend. "Uh . . . no."

Even Suzanne couldn't tell. "Maybe it's like stew; it has to cook for a while."

Gloria threw back her head and laughed.

Suzanne shook her head. "What are you guys talking about?"

"I'll tell you later." The boat swayed and rocked in the water. Arleta put her hand over her heart. No, she didn't feel any different there either. "What is the point of this tour?"

Gilligan turned slightly sideways. "A boat

ride is the point."

"We're not going to stop on an island or whiz past a historical building or something?"

Gilligan shook his head. "No ma'am, but we are about to come up to the best part of the tour."

Suzanne rubbed her shoulders.

"Let's huddle," suggested Arleta.

The three women sat on one bench, watching the glow left by the setting sun. The captain turned off the engine. Gilligan turned to face them, leaning against the wheel. "This is why I do night tours, ladies. Enjoy."

The water rippled against the boat, creating soothing rhythms. The afterglow of the sunset faded on the horizon. The calm that surrounded them seemed fuller, to contain the unnamed thing that now had a name.

"Come on, you must have seen her." Xabier trotted behind Tiffany, who appeared to be in training for the one-hundred-yard dash that was run in four-inch heels. "She's not in her room."

Xabier and Kindra, minus their wigs, had caught Tiffany on her way to Dustin's old office. Kindra had tried to wipe off the makeup in the lobby bathroom, but Xabier had been in a hurry to find his mom. The makeup made her face hot . . . or maybe it was the running around.

Tiffany turned her head but kept up race speed. "Look, sweetie, I'd love to help you, but I am doing more than just standing at the front desk taking notes on who has walked through the lobby. I have a lot on my plate." She stopped suddenly and elbowed Xabier. "Especially since I'm going to be a partner now."

She opened the office door, walked across the carpet, and placed her coffee mug on the desk.

Kindra followed Xabier into the office.

Using a high-legged kick she must have learned at dance school, Tiffany removed her pumps. She rolled the office chair out from behind the desk and slumped down into it.

Xabier's hand slipped into Kindra's as though it were the most natural thing in the world. They were partners too, working together to get to the bottom of this.

"Tiff, my mom could be in danger."

Tiffany swiveled in the office chair. She grabbed the coffee cup and took a long sip watching Xabier over the rim of the mug. "Am I going to be, like, in debt to you forever if you give me half ownership of the hotel?"

Tiffany seemed to have taken to the idea of owning a hotel. She rose and yanked open a file drawer. She took out a stack of papers and proceeded to run them through the shredder.

"Tiff, come on. This is my mom."

Judging from the piles of shredded paper, Tiffany was destroying a lot of documents. Why was she in such a hurry to get rid of so much paperwork?

Tiffany sat back down in the chair. She pounded on its arm and stared at the ceiling, making a clicking noise with her tongue. "Try the bellboy on shift. His name is Jason. He's pretty tuned into the comings and goings of people."

"Watch your step now, ladies." Gilligan's meaty hand grasped Arleta's as she stepped onto the pier. Her legs wobbled. *Hello, dry land.* This must be an underutilized part of the hotel. She squinted to discern Suzanne's features though she waited only a few feet away. The nearest street lamp was close to the backside of the discount bait shop about forty yards away.

This part of the dock housed larger boats separate from the gondolas. A string of maybe ten or fifteen boats were parked along the pier. Gilligan had docked next to a boat named *Jackpot.* Beyond the dock was what looked like a greenhouse or atrium that connected to the Wind-Up.

Arleta did a Charleston step on the pier and waved her arms. "I'm in the mood for cake, a celebration." She was still waiting for that *different* feeling to kick in, but she did feel wide awake, like she could go all night.

"That sounds like fun. Maybe we can find Kindra and Ginger." Suzanne looked at Gloria as Captain George helped her out of the boat. "You want to come with us?"

Gloria slipped back into her gloves and crossed her arms. "I am afraid I am out of energy. I have to do life in short spurts."

Arleta wrapped her arms around Gloria's shoulder and squeezed. "Am I glowing yet? I want to glow like you do."

"Be patient." Fatigue weighted her voice. She patted Arleta's hand with fleece-covered fingers. "Thanks for letting me be a part of this," she whispered close to Arleta's ear.

Arleta's hand warmed where Gloria covered it with her glove, and her breath brushed the older woman's ear.

Gloria slipped from the embrace, waved good-bye, and walked toward the well-lit garden that the two hotels shared. Empty gondola boats lolled in the smooth water. The chatter and laughter of clusters of people barely reached Suzanne and Arleta on the dark side of the hotel.

Gloria turned toward the side entrance of the Wind-Up, and then disappeared behind a lattice flourishing with ivy and small white flowers.

Gilligan, who had been bustling around his boat, walked past them. He saluted. "Have a good night now, ladies."

Both Suzanne and Arleta nodded. Arleta didn't say anything until the captain's footsteps faded.

Lack of light made her stumble when she moved forward. "Where are we going to find cake at this hour anyway?"

Suzanne caught her at the elbow. "This city never shuts down, remember. I'm sure we can find cake."

They padded past the unused greenhouse or atrium or whatever it had been. Now it looked like a giant storage bin. Arleta saw boxes through dusty windows. She stopped. "Did you see a light flash in there?"

TWENTY-FOUR

Gloria Clydell stuck her key in the lock of her hotel door. She stepped into the room and, without turning on the light, took off her coat and hat, crawled onto the bed, and pulled the pillow close to her stomach. Her hands ached, her joints hurt, and her breathing was labored even though she had only walked a short distance. Warm tears slid down her cheek.

I'm tired, Lord.

She pulled the covers around her. The boat ride and visit had been good. That's what she needed to focus on. Arleta was a sweet lady. Just when the constant pain and despair got the better of her, God gave her the reminder that there was still a reason to be here. She turned over on her back, elevating her head with a pillow, waiting for sleep, that blissful place of floating and drifting when the heaviness of her muscles made the pain subside.

In the dark, she stared at the ceiling. Something felt . . . off. She couldn't pinpoint it. She sat up and traced the outline of furniture in the near darkness.

She lay back down. *Sleep, Gloria, just sleep.* Maybe she should have just gone for cake with the ladies. Kindra was in good hands with mentors like that. Her teeth clenched. Hadn't she prayed that Xabier would find a male mentor? Turning on her side, she drew her legs up toward her stomach. *Shut the door on that thought.* She needed to take her own advice and focus on the gift of the moment she had been given, not what had been taken from her. She had her son and hopefully would see him soon. Dustin's messes continued to haunt them even after his death. It was hard to see the blessing in that.

She jerked at a noise, almost indiscernible, like a hand brushing over silk. Her body tensed. Without sitting up, she surveyed the room. The outlines hadn't changed. She turned and reached for the lamp by the bed.

A thud and then footsteps. Hard steel clamped on her shoulder. Her hand slipped from the light without being able to turn it on.

■ ■ ■ ■

"Somebody is in there." Arleta put her face close to the murky atrium window. "I saw a bouncing light." Her nose twitched from the dust she had stirred up.

"I thought we were going to go get cake," Suzanne said.

"Let's just look real quick. The place is probably chock full of all kinds of treasures that people have tossed." Arleta trotted to a glass door. Suzanne still hadn't moved. "Aren't we all about finding treasures?"

Suzanne shrugged. "Okay, you talked me into it."

Arleta eased the door open. "I bet this was beautiful in its day. Can't you just see the plants hanging from the roof?"

A huge chandelier, long past its luster, rested at an angle in a corner. The room was two-thirds dust and one-third card-board boxes. A mattress leaned against one of the glass walls. Hard-sided orange and avocado suitcases served as accents in the salute to the seventies' décor.

Suzanne sneezed. "Everybody needs a junk drawer and a junk room. I guess hotels need them too."

Suzanne followed Arleta as she shuffled

toward a wooden door. Dust clouds surrounded their feet. She twisted the knob. The second room was about the same size but with wooden instead of glass walls. Small windows, close to the ceiling, lined two of the walls. Broken chairs, an orange shag rug, and empty soda cans completed the arrangement. Several sets of fresh footprints appeared in the dust.

Arleta walked over to a counter where a soft-sided suitcase rested. "No dust on this. They must have put it in here recently."

"Why would someone abandon their suitcase?"

Arleta shrugged. Something white and clean nestled in the corner caught her eye. Among cardboard boxes, broken chairs, and a yellow washing machine was a tiny boat. It looked brand-new and dust free. Arleta leaned down to pick it up. The boat didn't budge. She pulled a little harder.

"Is it wedged in there?"

"It should just come out." She got down on her knees. "It looks like one of those boats that those squirrels are pulled by." Her eyes followed the lines of the boat to the hand that held onto it. Her gaze traveled up to two beady eyes surrounded by pale skin and fuzzy hair.

"It's mine," said the man. "You can't have it."

Suzanne placed a hand on Arleta's shoulder and pointed a finger with her free hand. "I know who you are. I saw your picture in the lobby with that squirrel."

The man erupted out of his hiding spot, clutching the boat like a football. He barreled into Arleta, knocking her over. She fell backward, hitting concrete. Her teeth clacked together. Pain radiated from the impact to her shoulder. Blackness and then intense light flashed through her brain. With the wind knocked out of her, it took a moment to recover and absorb what was happening. She rolled to her side. Her shoulder pain flared.

Two new sets of footprints leading to the exit were evident in the dusty floor. Now she remembered. Suzanne had said something about not hurting her friend and then raced after the man with the boat.

Arleta turned slightly and pushed herself to her feet. She swayed. Still a little dizzy there. The only thing that reduced the pain in her shoulder was to focus on the ache in her hip, which was even more intense. *Someday I'm going to decide I'm too old for cops and robbers.* She limped toward the open wooden door. *But not today.*

Suzanne might need her help. Still favoring one leg, she dragged herself through the glass door and outside to the pier. Suzanne was by the Little Italy terrace crawling into a gondola boat. The man with the toy boat was already paddling out toward the open water.

Arleta's feet pounded on wooden boards, trying to catch up with Suzanne. The man stopped paddling and bent forward, probably out of breath. Suzanne was now in the boat, pushing her oar through the water. The distance between them narrowed. Thirty feet. Twenty.

With a backward glance, the man resumed his rowing. He headed toward the shore by the park and the golf course, but Suzanne was gaining on him as she sliced through the water with strong, even strokes.

Arleta headed down the pier and across the grass where the squirrel man was likely to dock. He banged the gondola against the high piles and crawled onto the beach, still gripping his little boat. Arleta jumped in front of him obstructing his likely escape route on the path into the park. He sashayed first one direction, then another. She stepped side to side, mirroring his every move.

The man glanced back toward the water

where Suzanne was within ten feet of bumping against his abandoned gondola. They had him.

His head swung like a pendulum from Arleta and then back out to the lake. Suzanne climbed out of her own boat into the shallow water.

He met Arleta's gaze. Pain shot down her hip. Involuntarily, she bent forward. When she looked up again Simpson torpedoed toward her, clutching his boat. *Here we go again.* The pain from the previous tackle still hadn't subsided. He was going to do it again, knock her over.

He closed in on her. Her shoulder burned. Her hip felt like it was on fire. *I can't go through that again.* She stepped to one side. Simpson barely hesitated and ran past her into the park.

"What gives?" Suzanne stalked toward her, hands in the air. "You could have stopped him." She gasped for air.

Arleta put a fist on her bony hip. "I'm kind of brittle."

Suzanne tugged on her wet pant legs. "Let's go get him for Ginger. Looks like he's headed through the park into the golf course."

Twenty-Five

Ice formed in Kindra's veins as Xabier took her phone away from his ear and pressed it against his chest. He didn't have to say a word. The glazing of the eyes and an expression like a mask of gauze told her what was up. Frankenstein and his buddy must have Gloria. How else would they have known to call Kindra's cell? "What do they want?"

In the courtyard the two hotels shared, Xabier turned toward the trellis that overflowed with ivy. He clenched and unclenched his fists. "Dad told them about some cash he had stashed away in his office. They said they would settle for that."

"We have to get help." Her hand hovered inches from his back. She wanted to touch him, to offer support, but his actions just seemed so impulsive sometimes.

"We don't have time." He pulled his hair at the temples. "This is my mom we're talking about."

"I know that. I don't want her to be hurt either," Kindra said. "It just seems like you need to quit being such a Lone Ranger trying to solve this thing by yourself. Look how this has escalated."

"They have her out at the golf course. I need to be on the second hole in fifteen minutes."

"Can't we just call the police?" A group of people walking into the Wind-Up stopped and stared at them. Kindra sank back toward the ivy-laden lattice. She hadn't meant to shout.

Xabier lowered his voice. "They have my mom. I can fix this by myself." His stare was intense. "Are you with me or not?"

A picture of a nine-year-old boy, shivering on a park bench and having to find his way home by himself materialized in her head. "I'm with you." He needed someone to be on his side. His trust was so broken, he thought he had to do everything himself.

He headed for the side entrance of the hotel. "Dad kept a gun with his money stash."

A gun. Her breath caught. What exactly had she gotten herself into? "Xabier, I don't think —"

"I am going to get my mom back one way or another." He held the door for her. "She is the last person on earth who deserves to go through this."

While Xabier went to Dustin's office to find the money and the gun, Kindra waited in the hallway and tried Suzanne on her cell. Xabier said no police, but he hadn't said anything about friends. No answer, no way to leave a message. Suzanne must be busy. She dialed Earl's cell. Ginger would probably be with him, or he would know where to find her.

It rang once, twice. Her hand tensed on the phone after the third ring. *Come on, Ginger or Earl, pick up.* "This is Earl's message machine, not the real thing. Leave a message. I'll get back to you."

Kindra pressed her body against the wall and rolled so she could peer inside the office. Xabier came toward the door holding an envelope. Had he tucked the gun in his belt or decided not to take it? She pressed the phone against her ear. "Ginger, Earl, get over to the second hole of the golf course. It's an emergency."

Xabier tapped her phone with a finger. "You weren't calling the cops, were you?"

"No." And that was the truth.

They raced through the dark park holding hands, past the swing set where Xabier had kissed her for the first time. When she'd gotten on the plane in Three Horses, she never would have thought her trip would end up this way, running toward danger with a guy she cared about. Egghead Kindra on her way to a potential shootout, and she thought that she was just going to find some designer shoes on sale. *God, am I doing the right thing?*

"You're awful quiet."

"I'm praying."

He stopped, letting go of her hand.

"Don't you think it would be a good time to pray?" She leaned over, breathing heavily.

"When I was little, I prayed that my father wouldn't leave us." He dug at the ground with his toe.

Why did she like him so much? They were in totally different places with their faith . . . if he had any left at all. "Your father was the one who messed up . . . not God."

"My mom's been saying that kind stuff for years." He tugged on her sleeve. "If we don't hurry, I won't be able to hear it ever again." He sprinted down a paved trail past large trees, benches, and playground equipment. He picked up the pace even more.

Kindra jogged behind him. The distance between them increased. She leaned forward, pushing her leg muscles beyond the rising ache.

As they neared the slides, his sprint

became a jog, then he halted. His words came out between gasping breaths. "Do you want me to be a big fake? Every time I go into a church, my stomach gets tight."

"I'm still going to pray that God helps us get your mom back safe." *So she can keep telling you how much God loves you.*

He squeezed her hand. "You do that. I haven't been able to pray for years."

Their feet pounded on the walking trail toward the far end of the park, surrounded by the quiet of the night. By the time they stepped from the hard-pack earth of the path onto the lush grass of the fairway, they were both out of breath.

"What exactly is your plan?" She couldn't bring herself to ask if he had the gun.

"I don't have a plan. I'll make it up as I go. I just know I am going to get my mom back. I want these guys to pay."

Xabier spoke with conviction, but making things up as you go had never worked for Kindra. She attempted to discern the layout of the golf course. A brick clubhouse with a single light was all she could clearly identify. Three golf carts were parked on the concrete slab outside the clubhouse.

Xabier strode a few feet in front of her. "I wish we had a flashlight."

Kindra clicked her purse open and felt for

Earl's Pepper Light. "I think I have something that will work." She clicked on the light and swung it across the landscape.

A bridge over a small creek came into view. Just across the bridge, the flag for hole number one jutted out of the earth. The second hole must be on the other side of the rolling hill.

"Nice flashlight. It throws a good-size beam."

"Thanks, a friend of mine invented it." She slipped it into his hand. "The other end is pepper spray. That might come in handy too."

"You keep it." He patted his jacket pocket. "I already have something. Let's grab one of those golf carts and find the second hole."

Kindra's resolve lagged as Xabier pulled her toward the golf cart. He had brought the gun. Why hadn't she just called the police? That's what the still, small voice in her head had told her to do. Her attraction to Xabier made sound judgment pack its bags and leave town. Xabier took her hand and helped her into the golf cart. The warmth of his touch subdued her fear . . . a little.

After climbing in on the driver's side of the cart, he kissed her forehead. "Thank you . . . for helping me."

"You're welcome." She closed her eyes, unable to shake off the rising panic that corseted her rib cage.

The cart lurched forward, and Xabier steered toward the bridge. They rolled over the wooden bridge and up the grassy hill. When they came down on the other side, close to a rim of trees, a second flag came into view. A little farther up the hill a sign indicated the third hole was through the trees.

Xabier killed the motor. "This is it," he whispered. "The second hole."

Kindra crossed her arms against the nighttime cold. Xabier pulled his own jacket off and placed it over her shoulders. Why did he have to be so nice? What a special guy. She whispered a muffled "Thank you."

Please, God, just get us both out of here alive.

Xabier crawled out of the cart. Kindra followed. She swept the flashlight across the green, past a sand trap and toward the tree line. Kindra's pulse drummed in her ears. Her throat constricted. Her face brushed against the silk of Xabier's shirt. He grabbed her hand.

She saw a flash of color by the trees.

Xabier let go of her hand. His back straightened.

A voice boomed from somewhere in the trees. "Leave the money and you can have her."

Kindra steadied the flashlight. "It came from up there somewhere."

They raced down the tiny hill across the sand trap. Twice, they fell. Xabier helped Kindra to her feet, pulling her up by both her hands. Her shoes filled with sand, tiny barbs against the soles of her feet. She ran up the hill behind him, her breath ragged and raspy, her heart pounding.

"Where is she?" Xabier paced by the edge of the trees.

"Put the money on the ground and back away."

The voice was coming from somewhere in the trees, but where? The flashlight, still on, pressed against her leg. Kindra started to spotlight the area, then stopped. Better not risk making them angry.

"Where is my mother?" Xabier's voice cracked.

Silence accentuated her breathing. And then, the distinctive click of a pistol slide being pulled back. Her blood iced, and her muscles tensed.

Footsteps breaking branches. She detected a shadow movement in the trees.

"I don't think you are in a position to

demand anything, Mr. Clydell." The voice was closer now. "Put the envelope down and walk back twenty steps."

Xabier placed the envelope in the grass and walked backward. Kindra gripped his arm. Her eyes fixed on the envelope. She curled her fingers into a fist.

A man burst out of the trees from a different place than the voice had come from. Even though he was more shadow than discernable features, he was clearly the shorter, rounder man.

Xabier lurched, then froze. He must have seen the glint of metal in the man's hand. The man picked up the envelope, shone a tiny pen light into it, and disappeared.

They watched the trees. She grabbed his hand. Her breathing and his filled the air.

A mechanical noise, a low-level electrical hum, shattered the silence. Two headlights appeared on the path that lead through the clump of trees to hole number three. A cart with a passenger rolled onto the green and slammed to a stop. The passenger swung forward, then hit the back of the seat.

Xabier moaned.

Gloria lifted her head and gazed up at her son. "I was afraid I would never see you again." He rushed toward her, placing his forehead against his mom's.

Her hands were tied behind her back. The thugs must have set the cart in motion assuming she would be able to brake but not steer.

Kindra rifled through her purse for her pocketknife and handed it to Xabier. He pulled away from his mom after brushing her cheek with his hand.

As Xabier sawed through the rope, Kindra pulled it off. Gloria's hands were cold to the touch. When she placed her hand on Gloria's shoulder, the older woman was shivering.

"Mom, I —" A furtive glance toward Kindra indicated that he was embarrassed by the overflow of emotion.

Kindra reached over and squeezed his hand. "You got your mom back."

"Where are they?" He pulled himself free of Kindra's grasp and stalked toward the trees. Xabier was back in Lone Ranger mode.

Kindra placed an arm around Gloria's back and helped her to her feet.

"Xabier, come on. Let's just go. The police will handle it. You don't have to. They can get the money back and catch those guys."

Xabier paced along the tree line.

"Please, son. Don't try and do this yourself." Gloria shivered so violently that she was almost vibrating against Kindra.

"It's not the money." Xabier paced. "It's what they did to you. It's what Dad continues to do to us even after he's dead. This is his debt."

Gloria's entire body trembled from the sheer effort of having to stand up. Kindra pulled her a little closer and planted her own feet for balance.

"Xabier, for your mom, let's go. We need to get her to a warm place."

He turned to face her. She'd seen that same dark look the night he'd been so angry at his dad.

Gloria stumbled, and Kindra caught her.

"Don't let your life be about revenge and bitterness. Let God and the police take care of it." Gloria spoke to the ground, taking a wheezing shallow breath after each word.

"God and the police, both very dependable." His words dripped with sarcasm. "I depend on me."

Kindra shook her head. "I'm getting your mom back to the hotel. That's what you said you came out here for." She placed the Pepper Light in his hand and pulled her cell out of her purse. "You might need these."

She took a step forward and headed toward the sand trap. Gloria was still leaning against her and seemed to be getting heavier with each step. Kindra held her close and prayed for strength. After they crossed the sand trap, she helped Gloria into the golf cart.

Xabier still stood by the second golf cart. *Come on, Xabier, quit trying to do everything yourself.*

Gloria moaned. She bent her head and crossed her hands over her body.

Move, Xabier, move. Come toward us.

Kindra stepped into the driver's side and turned the key. She moved in slow motion hoping that she would see Xabier head toward them out of the corner of her eye. Hoping that she would hear the sound of his feet mushing through the sand.

Gloria leaned against Kindra. Her breathing sounded as if it was filtered through steel mesh. When she glanced up the hill one more time, Xabier was out of sight.

"That's it, we're lost." Ginger held the map of the golf course an inch from her face. "How hard can it be to find the second hole?"

"It's dark out here, woman." Earl tapped his thumbs on the steering wheel of the golf cart. "We came in the wrong entrance. How was I supposed to know there were two clubhouses?"

Ginger slapped the map. "If *we* had looked at this thing in the first place, *we* would have seen that." They'd probably be half way to Death Valley by now had she not found the map under her seat and put on her navigator hat. Of course, Earl couldn't bring himself to actually study the map. In all the numerous road trips they'd taken when their children were little, she had no memories of him ever looking at a map. Lots of memories of being lost, mind you. "Kindra needs us." That was the bottom line and the reason for her testiness. Her friend was in danger, and they were muddling around on the course like two stooges.

Earl held out an open hand. He sighed heavily on purpose so she could hear it, and had there been more light, Ginger was pretty sure she would have seen him roll his eyes. "Let me see the map."

Ginger's jaw dropped. She made a gurgling noise and shook her head. "Earl Salinski, you surprise the socks off me sometimes."

"Old dogs can learn new tricks."

She ruffled the hair at the back of his head. "Sweet old hound dogs."

"I know how worried you are about Kindra."

In the wake of Earl's sensitivity, her tirade

just seemed silly. "Sorry I blasted you."

He slid the map from her fingers, leaned toward her, and yanked on one of her curls. "Old poodles can learn new tricks too."

"Let's just find my friend." She pressed her head close to his as he shone the Pepper Light on the map.

"Okay, the other clubhouse is right there." He swept the light across the landscape. "Does that look like a building to you?"

Ginger leaned forward and squinted. It looked like a dark stain to her. "Yes, I guess." She crossed her arms.

"Get that worried look off your face. We will find her."

"In her message, she sounded . . . afraid." She hooked one curl behind her ear as she squinted into the darkness.

Earl putt-putted the golf cart over a hill. A top speed of fifteen miles an hour did nothing for her anxiety.

Somewhere to the left of them in the dark, she heard noises. Ginger grabbed another Pepper Light out of her purse and clicked it on. Was she seeing right? "Suzanne?"

"Suzanne?" Earl slowed the cart. "I thought you said we were meeting Kindra out here?"

Ginger shone the flashlight in the same place. This time, Arleta ran through the band of light. It was just a flash of an image and some distance away, but she recognized that thin, perfect-posture woman anywhere. "Over there, go over there."

"I thought we were trying to find the second hole."

"The plan has changed. Go that way."

They rolled down a hill toward a small pond and a sand trap.

Ginger stood up in the golf cart. "Suzanne."

Somewhere in the darkness a man screamed as if in pain.

"Did you hear that?" Ginger patted Earl on the shoulder with a fist. "Let's go toward that noise."

Earl groaned. "Can you make a decision and stick with it?" He turned the wheel in the direction of the noise. "We're both going to end up with whiplash."

Lumbering through the grass, Earl closed in on the origin of the noise. A man shouted a curse. A second voice let out a smorgasbord of swearing.

They were nearly on top of the second golf cart before it came into view from the band of light created by the Pepper Light. The scene was like something in a children's book, the ones where you had to make up a story about what happened based on what you saw in the picture.

Ginger spotlighted the bits and pieces of images with her Pepper Light. A man lay face down on the ground. What must have been a child's toy boat was scattered in pieces not too far from the man. Two men paced beside a golf cart. One of them had to be approaching seven feet in height. He had geometric features, square shoulders, square cheek bones. The other man resembled an actor playing a mafia hit man.

The man on the ground had been hit by the golf cart, and his toy boat had gotten the brunt of it.

The shorter man, Mr. Mafia, bustled around the golf cart. The large man leaned over the body on the grass. When Ginger and Earl came up on him, he jerked his head up and stumbled backward.

What was the proper etiquette in this situation? They had obviously nearly driven into a crime in progress. "Hi," said Ginger. "Nice evening."

"We're just out doing some late-night golfing." Earl's voice was very Sunday afternoon tea party, would-you-like-butter-with-your-biscuit in tone.

Good, Earl had decided to go with the ruse. *Thank you, dear husband.*

Mr. Mafia reached behind his back toward

his waistband. Instinct told Ginger he wasn't hiking his pants up. Probably had a gun tucked in his waistband.

The tall man thrust his chin up and shook his head. The other man pulled an empty hand from behind his back. Whatever these guys were up to, it wasn't good.

Earl chuckled. "I'm afraid we have just gotten a little lost."

The taller man reached down and gathered up the small unconscious man like he was a feather pillow. He lifted the man so his face was visible.

Ginger stifled a gasp. *Mr. Simpson.*

The fat, short man spoke out of the side of his mouth. "Our friend here has had a bit much to drink. We were just headed over to the tenth hole."

A splotch of blood on Mr. Simpson's forehead came into view as Ginger jerked the flashlight from one face to another.

Ginger stood up in the golf cart. "That doesn't look like too much to drink to me." She leaped out of the cart and stalked toward them.

The big man dropped Mr. Simpson and lunged toward her.

She froze. A man that size could clobber her with a single blow.

Earl climbed out of the cart and stood

beside her. She squared her shoulders. They could take on these guys.

Mr. Mafia closed the distance between them. She saw the bulge of a weapon in his waistband.

Her mouth went dry. She took a step back. Maybe fighting with these guys wasn't such a good idea.

Mr. Simpson stirred.

His movement triggered looks and nods between the two thugs. The big one's attention was drawn to something up the hill. He tugged Mr. Mafia's sleeve, and they sprinted back toward the other cart. By the time Mr. Mafia got to the cart, the big man was already behind the wheel.

Guns or no guns, she wasn't about to let these criminals get away. Ginger raced back to their cart and hopped in the driver's side, pressing the accelerator to the floor. She zoomed toward her husband. "Hop in, Earl," she yelled.

Mr. Simpson lifted his head. His eyes were swimming. As they sped past the crushed boat, the glint of jewelry caught Ginger's eye. One criminal at a time. They had a few minutes before Simpson became coherent.

Earl leaned out of the cart as they sped past Mr. Simpson. Mr. Simpson groaned and clutched his face.

"What did you do?"

Earl held up the Pepper Light. "Just a little insurance that he'll be there when we get back."

"You think of everything."

Ginger glanced back to see what the criminals had been alarmed by. Suzanne, Arleta, and a man she didn't recognize who lagged behind were closing in on foot. Five to two. Those were better odds. She pushed the accelerator to the floor.

Her cart traversed across the green for what seemed like several minutes. Ginger was tempted to jump out and run up the hill. It felt like they were moving backward. The other cart disappeared over the top of a hill.

She bounced in her seat. "Can't this thing go any faster?"

"This isn't a Corvette."

They rolled to the top of a hill. The other cart was nearly to the end of the fairway, which connected to a path. Once they left the golf course, they could scatter almost anywhere into the darkness. Chasing them on foot through the city would be futile. She and Earl had to catch them now.

Ginger pressed the accelerator to the floor. She rocked her torso forward and back as if that would make the cart go faster. "Come on, you old thing."

The men turned onto the path. Their cart puttered toward a fence with an open gate.

Earl gripped the tiny windshield.

"Come on. Go, go, go!" They were over halfway down the hill. She wanted to glance over her shoulder, to see if her backup had made it, but there was no time.

The men were within twenty feet of the gate when she saw a flash of red lights and heard a siren. A police car blocked the gate, and another pulled up behind it.

Ginger steered the cart out onto the path.

The two thugs held their hands up as the police came toward them.

Arleta and Suzanne dragged a wobbling Mr. Simpson down the hill with the help of the man, who was also a police officer.

Ginger crawled out of the cart, shaking her head. "How did the police know to come here?"

Xabier stepped from out of the shadows that surrounded the police cars.

Twenty-Six

Kindra held her breath as the sun climbed higher in the sky above the hotels and shopping malls. Morning light spilled over the parking lot filled with garage sale vendors waking up for one more day of selling.

The sidewalks below looked cold and abandoned. Hours before, they had been neon bright and bursting with noise. Only a few cars crawled along the streets that were not shut off for the garage sales. She leaned against the brick wall of the rooftop garden, inhaling the smell of lilac. Dew, like transparent jewels, shimmered on some of the leaves and flowers. Sunday morning in Calamity, Nevada. God was here too.

Footsteps, distinctive in the morning silence, sounded on the stairs that led up to the garden. She turned as Xabier's head emerged.

"Thanks for meeting me up here." Already her throat had gone dry. She laced her fingers together, pressing knuckle against knuckle. She had had a night to think, and she knew what she needed to do. *Please God, give me the strength I need.*

He shrugged. "Thank you for taking care of my mom . . . when I couldn't. I just talked to her. She's doing okay."

Xabier could show up in a garbage sack with a banana peel on his head and he would be handsome, but he was truly endearing in his oversized royal blue T-shirt and tan khakis with pockets on the legs. Maybe it was sort of that shy-guy way he had of hanging his head and hunching his shoulders.

He pulled a white flower off one of the bushes and then moved toward her. He stood beside her, resting his elbow on the brick fence and twisting the flower in his fingers. Their shoulders touched.

She wasn't sure where to start. She had had an elaborate speech scripted out in her head. Of course, all that flew out the window when she saw Xabier.

"So you fly out later today, huh?"

"Yep, back to Montana. The bad guys are in jail, thanks to you. Suzanne and Arleta are meeting me in few minutes so we can celebrate . . . a lot of things."

"I don't want you to go." He slipped the

flower into her hand, brushing his fingers over her palm. "Let's run away and get married. There's like a ton of places you can do it in this state."

She jerked her head back. *Whoa. That came out of nowhere.* "Xabier, I —" She had the sensation of turning in circles in a warm, swirling pool of water, slowly going under, but too dizzy and entranced by the comfort to care.

He cupped the bottom of her hand.

"And then what would we do after we were married?" She had been prepared for almost anything, but not a marriage proposal.

"I don't know." He raised his hands in the air and stepped back. "Sell my half of the hotel once all this is cleared up. We could go live in London. They have theaters everywhere there."

Her checklist said that she should date a guy at least a year before she thought about getting married. No matter how she did the math, three days didn't come close to qualifying. They hadn't even had a real date. "And after that? What do we do when the money runs out?"

He shook his head as if he couldn't comprehend her question. In a way, he couldn't. "Why do you have to script your life out for the next forty years? No matter what kind of plan you make, things will happen that spin you in a totally different direction. Believe me, I know. Doesn't what I said sound like fun? I'm not asking you to live with me without marriage. I respect your beliefs. I want to marry you."

She strode over to a bench and ran her hand over the cool metal. "But Xabier, my beliefs aren't your beliefs." What a coward she was. She didn't even look at him when she drove the knife through his heart.

"I called the police last night. I'm not trying to do everything on my own anymore. Isn't that a good start?" he pleaded.

When she finally lifted her head and looked at him, she saw sadness in his eyes. She'd done that. She'd inflicted that wound.

She opened her hand. The flower he had given her was crushed. "That was a big step. But it's not —"

Xabier swayed back and forth, studied a plant, and then stared at the ground. Through an act of will or maybe it was just an act, he smiled and did a dance step that involved turning in a half circle. "I know." He ran his fingers through his hair and leaned close to her. "I grew up in the church, remember? You guys like to marry your own kind and all that."

She giggled. "Yeah, our own kind." She sure was going to miss this guy. He was worried about her pain and willing to turn into a clown to get her past it.

"I like to make you laugh. Wish I could hear that for the rest of my life."

"I got my checklist. I have to finish college and then —"

"— you need to meet a nice Christian guy." His shoulder drooped. "I don't know if that will ever be me."

She looked into his dark brown eyes. "You're something special, Xabier Knight."

"Not special enough to get the girl of my dreams." His voice was tinged with bitterness, but he managed another smile for her.

Invisible weight pressed on her shoulders, and she wanted to collapse into a chair. She'd deceived him into thinking there could be more between them because being with him felt so good. The wounded look in his eyes nearly crushed her. "I didn't mean to be just one more cruel Christian who led you on and let you down."

"I don't think you're cruel." He turned his back to her and walked toward a potted plant on a pedestal. "Would you do one thing for me?"

"Sure."

"Would you put 'be more spontaneous'

on that list of yours 'cause I think you need that."

"I'll do that. Would you do something for me? Keep hanging out with your mom? She needs you and you need her."

" 'Cause you're just secretly hoping that I'll come around spiritually. I bet you and my mom talked about how you're going to pray for me. 'Poor prodigal son Xabier. We'll pray him into the kingdom.' "

His voice had become a bit mocking. She had to hand it to him though. He had described the scene almost exactly as it had happened. Were Christians that predictable? "Can't pull the spandex over your eyes, can we?"

Xabier shoved his hands in his pockets.

A couple came up through the entrance. They glanced at Xabier and Kindra and then headed toward the other side of the garden, holding hands and leaning close to each other. Morning light warmed Kindra's skin. She closed her eyes. *This garden should be the place where people fall in love, not where they break up.*

Xabier pulled her close and kissed her on the cheek. "Why don't you go be with your friends?"

"But I want —" What she wanted was to not feel so rotten for the horrible way she had deceived him. He was the better person. "It's my fault. I hurt you."

He shrugged, but she saw the pain in his eyes. "It's not that I don't believe in God."

"Maybe you will find your way back to Him."

"Maybe, but not today. I won't lie to you." He twirled her out of the embrace in a move from a ballroom dance and then stepped toward her. Like butterfly wings, his hand brushed over her arm. "Turn your back, and I'll be gone."

"Looks like we have a triple header this morning." Detective Jacobson waved a clipboard at Mallory.

"No thanks to the Calamity PD, huh?" Mallory took the clipboard and filed through the stack of paperwork.

Jacobson shrugged. "If the Salinski woman wants to play junior detective, it saves us man-hours."

Early-morning activity in the police station was at a minimum. A few officers sat in carrels typing up reports or talking on the phone. Commander Laughlin wouldn't be in for another hour.

All the witness statements had been taken for both Simpson and the two other men. Nevada law allowed them to hold a suspect for twenty-four hours without charging him with anything. Mallory had opted to wait until morning to question them when she was more alert. Sometimes, too, a night in jail made a suspect more likely to see the error of his ways.

Detective Jacobson looked fresh and effervescent. On her way out the door this morning, Mallory had dared herself a glance in the mirror, conjuring up comparisons to things that had been run over with steamrollers. "Who's behind door number one?"

"Confirmed jewelry thief, Mr. Alex Simpson."

Mallory's head cleared. Her thoughts sharpened like that moment in third grade when she knew she could recite the entire multiplication table. This was going to be easier than she had imagined. "He fessed up?"

"I don't think being on the run suited him." Jacobson smiled. "Being run over helped too. People from the hotel have already come in to identify the jewelry. He didn't give up anything on his relationship with Dustin Clydell."

"And door number two?"

"We pulled sheets on our golf-cart guys." Jacobson flipped through the papers on

Mallory's clipboard and pointed to one. "The first guy is Fred Danske. He's a bouncer from Vegas with a history of assault."

"The other guy?"

"Still down in the holding cell. Milo Warren, recently employed as a used car salesman in Vegas, moved here six months ago from Los Angeles. Left California because of all the back child support he owed." Jacobson pointed to an item on the sheet. "Due to appear in court for beating up a fellow blackjack player."

"Everyone needs a hobby." Last night when she'd gotten the call from the patrol officer, she'd been given the *Reader's Digest* version of the reason for the men's being taken into custody. Before she could formulate lines of questioning for Danske and Warren, she needed to get some details, read over witness statements. Simpson would be the easy one; she'd been thinking about what she would ask him since the Salinski woman had pointed the finger at him as the thief. Now to figure out what he had to do with Dustin's death. "Give me twenty minutes to review this?"

"I need to grab coffee and a doughnut." Jacobson put her hand over her mouth. "Oh, sorry."

"Don't worry about it," Mallory said. "Eat all the doughnuts you want. I'm the one with the food issues."

Twenty minutes later, Mallory headed down the hallway toward interrogation room number two with Jacobson, doughnut-breath woman, right behind her. The room was painted a color somewhere between pink and peach. A hue that was designed to have a calming effect on all who gazed at it . . . or at least that was what the decorator had promised.

Across the room, Fred Danske slouched in the interrogation chair. His skin had a yellow tinge. He gazed at them with watery eyes. The night in jail had not done him good. Exactly what Mallory had hoped for. The chair disappeared beneath his massive body.

Jacobson took the chair across the table from Danske. Mallory chose a position against the far wall. She deliberately stared at him long enough to make him uncomfortable. He scooted his chair up to the table, put his hands on it, then on his lap and then back on the table.

Jacobson smiled at the suspect, and he smiled back. "You like to play golf, Mr. Danske?"

Danske shrugged. "I hit a few balls, swing

a stick from time to time."

"At night." Mallory made both words sound like hammer blows on steel.

Danske jerked his gaze toward Mallory. He leaned back in his chair, lifting his chin. Despite the bravado, she could read fear in his eyes.

Then he looked back at Jacobson. He grinned, resting elbows on the table and leaning toward her.

Done with enough subtlety, good cop–bad cop really did work.

"Look, I was just hired by a guy in Vegas to get Dustin Clydell to pay up."

"Dustin Clydell owed Eternal Nirvana one million dollars. That's a pretty big chunk of money." Mallory crossed her arms.

Danske shrugged. "Clydell signed on the dotted line."

"There was only twenty thousand in the envelope Xabier Knight gave you." Jacobson rubbed a page in her notebook with her thumb.

Fred raised an eyebrow and sucked on the inside of his cheek.

"Did your employer tell you that threatening physical harm to Dustin and his son was okay?" Mallory had a feeling that at some point Danske had acted on his own for his own benefit.

Fred rested his elbows on the table and leaned closer to Jacobson. "I never been interviewed by two lady cops before." Danske licked two fingers and smoothed the hair by his forehead.

From where she stood, Mallory could see the back of Jacobson's neck turn red, but her partner offered the suspect a neutral response, neither a smile nor a scowl, just a lifting of her head. The salaciousness of his remark irked Mallory. An armor of self-control kept Danske from seeing her anger. Rule number one of an interrogation was never let the suspect get the upper hand emotionally.

Jacobson rested her hands flat on the table and gazed demurely at Danske. "There is a first time for everything." Her voice was steady and firm. "Now why don't you tell us who hired you and why?"

For a Yale girl, Jacobson had developed some solid street smarts when it came to moving an interrogation forward.

"Man came into the bar, wanted me to lean on this guy down in Calamity. Showed me the bill. He looked legit. I needed the cash. When Clydell" — he cleared his throat — "expired, the man said to lean on the kid."

"Did you have anything to do with Mr.

Clydell's . . . expiration?"

"Why would I kill the guy who was gonna put money in my pocket? His death made things harder for me. I got paid one-third of the promised money up front. I got the other two-thirds if I delivered."

Assuming that Mr. Danske hadn't simply lost his temper and killed Dustin Clydell, which she guessed he had the personality and physical strength to do, his explanation made sense. "What kind of business is Eternal Nirvana?"

The suspect did a spastic half shake of his head, puckering his lips.

"How do you know Milo Warren?"

"Bought a car from him back in the day. He was in the bar that night. When the guy hired me, he said I might need some help. I knew Milo was looking for some quick cash . . . gambling debt, law breathing down his neck about child support."

Jacobson made doodle circles in her notebook. "I don't suppose you know the name of the man who hired you."

"I got a contact phone number. I can give it to you, but I've only talked to a middle man. No skin off my teeth. Doesn't really look like I'm going to get my money anyway."

Mallory stepped toward the table. "Is that

why you decided to get the twenty thousand from Clydell's son and put it in your own pocket?"

Danske sat back in his chair. His fascination with the ceiling increased by the second. He didn't need to say anything. That had to be what happened. No business would endorse kidnapping.

"Thank you for being so forthright with us, Mr. Danske," Jacobson said.

"You're welcome." His voice smoldered, and he kept his gaze on Jacobson.

"It would be hard to spend the money in jail anyway." Mallory stepped toward the table. "At the very least you'll be charged with abduction."

Ginger caught a glimpse of herself in the lobby mirror. She was no celebrity, but she looked quite fetching in her periwinkle workout suit. Light blue set off her eyes and hair color. Working out with Victoria Stone seemed a fitting way to finish up their trip to Calamity — ending on a good note, after all that had gone wrong, would give her something positive to share with friends when she got home.

They'd spent half the night at the police station giving statements. When she woke up in the hotel room, Earl was gone. No matter, they had agreed to meet for lunch before they had to catch their late-afternoon flight. He had said something about tracking down Fiona Truman to apologize for being pushy.

She patted a wayward curl back into place and smiled. Helping catch those two terrible men, who no doubt had killed Dustin Clydell, contributed to her high spirits. As she made her way across the lobby toward the spa, the sense of victory gave a rocket boost to her stride. Mallory didn't think she and Earl were involved anymore. Things were working out.

Ginger stopped short. Earl sauntered toward the restaurant without looking in her direction. He was supposed to be meeting Fiona in the basement coffee shop. What was he doing here?

"Earl?" He didn't turn around. The peacock feather in his straw cowboy hat bobbed slightly. She trotted toward him and grabbed his arm. "Hey, sweetheart."

Earl swung around, only it wasn't Earl. Same hat, same build, even the same walk. But this man had a large nose and glasses and more wrinkles than a Shar-Pei puppy.

The man studied her head to toe. "Well, hey, sweetheart, right back to you." He tipped his hat to her. "May I help you?"

Her cheeks warmed. "I'm sorry. I thought you were somebody else."

"No problem, ma'am."

"Were you . . . did you have anything to do with the Invention Expo that just got shut down here?"

"Why, yes I did. Angus Melbourne is my name." He pulled a business card out of his wallet. "I'm with Wesson Electronics out of Dallas. We're always looking for innovative ideas to support."

Ginger stared down at the business card. From a distance, Angus could have been Earl's twin. Sometimes what you saw wasn't really what you saw. It took faith.

"Did you have any inventions you wanted to pitch to me?"

Ginger shook her head.

"You thought I was some fellow named Earl."

"He's my husband." Ginger shook her head. She was reeling. "You just look so much like him."

"They say everybody has their twin, don't they?"

"Yeah, that's what they say." She couldn't stop shaking her head. This was amazing.

Angus nodded for a moment while Ginger stared at him. "Sorry I couldn't be Earl."

"That's all right. I like the one I have . . .

a lot. It was nice meeting you, Angus Melbourne."

Angus pushed through the restaurant doors.

Ginger made her way back toward the spa. The sign that advertised Binky the water-skiing squirrel was still posted. The new Binky had one final appearance this afternoon. Binky had a twin. Earl had a twin. Everybody had a twin.

When Ginger entered the spa, Victoria was waiting for her by the treadmill. She'd chosen a workout suit in shades of purple.

The former child star raised her muscular arms. "Are you ready for the workout to end all workouts?"

TWENTY-SEVEN

Mallory caught Jacobson at her carrel where she was typing up the summary of the interview with Danske. "Did we bet on the Walt Disney thing?"

Jacobson looked up from her computer. "No, why?"

Mallory sat on the corner of Jacobson's tidy desk. She had a hard time containing her excitement. "Do you want to bet now?"

"Steak dinner with ham for dessert."

"Box of doughnuts and a trip to the fast food place of my choice." Mallory took a sip of her coffee, enjoying the slightly bitter taste that suggested an extra zing of energy for the Simpson interview.

Jacobson stretched and twisted in her office chair. "Are you giving up on the diet?"

"Just taking a break. I keep cheating anyway. Why not just do it officially and for a good reason?"

"Deal. What did you find out?"

"Took some doing, but I just got off the phone with the receptionist at Eternal Nirvana. Told her I was interested in signing up."

"Signing up for what?"

"Immortality. It's for sale." Mallory stood up and rested her hand on top of the carrel. She liked days when things worked out right. "Eternal Nirvana freezes people for future thawing. Dustin Clydell had invested a million dollars in cryonics — as a business partner and future recipient. Clydell must have figured if Walt did it, he could do it too. He really believed his money could give him life everlasting, and he bet the hotel on it."

"You can't buy eternal life. Only God gives it freely." Jacobson flipped through her notebook.

The remark took Mallory by surprise. Jacobson hadn't ever said anything about her religious beliefs. "A million bucks seems like a lot of money for something that may or may not work. That might be why they hired the amateur thugs instead of using legal means to get the money. Eternal Nirvana didn't want the bad publicity."

"It's an urban legend that Walt Disney did that. But you called it right. The note did matter. I wanted to toss it." Jacobson clicked some keys on her computer. Without looking away from the screen she said, "You're good."

"No, I'm old. Gut instinct is something you learn over time."

Jacobson rose to her feet. "That's why I hang out with you. Detective Mallory, I think that your investigative techniques are second to none." Her gaze was unwavering.

Mallory was unaccustomed to compliments . . . from anyone. "You know, maybe I should listen to you more than I listen to the voice in my head. 'Cause you're a lot nicer." She'd probably eat less if she quit listening to that voice too. "Let's not get mushy here. Alex Simpson is next on our dance card."

A ghost of a smile crossed Jacobson's lips. "You have to quit thinking I'm perfect. Why don't you come over to my house some Saturday afternoon? I'll clear a path through the toys and dust bunnies, and we'll do coffee."

Coffee for social reasons. She'd never done that with a partner. "You're not doing this because I'm so pathetic and alone?"

"You're not alone. You have a cat."

"Okay, once this is all wrapped up, we'll do coffee and not talk shop."

Jacobson slammed her notebook shut.

"Let's go get this Simpson interview done."

Ginger's leg muscles ached as she pounded the treadmill. She thought she was in good shape. But Victoria had the stamina of a twenty-year-old and the strength of an Olympic weightlifter.

Still trotting, Victoria leaned to check the monitor on Ginger's treadmill.

"Why don't you try to rev it up a notch?"

Ginger spoke between wheezing breaths. "I think . . . I think . . . I am going . . . fast . . . enough." She touched her neck. Her pulse pounded against her fingers at a scary pace. *Don't give into peer pressure. Keep it up, and they'll be carrying you out on a stretcher.* She clicked the treadmill down to a slow walk.

Victoria ran, chin held high. "Ahh, come on, you aren't slowing down on me, are you?"

This wasn't fun. They were supposed to be having a girlfriend bonding time. "I just . . . need to catch my breath." How could you get close to someone who turned everything into a competition?

Victoria shrugged. "Suit yourself." She pressed a button on her control panel and broke into an all-out stationary sprint. "Shall we do weights next?" she shouted over the pounding of her feet and the mechanical grind of the treadmill.

"Weights?" Ginger slowed to a stop. "How about a cool down?" She stepped off the treadmill. "And didn't you say something about a massage and spa?"

Victoria threw back her head and laughed. "I like to go an hour to an hour and a half before I reward myself. The thought of the massage motivates me."

"Don't your muscles get sore?"

Victoria ran with large, even strides, arms pumping. "I do get some back stiffness. The doctor gave me a muscle relaxant that takes care of it." Victoria clapped her hands together. "Come on, Ginger, push yourself."

Ginger stepped back on the treadmill and increased to a comfortable walking speed. She was not about to give into this kind of intimidation. Victoria didn't want to be her friend; she wanted to torment her.

"Mr. Simpson, can you tell me what you know about the murder of Dustin Clydell?" Jacobson sat in a chair opposite Alex Simpson.

"I didn't kill him."

Mallory paced behind Jacobson, hands shoved in her pockets. She stopped suddenly and looked right at Simpson. "You were stealing jewelry from the guests in the hotel, and Dustin found out . . . or did you have some kind of business arrangement?"

He turned sideways, posture stiff, lips pressed together.

"Mr. Simpson, we are willing to believe you didn't kill him, but you have to help us here." Jacobson tempered her voice so there was just the right amount of gentleness.

Simpson turned to face Jacobson. "I don't know what Martha told you, but I loved Binky. Do you think I would stuff him down anyone's throat?"

Mallory moved in, placing her palms on the table and leaning toward Simpson. "Did you hit Ginger Salinski and put her in a gondola boat?"

Simpson rubbed his nose and stared at the ceiling. He sniffled. His pulse visibly pounded on the side of his neck. *Gotcha.*

Mallory slammed a palm on the table. "You told us you took the jewelry, Mr. Simpson, and we know you've been stealing from other hotels where Binky made his appearances." They hadn't verified that yet, but sometimes in an interrogation you had to push things. "Did you kill Dustin because he was on to you, or were you partners with him? Did he want a bigger cut?" They still didn't know where the windfall Dustin had bragged about to Tiffany was coming from.

He made eye contact with Mallory and spoke very slowly. "I . . . didn't . . . kill . . . him."

Mallory stood up straight and backed away. "This is your chance to save yourself from a murder trial." Some of the wind had been knocked out of her sail. It was almost impossible to tell a lie and hold eye contact like Simpson had done. He hadn't even blinked.

"Dustin figured out I was the one doing the thefts. He caught Binky stealing a key; he took some of jewels off me."

"So you killed him?" Even Jacobson didn't sound convinced.

"No. No. No. I didn't kill him." Simpson threw his hands up. "Okay, so I hit the Salinski woman because she was about to find my jewels."

"Why didn't you take the jewels when you stole the bear suit from the evidence pile?"

Simpson scooted back his chair. "I never stole the bear suit."

Mallory leaned against the back wall. "Did you ransack Dustin's apartment looking for the jewels?" They were losing ground here.

"No, I never went to his apartment. I was pretty sure he put the necklaces in the bear suit because he had it on when he waved the jewelry at me and said he was going to turn me in. The first time I laid eyes on that suit without Dustin in it was when I saw the Salinski woman lift it out of that Dumpster."

Nothing in Simpson's body language or demeanor suggested he was lying. They were back at square zero. Unless they could press a confession out of Milo Warren, they were down to no suspects.

A gentle rapping on the door caused Mallory to jump. They wouldn't be interrupted unless it was important. "Yes?"

A female officer poked her head inside the interrogation room. "Sorry, detectives, but we located Edward Mastive, the guy Dustin Clydell had an appointment with the night he died. He's here in the station. He can answer your questions, but he's got to catch a flight in twenty minutes."

Twenty-Eight

Mallory approached the man with the shoulder-length hair and beaklike nose. Edward Mastive leaned against the police check-in counter and fluffed his mustache, which resembled a caterpillar on steroids. This was probably going to be another rabbit trail.

"I'm Detective Mallory." She held out a hand. "Thank you for taking time out of your schedule."

"This is a murder investigation. I just wanted to do my citizen's duty."

Mastive sounded so sincere that he had to be insincere. Besides, they had hunted him down. "How did you know Dustin?"

"I stayed at his hotel a couple times when I was working on a story."

So Mastive was some kind of writer. "Dustin Clydell contacted you before he died?"

"He didn't contact me after." Mastive tossed his hair. "Now that would be a story."

"According to what we just found out, he may have tried. He was working on freezing himself for later thawing. Was that what your meeting was about?"

"I canceled the meeting at the last minute, had another story I had to run down. He had only gotten hold of me a couple of hours earlier." Edward massaged his pockmarked chin. "He didn't say anything about being freeze-dried. This story gets juicier all the time. A guy who wants to be a human Popsicle gets bumped off . . . interesting."

"So why did he call you?"

"In addition to the tabloid I work for, I'm an acquisitions editor for a publishing company. We do memoirs of the famous and the infamous. He said he had some dirt on Victoria Stone, and he thought it would be worth quite a bit of money. I think he was fishing for a book deal."

"What kind of dirt?"

Edward tugged on his mustache. "That Victoria Stone wasn't who she said she was."

"Hey, Belgian chocolate is still on sale." Kindra pulled Suzanne and Arleta toward the candy shop. "We can't leave Calamity without some discounted European chocolate."

Arleta slapped her thigh. "That sounds

like a good way to celebrate the new me."

Inside the shop, Kindra absorbed the sweet smell. Her mouth watered. Chocolate and coffee with friends would be a good way to end a trip that had been full of surprises. Maybe once they got into celebration mode, she wouldn't think about Xabier so much.

"What do you say, ladies? Should we treat ourselves? The truffles look pretty good." Suzanne wrapped her hands through the other two women's elbows.

The clerk was a middle-aged woman with a round face, round body, and circular glasses. She pulled her straight, brown hair into a ponytail. Her white apron was stained with brush strokes of chocolate and red frosting.

"Is the Belgian chocolate still on sale?"

"I don't have any left except —" She turned slightly and tapped her lips with her fingers. "The night Dustin Clydell died he put in a huge order for Belgian chocolate in a specially wrapped box. Never got picked up."

Kindra bounced three times and tilted her head. "It'll still taste fresh, right?"

The woman nodded. "I'll even give it to you at a greater discount since it's in Dustin's customized box." She raised a hand and then turned and disappeared through a door, returning a moment later with a huge, foil-wrapped box.

"Wow, Dustin really liked chocolate."

"He wasn't much of a sweet tooth." The clerk set the box on the high counter. "It was a gift for someone. He had made arrangements to pick it up the night he met with his demise. He was very specific about it, supplied the card and the box that they were to be put in."

Kindra stood on tiptoe to view the box. "Who was it for?"

Suzanne gave Kindra's arm a warning squeeze. "I'm sure that's private."

"Yeah, but the guy's dead, so private doesn't count anymore."

Arleta popped a sample candy in her mouth. "She has a point."

"Wonder no more. I already checked the card after he died. I didn't think privacy rules applied either." The clerk shoved the box toward Arleta. "He had the chocolates made up for Victoria Stone."

Ginger relaxed into the individual spa bath. Her tired muscles had turned to marshmallows. Herbal smells, the strongest of which was peppermint, swirled around her.

"How are you doing?" Victoria's voice

floated lazily over to her from the massage table a few feet away. Her words were smushed because her face was pressed against the table.

Ginger slipped deeper into the bath until her chin touched the water. "This makes it all seem so worth it. But I'm going to smell like a candy cane."

Victoria laughed. "That's the peppermint; it masks the bitter smell of the valerian in the bath, which relaxes your muscles." Before she left, the massage therapist had placed scented towels over Victoria's back and advised her to be still for twenty minutes.

Ginger sighed. "It's making me kind of sleepy."

"We can do a mud-pack treatment too. It's on me."

"I have to meet my husband for lunch around one."

"Oh," Victoria said. "I never had one of those."

Ginger's head jerked up. Something clicked in her brain. Her friend at the Southern Belle wedding chapel had said her husband had married Victoria and her third husband. Her body tensed. How could someone be married and not married?

"Something wrong?" Victoria turned her

head sideways. Her face was flushed red from the heat in the room.

"No," said Ginger. *Everyone has their twin.* The water seemed suddenly colder, the room drafty. Her thoughts jumbled and crashed into one another like socks in a dryer. Ginger cleared her throat. "So you never told me. Why were you waiting for Dustin the night he died?"

TWENTY-NINE

Three members of the BHN swarmed toward Earl, nearly knocking Fiona Truman off her feet. Fiona braced a hand on the coffee shop window.

Kindra held a box of chocolates with no cover. She bounced as though she had springs in her tennis shoes. The chocolates jiggled. "Where is she? Where's Ginger?"

Earl placed a calming hand on Kindra's shoulder. What was all the hoopla about? You'd think Ginger's friends were thundering toward a half-price sale. "She's working out with Victoria Stone. Why?"

Suzanne slapped her forehead with the papers she held in her hand. Arleta gasped and Kindra shook her head and repeated, "Oh no."

"What are you worried about? I'm meeting her for lunch" — he checked his watch — "in half an hour." The talk with Fiona had taken longer than he expected. Letting go of a dream had not been easy, but Fiona had been moved by his apology.

Arleta crossed her thin arms. "I don't think we should wait."

Their cryptic panic made his own fear meter rise. "What are you talking about?"

Suzanne shoved the papers toward Earl. "Look what we found in a box of candy meant for Victoria Stone."

The first piece of paper was an article from a 1968 Nevada newspaper. It featured a picture of a teen girl in a swimsuit with the headline "Veronica Stone Wins Local Meet." "Veronica?" The other two papers were birth certificates for two babies, Veronica and Victoria, both born on June 7, 1950. "Twins?"

"We think Victoria is really Veronica. Dustin was going to give these things to her the night he died. Maybe in exchange for money. But something must have happened."

"Ginger did say that she met Victoria when she was waiting to meet with Dustin . . . the night he died. But why would she . . ."

"What if Dustin upped the price and it made her mad, or what if he got a better offer for the secret from someone else?" Kindra flapped her hands and bounced.

Arleta pressed her face close to Earl's. "What part of the spa is Ginger in?"

"She said she was going to work out, and then they were going to do a massage or something."

Fiona nodded. "I bet Victoria took her to the executive rooms. You pay extra for exclusive access." She snapped open her purse. "I have a card key."

Earl held up a hand. "Let's not jump to conclusions." Who was he kidding? His mind was already racing with the possibilities of what could happen to his sweet Ginger. The woman had a gift for getting herself into danger. "We're not going to accuse. Let's just go over there and make sure she's okay." He waved the papers. "We can turn these over to the police."

Five minutes later, they stood at the greeters counter of the spa. A woman in a tight-fitting pink smock crossed her arms over her chest, where a name tag identified her as Pauline. "I'm sorry, but Ms. Stone and her friend requested that they not be disturbed."

"I just need to talk to my wife," Earl said. The urgency in his voice betrayed him. His wife was in danger. A low-level tensing at the core of his being told him it was true.

"Our clients pay a great deal of money for

their privacy." Pauline's expression was unflinching stone.

Earl stepped past the counter. "I just need to make sure she's okay."

Pauline clamped a hand on Earl's biceps and squeezed. A tinge of pain shot up his arm. *The lady has some strength in her fingers.* "They asked not to be disturbed."

Right now, he didn't like Pauline very much. Her voice had echoes of Mrs. Huntguard, his third grade teacher, a woman who was fond of rulers and the phrase "Discipline is the key to learning."

Behind him, Fiona whispered something to Kindra.

Kindra touched his back. "Earl, how about we just wait until Ginger comes out?"

Earl swung around. "What?"

"I think she's right." Arleta raised her eyebrows in some sort of microscopic signal that he was supposed to understand.

These women and their signals. What did she mean with that little spasm of her brows? Why were they giving up so easily? They'd just been in a panic five minutes ago.

Suzanne did the thing where she made her eyes bigger and her lips flat. "Why don't we do that?"

She squeezed out her words like toothpaste through a tube. They were all signaling him. He had no idea what was going on, but he was outnumbered.

Fiona slipped between Earl and the pink lady. "Thanks, Pauline."

Pauline lit up like a light bulb when Fiona noticed her. "No problem, Miss Truman."

Suzanne and Arleta took positions on either side of Earl and wrapped their arms through his.

"Let's just wait." Kindra trailed behind them while Fiona hung back.

What choice did he have? They escorted him out of the spa back into the hallway.

When he was sure that Pauline couldn't hear them, he demanded, "What?"

"We can't force our way in." Kindra peered up at him. "Pauline will just call security. Fiona's going to let us know when the coast is clear."

"Okay." The plan made sense, but he couldn't let go of the feeling that the clock was ticking.

Earl paced the carpet. His wife needed his help. The tightness in his chest told him that. The women leaned against the wall and stared at the floor. He appreciated Fiona's assistance, though her commitment to give this much help to people she didn't know perplexed him.

Fiona poked her head out into the hallway. "Now."

They raced back into the spa. Pauline was across the room and behind glass where she was busy helping a client with a weight machine.

"This way." Fiona led them down a tiled hallway. They turned a corner and faced a closed door. Fiona swiped her card and pushed the door open. They entered a hallway that featured a series of chrome doors. Fiona pointed up. "The amber light above the door indicates the room is occupied."

Two of the bulbs glowed.

Fiona swiped the card over the first door and eased it open. A woman mumbled a protest. Fiona's shoulders jerked up. "Oh, sorry."

Earl took two big strides to the last door. "She's got to be in here."

Fiona swiped the card. "I'm anxious to meet your wife, this Ginger Salinski."

What an odd thing to say.

Fiona pushed the door open. Earl peeked in.

The room contained two padded, bed-sized tables, a table with candles, and two bathtubs. Soft instrumental music piped in from some unseen speaker. Towels were neatly folded on one table along with an assortment of massage oils and lotions . . . and no Ginger.

THIRTY

Something warm brushed over Ginger's cheek, just a fleeting touch. A bug maybe? Her head swam. She couldn't process. Her limbs were like wet rags. What was it? She couldn't remember the word. Oh yeah. A hand. A hand touched her cheek.

Then a voice twirled through the air. "My problem here is that I have to make this look like an accident."

Noises. Shuffling. Her head dropped forward and then jerked back. She swayed and slipped deeper into her spa tub. Her chin grazed the surface of the water.

The voice had been Victoria's. But she wasn't really Victoria, was she? She had to be a look-alike, a twin.

She couldn't lift her head, but she could look around.

Her last memory was of lying in the spa bath. She'd been relaxed and tired from the workout. When she asked Victoria the question, she hadn't seemed upset, said something about her and Dustin exchanging smoothie recipes and watching old movies. It all made sense. Her suspicions were way off base. She had drifted off to sleep . . . smelled the strong scent of peppermint.

What was Victoria talking about? Making what look like an accident? She couldn't put the thoughts together. Couldn't make things fit. *God, help me.*

Victoria was dressed in her workout clothes. When had she done that? Some time had passed, and Ginger wasn't sure how she had spent it. Probably sleeping. Victoria lifted her chin. "I turned on a different amber light so I could get this job done without interruption. It's not like stupid Pauline pays attention to which light is on. She can barely count to two."

"Why?" The question sort of fell out of Ginger's mouth. It hadn't even really formed in her brain.

The woman who called herself Victoria slammed something on the dresser. "Because Victoria got everything. This all should have been mine anyway." She touched her chest. "I was talented too. No one cares if you're a great swimmer. So what if you can't sing?" The imposter tilted her head side to side and put a finger on either cheek. "But it was all about being cute."

That was way more of an answer than Ginger had expected. She swallowed. She had just wanted to know why she felt so drowsy. Now she remembered. Victoria had tossed something in her tub, strong scent of peppermint. She had been tired enough to drift off.

Victoria paced. "You want to know what? All those tap dancing lessons didn't do her a bit of good when the boat capsized." The imposter smirked. "I made it to shore. Everyone thought I was her. They wanted me to be her." Her hand massaged Ginger's shoulders. She leaned close and whispered in her ear. "A stolen life."

"Dustin?" Again, the question hadn't formed in her mind; it had simply spilled out. Her subconscious was working on things while her conscious mind nodded off.

Victoria dug her fingers into Ginger's shoulders. Fingernails prickled her skin. The pain roused her a bit.

"Dustin sold everything to the highest bidder. He thought he could get more for my secret from someone else." She wandered toward the dresser. She picked up a hand mirror turning her head side to side. "He just made me so mad. I saw his appointment with Edward Mastive in his Day-Timer when we were looking for the elevator code and I knew what was up. I knew I could find him waiting on the dark side of the pier where he did all his little secret deals."

Ginger nodded. Not because she agreed with Victoria, but because she didn't have the muscular control to shake her head.

Victoria trotted back over to the spa bath. "You're too smart. Nobody else figured it out." Her jaw tightened. "I still don't know what he did with the birth certificates. I looked everywhere, in his place, in his suit."

She smiled a saccharine-sweet smile as she swished her hand through the water. "I live in this hotel. I'll find it sooner or later." Victoria's face filled Ginger's vision. She whispered, "Just as long as no one but me knows."

Victoria's voice was bone chilling. The emotional coldness of the moment cleared Ginger's head. *She's going to kill me.*

THIRTY-ONE

Victoria held up a pill bottle. "Look at this. It's the muscle relaxant I told you about."

Ginger slipped even farther into the tub. She tilted her head. *I have to get out of here.* She leaned forward. The effect of the herb seemed to be wearing off, but fatigue weighted her limbs.

"After you put too much valerian in your bath, you were disoriented, and your muscles were so sore." Victoria slapped her cheek with theatrical exaggeration. "Silly me, I went and left my purse here, and you, you naughty girl, you found the pills I had been raving about. I'll do a little drama so Pauline is sure to remember when I left and when I came back looking for my purse." She forced Ginger's chin down and placed the pill in her mouth.

Ginger tried to push the pill out with her thick and fuzzy tongue.

Cold fingers clamped on her shoulders.

Victoria put her mouth close to Ginger's ear. "You just fell asleep and slipped into the water." Fingers dug into her like chilled butter knives. "You drown, quite by accident."

Ginger stiffened. She wiggled. Her hand jerked out of the bath, spraying water.

Pressure on her shoulders. Legs kicking. Face going under. Water surging against her ears. Kicking. Air. She needed air . . .

As the water encased her, she saw flashes of light. She twisted to one side, pushed herself to the surface for a moment. Gasping. Breath, precious breath.

Victoria grunted.

Weight came down even harder on Ginger's shoulders. She kicked. Strength ebbed away.

A muffled crash reverberated as she went under and water covered her face.

Earl Salinski pushed the door open with hulklike strength. It slammed against the wall.

Victoria's hand flew up, and she whirled around. Her eyes flamed with rage.

A foot stuck out of the spa tub. He'd recognize that foot anywhere.

How dare this woman try to hurt his Ginger.

He bolted toward the bathtub. Ginger's face appeared murky and distorted beneath the water. *No, please, no.* Grabbing her shoulders, he yanked her out of the water.

Something solid hit his head. Despite the searing pain, he gathered his wife close to him, cradling her in one arm. Victoria lifted her arm behind her, preparing to strike him again. His forearm jerked up to protect his head.

A blond head bobbed into view and then a gray one.

One of them yelled, "Oh no, you don't!"

Suzanne filled the doorway. Kindra had jumped on Victoria's back. A wooden candlestick rolled across the floor. The ladies could handle Victoria just fine.

While things crashed and banged behind him, he laid Ginger on the tile floor. Ginger's still body numbed him. She wasn't breathing. His precious wife wasn't breathing. Her chest was frozen, mouth slightly open. On autopilot, he placed his fingers on her neck. A faint pulse pushed against his fingers.

Suzanne kneeled on the floor beside him. "You got something?"

He nodded. He knew what he had to do, but it was nice to have someone beside him. Her proximity broke the paralysis that had made it hard for him to put thoughts together. He tilted Ginger's head and lifted her chin.

"Nose." Suzanne pressed her finger against her thumb, reminding Earl to pinch Ginger's nose.

Earl sealed his mouth over Ginger's and blew gently.

"You got breath into her. Her chest rose and fell."

Earl counted to five and breathed life into his wife again.

THIRTY-TWO

"Hello, Ginger, I'm so glad to meet you. I'm Crazy in Calamity. You have no idea how your blog has helped me already."

Ginger had a clear view of the ceiling. She must be dreaming. Like those dreams she used to have the night before the end of the season sales. Now Fiona Truman, the Shopping Channel lady, was talking to her. About to tell her about a good deal? No, that wasn't it. Fiona was Crazy in Calamity?

A warm hand touched her shoulder. That was Earl. She couldn't see him, but she could hear him. A moment before he had held her and said over and over, "I am so glad you are back."

That part of what had just happened was the clearest of all. She was resting on the floor of the private spa where Victoria had tried to drown her. Someone had put a bathrobe over her swimsuit.

"Did they catch — ?" she croaked.

"We have taken Veronica Stone into custody."

The lady detective showed her face. What was her name? Mallory.

Still a little dizzy, she sat up. All of them surrounded her, kneeling and sitting crosslegged: the detectives, Earl, Fiona a.k.a Crazy in Calamity, and her precious BHN friends.

"We owe you a debt of gratitude for catching Dustin's killer." That was the other lady detective.

Ginger sighed. "I'm sort of an accidental detective. All of this started because I was looking for my missing cat."

"You lost a cat?" asked Detective Mallory. "Is she gray with white toes?"

Epilogue
LIVIN' LARGE ON THE CHEAP

Tuesday, July 27

Strange Blessings

I am sitting here with my fuzzy slippers on, in Earl's lounge chair in my own house. The rest of the Bargain Hunters are in the kitchen getting tea. I hear them laughing. We had quite the adventure in Calamity. My world has righted itself and turned upside down at the same time. Earl's invention didn't quite get off the ground. We are still hopeful. Fiona Truman from the Shopping Channel thinks I should become one of those financial advisors, go on television, and sell CDs and books that explain how to live large on the cheap. She thinks she can make it happen. Maybe the money we made from that would help us get out from under this second mortgage and build our savings back up. I just don't know.

What I do know is that I love my husband. I want him to succeed. I love my Bargain Hunter friends. I know I could lose every material thing tomorrow and I would still be okay. Been there, done that. You can survive without a cell phone, purse, or credit card.

I sit here with this computer and my cat on my legs. I got my Phoebe back, and right now she's making my thighs fall asleep. What a nice feeling. The detective who took care of her for me has decided to get a cat of her own. She said taking care of Phoebe was the first step toward realizing she was too alone. Who would have thought my monster cat could be a good counselor?

I don't know what I will do about this Shopping Channel thing. I just know the blessing of loss clarifies things way more than the blessing of success and abundance. That's all for now, bargain hunters. Stay in touch.

ABOUT THE AUTHOR

Sharon Dunn loves coupons and punch cards and can hone in on the clearance rack in any store at a hundred yards. Like Ginger, Sharon had to learn that God was a better financial manager than she was. Giving Him control of the checkbook allows her to operate from a place of gratitude instead of fear. Sharon clips coupons and haunts the clearance racks, where she buys things for her three children and very tall husband. She would love to hear from her readers — visit her at www.sharondunnbooks.com. It won't cost a dime. Such a deal.